ALBA

Nichelle Kovacheff

Copyright © Nichelle Kovacheff 2022
All rights reserved. No part of this publication may be reproduced, stored or transmitted in any form or by any means, electronic, mechanical, photocopying, recording, scanning, or otherwise without written permission from the publisher. It is illegal to copy this book, post it to a website, or distribute it by any other means without permission.

This novel is entirely a work of fiction. The names, characters and incidents portrayed in it are the work of the author's imagination. Any resemblance to actual persons, living or dead, events or localities is entirely coincidental.

Trade Paperback ISBN 9781738740307
eBook ISBN 9781738740314

Cover design: Emma Brickstock
Cover image: (silhouette) Miftakhul Azis / Shutterstock

One

Alba sat in her villa's outer garden, her hair wrapped neatly on top of her head, a simple gold bracelet clinging to her arm. She wore a pale blue dress, one that had belonged to her mother. The setting sun cast a pink light through the clouds—marking her favorite time of day.

Her uncle called out to her, his sharp voice giving her a start. She knew that he couldn't see her from the terrace, which was why, long ago, she had chosen this spot to sit. Unlike her aunt, though, he rarely disturbed her peace, so she rose and took the stairs quickly.

At his shoulder was a slave girl around Alba's age with full lips, pale skin, and dark hair, her body rounded with curves. She had been well looked after in her previous master's house. "I present to you your body slave, Diana."

The receiving of a body slave was a symbol of entering womanhood. They were solely devoted to their master. To dress, shop for, and preen in preparation for marriage. The fact that her uncle was gifting her with one now could only mean one thing: he intended to find her a husband.

Her shoulders tensed at the thought. She wanted to tell her uncle to send this girl back, that she didn't need a body slave. But she knew her words would be futile. Instead, she bowed her head and said, "Thank you, Uncle."

"It has been pleasant having you as a guest in our villa these five long years."

In my father's house, she wanted to say, in the beautiful rooms my mother decorated.

"But as all things do, your time here has run its course, do you not agree?" Her face must have hardened because he took her hand and said, "Don't look so worried. We have arranged for you to attend the spring festivals with your cousin. Cheer up. Someone will take you."

As he dropped her hand and left her there with Diana, she fought to quell her agitation. Composing herself, she finally acknowledged Diana with a tight smile. "I'm afraid you've been placed with someone rather dull."

There was the smallest shift in Diana's large, dark eyes.

"Ah," Alba said coolly. "So they have told you about me." Of course her uncle and aunt had; they were never discreet when it came to Alba's past. "May I ask, what did they say?"

Diana shook her head, feigning ignorance.

"You can tell me." Alba tried to sound kind.

"That you spent a time in Thrace and that your parents have passed," she said. She had a sweet, melodic voice. A practiced voice.

"Both are true," Alba said. "My father's life was taken from him and my mother took hers. I spent five years during my youth in Thrace."

Diana swept her arm down the hall. "The bath has been prepared for you."

This girl was adept at changing the topic. What had her last master been like?

"I want you to know," Alba said before going with her, "there are some in this house that may play games, but I do not enjoy them. I promise to always be direct with you. If I want something, I'll ask for it. I'll never make you do anything that you are not comfortable with."

Diana gave her a small nod but did not meet Alba's eyes.

Alba

Their villa was one of the largest in Rome with a private bath to match. It could easily fit a dozen people and seemed a waste to fill it for only one. It was in a windowless room, the bowls atop the stone podiums lit. The flames licked the walls and danced across Alba's smooth skin as she stepped down into the warm water. Diana massaged her thick, dark hair into a lather, and Alba tilted her head back, feeling her hair swell around her. When she sat up, clicking footsteps filled the marbled room.

"Get my robe." The water sloshed over the edge as Alba stood quickly, her hair falling down her back.

"I was wondering what that smell was," her aunt Liana said. "If I'd have known you were bathing today, I would've come earlier."

Liana sat next to the bath with impeccable posture while her curly red wig was lifted from her head, her necklace and earrings removed. Liana's body slave was an older, sinewy woman, with craggy arms. She took great care with Liana's things, placing them on a stone ledge.

Her aunt had struggled with Alba's return to Rome the most. After becoming the head of one of Rome's most elite families, she was burdened with overseeing the upbringing of a thirteen-year-old girl. Liana and her husband had had no choice in the matter. Alba's parents had been greatly respected, and her father had been murdered while overseeing a task set down by the council. Casting Alba aside wasn't an option. It would only mar them in the eyes of the noble families.

"Your uncle has spoken with you?" Liana's eyes traveled down Alba as if assessing her.

"He has." Alba slid her gold sandals onto her feet.

"Good." Liana stood and grimaced as she stepped down into the water, just in case Alba had forgotten her displeasure at going in after her.

After all this time, her aunt still managed to get under her skin. Alba needed to shake off her words, her scathing glares. She tightened her sash around her waist, cutting through the atrium's white marbled columns and past the life-size statue of Apollo casually holding his lyre. When she reached the second floor, she swung her bedroom door shut and accidentally hit Diana. "Sorry!" Alba would have to get used to her new shadow, even in her bedroom. Her last refuge. She took a breath and sat on her bed, placing her hands beside her.

The villa was adorned with statues, urns, and intricate mosaics celebrating prominent figures in Roman history and the Gods. Her bed, dresser, and chest were simple but well made from warm oak and cherry.

Diana opened the wardrobe and then turned to Alba hesitantly.

"What? Speak," Alba said more harshly than she intended.

"Senator Marcus Crassus and his family have confirmed their attendance for your cousin's coming-out party tomorrow, and your uncle would like you to wear this." She held up a gold dress with a deep neckline and a low-cut back.

Alba shook her head in dismay. So he was quite serious about her finding a husband. They rarely gave her new dresses, only ones her cousin had worn out or were no longer in fashion. Who would want to marry her? As far as she knew most of the eligible men had been warned away from her after her time in Thrace. But there was no end to her aunt's scheming and no one to protect her from an ill sought-out match.

The senator's imminent arrival sent the villa into a frenzy. Marcus Crassus was one of the richest men in Rome, which meant that everything would have to be perfect while appearing effortless. No expense was spared, no detail overlooked. Every statue was polished, every cracked bust replaced, every marble floor shined and plant trimmed. Barrels of the finest wine had been stocked for the early evening, the quality deteriorating as their guests did. Even Diana had been sent to help with the flower arrangements.

Her aunt had been flitting in and out of Alba's room all day. "Alba,

I know you have absolutely no sense of style, but what do you think of these earrings with this necklace?"

Alba glanced at the massive sapphire and ruby earrings dangling from her aunt's fingertips. "I liked the other ones better."

Liana dropped the earrings in her slave's waiting palm. She had the nervous jitters that came with hosting a great event. Once it was done and branded a success, she would spend weeks dissecting it.

Alba's cousin Pomona came into the room. Her large eyes and long, jutting teeth made it seem as though she was constantly on the verge of asking a question. Liana had had her mind set on finding Pomona a husband, one that would align with their house's interests and political views. It was the sole reason they were hosting this expensive celebration, to mark Pomona's debut to the eligible men. Alba was an afterthought, but still a thought, and that scared her. To be stuck in a union with a man that she did not know made her very nervous. She didn't care what he looked like or what house he was born into as long as he was kind.

Liana adjusted her vibrant red wig. "Pomona, darling, don't just stand there. Do get ready."

In moments of weakness, Alba felt sorry for her cousin who was often severely scrutinized by her mother. Though Liana often covered much of her face in makeup, she had aged gracefully with sharp, pointed features. She was a very attractive woman, and Alba's uncle an attractive man with a strong jaw and broad forehead. Unfortunately, Pomona had inherited both of her parents' most intense features, so Liana insisted Pomona wear thick necklaces, wigs, and headpieces to distract from her face. She told Pomona to grin instead of smile because her thin lips would disappear entirely. Her cousin lacked her mother's natural poise and charm, and her nerves grew as the day unfolded.

"I'll need these." Pomona picked up Alba's only respectable pair of shoes and tossed hers on the bed. "Mine were giving me blisters."

Why did her aunt and cousin always come to Alba's room, which was by far the smallest, when getting ready? Alba excused herself and went out into the atrium, which was in the process of being transformed. A waft of smells, both sweet and savory, drifted up from the kitchens. Fruit was being laid out in colorful designs and knives sharpened to cut the meat into thin slices. A tiger was chained in the front garden, stalking back and forth. Tapestries were hung in the great hall and their most expensive paintings displayed. The dancers in their dazzling costumes paced out their routines. Fine, sheer veils dropped down around them, dividing one room from the next, creating depth, a sense of mystery, and most importantly privacy for conversations. Alba hoped nobody would bother the tiger.

A slave stopped to let Alba pass, their arm shaking from the weight of the tray. Alba glanced at the cascading heap of olives and pointed discreetly at one that had gone bad. The slave lowered their eyes in thanks. Earlier that day a slave had been caught mistakenly putting out soured wine and had been whipped in the courtyard as a warning to the others.

"Well?" her aunt said, coming up behind Alba as a veil of lace dropped down beside them.

"It looks nice," Pomona said on the way to her room, but Liana turned away from her daughter. She didn't want her opinion.

"It's magnificent," Alba said.

Her aunt nodded with approval.

"Perhaps," Alba continued, "you could open the windows and doors to the gardens and terrace to create movement and a breeze."

Her aunt regarded her a moment. "I shall have my nap now," she said, which meant that the slaves would have to go about their chores more quietly than usual.

In the early evening, Alba forced her feet into Pomona's shoes, which were difficult to walk in but not nearly as uncomfortable as the dress made her feel. She was used to wearing flowy, billowing dresses—not deep-cut, tightly fitting ones.

Liana popped her head into Alba's room and nodded at her to

follow. "Don't pull at it," Liana said, straightening one of Alba's straps. "Just let it sit."

Alba focused on walking normally as her feet pinched with every step. Liana's closest friends had gathered in the smaller, more intimate side parlor. Each time a new guest came in, her aunt glanced around, welcoming them.

Alba sat next to her aunt on the divan, and was nodding and smiling benignly when her aunt tapped her thigh. She wanted Alba to sit up straighter. No, Pomona was coming into the room. As usual, Liana had meticulously chosen everything her daughter wore, from the long peach gown to the massive headpiece. Alba moved to make room for her cousin.

Liana could be captivating to watch, the way she moved and spoke. She would shower others with false praise and carefully placed compliments. She knew just when to pause to draw out information and which questions to ask. It was an art and she was the master.

Alba had always craved a friend to experience these events with, but as usual Pomona had angled away from her. What she would give to have someone to talk to, laugh with, and confide in. But the mothers had warned their daughters away from her, making Alba's many early attempts stilted and all forced politeness. Alba never knew exactly what had been said about her on her return from Thrace, but there wasn't a doubt in her mind that her aunt hadn't tried to rebuke the rumors or come to her defense.

Because she had no one, these events were often tedious for Alba.

When the first prominent guests entered the villa, the women rose and took to their places in the atrium, their husbands joining them. The windows and doors had been thrown open to the gardens and terrace, which offered a welcome breeze. Alba retreated to the perimeter of the gathering, skirting the conversations, and trying to walk as little as possible in her shoes.

Marcus Crassus's entrance was greeted with fervor. Liana's charm was in full form as she introduced her daughter to his son Licinius. He was the younger, shorter version of his father, with a face chiseled from stone and a wig of light brown hair coiffed in swirling curls.

The other son, Publius, stood farther back with his mother, his hands clasped behind him. Tall and lanky, he had a dimpled chin and short, dark hair. After his introduction, he bowed out of the circle and retreated to the party's outskirts. Liana didn't bother trying to lure him back. She was after Licinius.

Many eyes darted toward them with the men angling themselves toward Marcus, each wanting their time with him.

Alba slipped behind a marbled pillar, momentarily shielded from view. She shifted her weight to give her foot some relief from the blister forming as two women's voices drifted toward her.

"It's uncanny, the resemblance she has to her mother."

Alba straightened against the column, feeling the cool marble on her bare back.

"It gave me quite a start when I first came in," the other woman said. "I thought it *was* Aurelia, but their mannerisms are very different."

"Well, of course, Alba lived with a savage family in a hut. I shudder to think what they did to her. The trauma she must have experienced."

Alba pressed farther into the column, hoping it would absorb her.

"It's a wonder they brought her back at all."

"Of course they brought her back, after all that her father did."

Beside her, the lanky Publius backed up into the harpist and offered a quick apology. Eager to avoid an awkward encounter with the son of Marcus Crassus, she moved from her hiding place back into the mouth of the party.

As the night wore on, the drunken laughter, silliness, and perversity started to grate on her. Perhaps she could slip away now that her aunt and uncle were preoccupied with their guests. She ducked beneath a veil, slipped off her shoes, and took the back staircase, which led her by the slaves' quarters. As she passed the men's baths, a low smacking noise drifted through the half-open door.

Alba realized something—that she had not seen Diana in quite some time. She took a breath and opened it all the way. Diana was being held against the statue of Poseidon, naked and still, by a man, tanned and muscular, who was thrusting into her from behind.

"Get off her!" Alba yelled.

The man took a step back, his chest glistening with sweat. He too was naked. Alba took a robe from the closest hook and passed it to Diana. The girl ran barefoot from the room, clutching it against her chest.

"How dare you," Alba said, her face growing warm with anger and embarrassment. She turned away from him. "She is my body slave."

"There must be a misunderstanding," the man said, coming around to try and face her. "The lady of the house offered her services to me this evening. I did not force myself on her. Would you stop moving? I've put a robe on."

"She was not hers to give," Alba said, making her way to the door.

"You must be Pomona?" he said.

"No." She turned sharply. "I am Alba of the Junii."

"Ah." His face softened as he took her in. "This was your father's house. It's a great pleasure to meet you. I am Julius Caesar."

He held his hand out for such a long time that she finally took it, raising her eyes to take him in. He had short, blond curls—real ones, unlike Marcus's and Licinius's—and a youthful smile even though he had to be at least ten years older than her.

He swept his hand toward the water. "Would you care to join me?"

"No," she said.

"A little joke," he said, but Alba was partway through the door.

No longer tired and ready for bed, she went out to the edge of the garden and tossed her shoes at the base of a statue. The tiger eyed the dancers from its perch. She needed a moment to collect herself, but when she turned, she almost collided with Marcus's son, Publius.

"Sorry," she said as they wobbled from side to side trying to pass one another.

"Shall we dance?" Publius said, making a joke of it by holding out his hand just as Liana passed by with his mother, Tertulla.

Alba fought the urge to recoil.

"Dislike for your aunt or my mother?" Publius asked.

Without realizing it, she had been glaring at their backs. "How did you know that she was my aunt?" Alba asked. They had never been introduced, though she had seen him at other events.

"Women at these things tend to travel in packs or with their family. As you are accompanied by neither, you must be a host with the luxury of excusing herself from conversation without offense. Now, what I don't know is your name."

"Alba of the Junii," she said, impressed by his deduction.

"Alba," he said, intrigued.

So her story had even made its way into his grand villa.

"Are you having a nice time?" she asked, wanting to redirect the conversation before he asked her a question she would not answer.

His brow furrowed, seemingly disappointed with this change to a pedantic topic. "I am."

Two girls came out onto the terrace in a fit of giggles, their wine spilling over the brim of their cups and splashing about their feet. They were followed by a man in a finely embroidered, pale green tunic.

"Publius." Julius held his hand out in greeting. "Good to see you, man."

"Good to see you, Julius," Publius said, taking it. "This is Alba of—"

"We've met." Julius's green eyes sparkled mischievously. "And I do sincerely hope that there are no hard feelings." He held his cup out to the side and bowed deeply.

"No hard feelings," she said, and it was the truth. A slave's purpose was to offer their services in whatever form they were asked. It was the norm—a barbaric norm, like the gladiator games, but still the norm and not something she had ever fully gotten used to after her time in Thrace.

"Now, before I become obliterated . . ." Julius pointed a swirling finger at her. "Are you going to join us at the games tomorrow?"

She nodded halfheartedly.

"Great," Julius said, ignoring her lack of enthusiasm and disappearing with the two girls through the terrace archway.

"You don't approve of the games?" Publius said.

"I do not favor them, no."

"Then why go?"

"You think I have a choice?"

"My mother often feigns headaches to get out of things she does not enjoy."

"It doesn't work like that in this house," she said. "May I ask, are you well acquainted with Julius?"

"To a degree."

"What kind of man is he?"

"He is an intelligent and skilled politician, very adept at getting what he wants. He has a way with the senate. Gives great speeches. And he is a devoted husband."

"He's married?"

"To a lovely girl, Cornelia. He had to marry when his father passed. After Sulla was victorious, they tried to make him divorce her, but he refused and left Rome to join the army. When Sulla died, Julius was able to come home, and he's been a force ever since."

Sulla. His name conjured an unpleasant image for Alba. A slight man with a rodentlike nose and a searching face. Most of their guests had indulged Alba as a young girl even if they did not like children, but he did not even acknowledge her. He had almost sat on her once at a dinner party when she was five years old, only to be saved by her timid mother.

There had been a bitter and deadly feud between Julius's uncle Marius and Sulla. When one of them took political ascendency, they would carry out bloody purges of their opponent's families.

Alba's parents had been careful not to take sides. Julius had come of age as Sulla was rising to power once again, and it was Julius's mother who had intervened, pledging the loyalty of her family, and in doing so saving him. Julius had been spared but banished from Rome and had only been able to return once Sulla had died.

Publius placed his finger on the cleft of his chin and tilted his head down so that it was closer to hers. "Would you accompany me to the games tomorrow?"

Had he not done his due diligence on her?

"I'm a poor partner, I'm afraid," she said. "I do not care for the blood or the violence."

"But that is what Rome was built on."

She would have to go anyway. "Fine, I'll go with you."

Two

Publius was waiting for Alba at the bottom of the great hall steps. Men and women from the night before staggered past them, clutching their heads and slaves for balance, mumbling that the midday games were much too early. The slaves started out ahead of them, most making their way on foot, Diana among them. As Alba approached, Publius's face strained with guilt.

He cleared his throat. "My father doesn't think it appropriate for you to accompany me."

"I thought you knew who I was," she said.

"I did—I do," he stammered. "My family is very particular when it comes to these things." He bowed his head. "I am sorry."

"I understand," she said. And she did. She knew what they thought of her. In their minds she was tainted, her virginity having been taken in Thrace. No one would believe otherwise. How could she have lived among those savages all those years and come back unscathed?

Publius reluctantly offered his arm to one of Pomona's acquaintances, the daughter of a magistrate. This meant that Alba would have to endure a tense carriage ride with her aunt and uncle.

"Well," Julius said, coming up beside her and straightening his robes, the marks from his sheets still etched into his tanned face. "I don't give a fuck where you were for five years."

His brashness startled her. "But they do," she said.

"As a man who has had many rumors spread about him, I heed them little . . . that is if I like the person." He held his arm out and led her toward a carriage. He was doing her a great kindness by offering to take her, and it was a welcome change to going with her aunt and uncle, but, as ever, she was on her guard. She stepped onto the ledge of the carriage and briefly met eyes with Liana. It was one thing to speak with Julius openly at a party, but another thing entirely to be alone with him.

Through the carriage window, she caught glimpses of people in the streets, going about their day. Scrubbing their clothes in the public fountains, bartering for fish, selling sturdy clay pots on makeshift tables. After a few minutes, she felt Julius's green eyes on her.

"What was it like living among savages?" His tone was different than the previous night. No longer playful and mischievous, but somber and direct.

Is that why he had offered to take her? To ask her the same questions she had been asked since her return. She would not answer him or anyone for that matter, for none could understand. There was no one sweeping statement that she could make to shed light on that time in her life. How to describe her bare feet, hardened from a summer outdoors as they hit the forest ground or her hands drawing milk from a goat's teat. Or the cocoon of kindness and warmth that had been living with the brothers and their mother Neme.

No, she would not even try.

"They say you were kidnapped by the Thracian family," he ventured. "But you weren't, were you?"

She could not ignore him entirely. "No," Alba said.

"I thought as much when I saw you in that dress last night," he said. "Your skin is unmarked. You were never mistreated."

She shook her head.

He was watching her closely now, so closely that she shifted in her seat. It was a warm morning and a light film of sweat was forming on her back.

"You enjoyed your time with them," he said, those green eyes studying her. "You grew to love them."

She swallowed, a small gulp. How was he doing this? Unravelling her, reading her face, her body, in a way no one had ever been able to do before.

"Yet you left them?" he said.

She fought to conceal the drape of sadness that fell over her face.

"Ah." A sparkle in his eye. "You were taken from them."

Making these deductions was a game to him, but it was not a game to her. She had loved that family, had dreamed of them for years after. She would not be interrogated like this. She bunched her dress in a fist and opened the carriage door, about to jump out and walk the rest of the way.

"Whoa," Julius said in shock as he grabbed her arm. "What're you doing?"

She was not like other women in his acquaintance. She would not acquiesce to these questions solely for his pleasure. "You ask me these questions as if it is a game," she said. "It is my life."

"I ask you these questions because I wish to know you better," he said, his hand still on her arm. "You intrigue me, Alba. I remember you as a small child. Before I was banished from Rome, your parents would host me at their villa in the days when you needed to be careful. Many were scared, bowing down before Sulla's rule, but your father was able to see past such things. He was a clever man. It was he who helped me slip from the city."

Now it was Alba who regarded him.

"Please," Julius said, giving her arm a gentle tug.

She pulled the door shut.

"I do have one last observation if you'll indulge me," he said, and his face softened. "That you fell in love with one of the boys."

"I was only thirteen when I left," she said.

"My wife was thirteen when she married me."

She stared at him for a minute, stunned. She turned toward the window again, but this time she did not see what was in front of her. Her thoughts drifted back to the brothers and Neme.

THREE

Ten Years Earlier

Her father's convoy had been traveling for several weeks, sent by Pompey, a keen commander under the dictator Sulla, to recruit new soldiers for the Roman army. Sulla had recently taken the republic by force and with that had implemented many changes. An overnight shift in the political powers. As their convoy went from village to village, they were met with faces filled with dread, unwanted as they plucked young boys from their families.

Alba watched from the carriage as the young boys were taken from weeping arms. Boys her age that would be used to restock the Roman legions.

"Why so young?" she asked her father as he came for a moment to stand by her window. Being a big man, he hunched to better see her. His dark hair, rich and wavy like Alba's, was badly in need a trim.

"That is what Pompey wants," he said.

The dissatisfaction with his answer must have shown on her face.

"They are more malleable at that age," he said in a low voice. "There is less to unlearn. They are not yet as bitter or resentful of us."

His gaze fell upon a group of villagers, glaring at them from outside their hovels.

As her father mounted his horse, she thought back to that frigid day when they had left on their journey, her mother tucking the loose strands of Alba's hair under her cloak. Her father had not wanted to bring her, the only female in the party, as he had to travel through unstable lands with warring tribes. But her mother, whose mental state had waned throughout the years, had deteriorated that winter, and she had become cyclical in her thoughts. Her father was a kind and patient man, but it was clear to Alba that when he interacted with her mother it was not a relationship of equals. It might have been if her mother had been stronger. But she was needy and repetitive, and her father's patience waned.

Alba's aunt and uncle had taken it upon themselves to move into their villa to watch over her mother in her fragile state. Alba's father saw through their guise. It was not a kindness. Their villa was situated in the heart of Rome, and it was renowned for hosting coveted guests, the results of relationships he'd cultivated over years of interactions. Her father and his brother had a complex relationship, an understanding of one another, but her father despised his brother's wife.

While next to the fire that night, Alba started to doze off, resting against her father's arm.

"You have a good mind, Alba, a strong mind," he said, his voice cutting through the darkness. It was somber and tinged with sadness. "I wish that your mother and I could have given you siblings."

"Why do you wish that?" she asked softly.

"So that you had someone else to look out for you."

With all the tenacity of an eight-year-old who had been sheltered her whole life, she said, "I will look out for myself."

He peered down at her. "I hope that your spirit is a blessing and not a curse. Not something others will try to break."

She did not know what he meant by that.

The road they traveled was ill kept, full of too many divots to count, and from within the carriage, Alba had to brace herself at times.

Around midday they stopped abruptly. Had they hit another rut? Or were changing the horse again. She reached for the door but was thrown to the floor as the horse took off with her carriage in tow. She slammed against the wall again and again, the carriage being dragged as the horse fought to break loose of its halter.

There was a jerk and the carriage slid a few feet as it flipped onto its side. She lay there for a moment, her back sore from the pummeling, before climbing through the window above her.

Perched on the carriage, she watched with confusion as men with bare chests and crude weapons ran swiftly toward their convoy. Her father's men, bulky and stiff in their layers of armor, desperately struggled to get into defensive formation.

Paralyzed with horror, she searched for her father's face in the mass of sweaty bodies.

Out of the flailing limbs, he emerged. Had he been looking for her? He was yelling at her. What was he saying? And then she caught it. *Run, run*, over and over.

Amid the chaos and death, he had sought her out. She teetered on the spot, drawn to him, this final kindness. She wanted to hold his face in her palms, but she knew that she could not. Her father's men were being cut down all around them, and if she ran toward him, it would only cause him further peril. She slid down the side of the carriage.

Into the forest she ran. Her dress caught and tore, her sandals fell apart, and the soles of her feet became raw with pain as they slapped against the roots and rocks. Adrenaline and fear pulsed her forward until the yells faded away to silence and she stopped, realizing she was alone in the forest with no idea where she was.

She made her way down a steep riverbank. The water was high from the late spring runoff. As she drank from it, hunger crept through her. Which berries were the ones her father had said were safe to eat? She could probably recognize the mushrooms.

A rabbit rolled down the muddy bank in front of her, its hind legs caught in a snare. It frantically thumped free and scampered off just as the boy pursuing it slid down the bank. His hair was the color of eggshells and his face gaunt.

"Damn it!" he spat, and then went still, realizing Alba was there. He eyed her dress and hair, his gaze lingering on her necklace. "You from that convoy that got slaughtered?"

"Slaughtered?" A slice of pain cut through her as she thought of her father and the image of him through the flailing bodies.

"You're from Rome," he said with a hint of excitement. "Come with me."

"No," she said, suddenly keenly aware that she was in unknown and unsafe territory.

"Listen, you little whore—"

He reached for her arm, and she flinched, stepping back into the cool water. When he glanced warily at the ripples, giving himself away, she took another step.

"You can't stay there all day," he said.

He was right, her feet were going numb. She started to swim, being pushed along by the current, and as her arms and legs seized, she kept kicking, careful as she skimmed over a long rock close to the surface and then pushed herself around a massive log as she made her way to the other side. She staggered out onto the slippery mud with wobbly legs and sat, shivering and shaky, catching her breath.

The boy was gone, his footprints making their way down the bank. She needed to keep moving.

Her mother had encouraged her to pray to the Gods when she was having trouble with something. But speak in mumbles, she had said, because someone is always listening. So Alba took a moment and shut her eyes. She whispered to the Gods while untangling the gold necklace her mother had given her from her hair. They would see her from danger. Her stomach rumbled, the Gods and some common sense.

A loud squeal startled her, and a boar with mighty little tusks charged her way. Before she could react, another boy, this one with wild brown hair, chased after it, clutching a spear. He pierced the boar's throat, and it collapsed, wheezing and twitching to the ground. The boy pulled a knife from a pouch in his thigh and slit its throat.

Another boar squealed out of the forest, rearing its tusks at the boy.

"Watch out!" Alba yelled.

The boy narrowly avoided it by jumping back into the water. The distressed boar sniffed the dead boar and then cried out and ran off into the bush.

In a panic, the boy started to wheel his arms trying to get out of the river.

"Calm down," Alba said, and went in after the boy, offering him her hand. If he wasn't careful, he could get caught in the current, but he didn't take her hand. He managed to get a grip with his feet and waded out. His stomach rose and fell as he leaned over the boar. He must have been tracking it for some time. He too had a scrawny frame, but his limbs were toned and his face full. He was well fed.

"You do not thank the goddess Diana?" Alba said as he tied the boar's legs together.

"For what?" He tightened the rope. "I'm the one who caught it." He pulled the boar onto a large fur and dragged it along the riverbank.

"What will you do with it?" Alba asked.

"Eat some, trade the rest."

"Trade it for what?"

"Salt, cloth."

She held out her necklace. "How much would this be worth?"

He stopped to look at it. His eyes were as blue as the sky. "More salt than I could carry."

"If I gave it to you, would you help me get back to Rome?" she asked.

"Back to Rome?" His eyes fell on her tattered dress, taking in the fine fabric, a soft purple that shimmered in the sun. "Piece of advice. Tell no one you are Roman. And Rome"—he pointed with his spear—"is back the way you came." Then he headed off, dragging the boar behind him, leaving an indent in the mud.

She clutched her forearms, rubbing them to try and stop the shaking. She had no idea how to get back to Rome. She only knew that she was somewhere in Thrace.

She did the only thing she could think of—she hurried to catch up with the boy. Though he was laden down with his kill, he moved quickly, and she caught him just as he was disappearing into the undergrowth.

She snapped a branch of berries from a bush but didn't eat them, not wanting to lose him in the dense forest. He left the animal at the edge of a modest clearing where a circular thatched-roof structure made with wood, stones, and grass stood. A goat was tied to a tree stump, and it perked up and baaed as they approached.

A tall, large-boned woman came out of the hut. Her gait was methodical and slow, her knees turned severely inward.

"Well done, Alex," she said. Then her gaze went over his shoulder. "Who's this?"

"I don't know. She followed me here," he said.

The woman eyed Alba's clothing. She snapped some twigs and placed them on the warm coals, sweeping her long hair back and kneeling. She blew gently until they ignited. As she added sticks, Alba noticed that her hands were like a man's, her fingers thick and her knuckles broad.

"Would you be so kind as to tell me how get to Rome?" Alba said.

"Rome?" the woman said, her voice dropping with panic. She turned to Alex. "She must go."

"Please," Alba said. "I don't know the way."

"How old are you?" the woman asked.

"Almost eight."

"Old enough to fend for yourself," Alex said as he threw a rope around a branch and began to hoist the boar up. When he struggled, his mother stood to help, but another boy appeared at his side, and together they pulled until it dangled down, the beast's tongue hanging from its mouth.

This new boy had the same dark hair, tanned skin, and clear blue eyes as his brother, but his nose was flat like the tip of an arrow and his face serious. A few inches taller, he had his hair pulled back in a messy knot. He took a step back. "Why're you wet?"

When Alex didn't respond, Alba said, "He fell in the water."

"Who're you?" the bigger boy asked, but before she could answer, he touched the medallion on her necklace. "You're Roman."

Just then, the boy with the eggshell hair came into the clearing. Up close, Alba noticed welts on his neck. A sacklike tunic covered his arms and back while the other two boys had bare chests.

"What do you want, Saul?" the bigger boy said.

"The girl," Saul said, eying the boar hungrily.

"Why would you want her?"

"For my old man, Zos."

"No," Alex said.

"Max." Saul appealed to the bigger boy. "Let me unburden you."

"Get lost," Alex said.

"Max?" Saul said again, ignoring Alex.

Max hacked off a leg from the boar. "Here." Max threw the leg into Saul's clumsy hands. "Take it and go."

As Saul scowled and slumped off into the forest, Alex slid a rod through the other thigh and placed it over the fire. It surprised Alba that the boys' mother was so passive during the exchange. The women in her halls would have spoken on their son's behalf at their age.

Alba started to pick the berries off the branch she was holding.

"Those are poisonous," Max said.

"How do you know?" Alba said.

"The dark indents."

Disappointed, she tossed them into the bush.

"Is my being Roman a problem?" she asked.

"Quite a large one," Alex said, giving her a sidelong look.

They were clever boys. They would know what her father's convoy was doing in these parts.

"It's for your protection. That is why we take your sons. To protect your land," she said, thinking back to the words her father's men had spoken to the village people. "They're able to come back when they have done their time."

"To the family they no longer know?" Alex said.

The sun was sinking on the horizon. "Please, may I stay the night?" Alba asked.

None of them answered her, but they did not ask her to leave when she tentatively sat by the fire either.

It took what seemed like ages for the thigh to cook, and Alba wasn't used to waiting for a meal. Alex, Max, and their mother came and went, paying no attention to her. Finally, they sat on logs that had been fashioned into seats. Max lifted the meat carefully from its holder and placed it on a wooden board. He sliced it into pieces and passed it out to his mother and brother. Alba reached forward slowly, waiting to be reprimanded or stopped, but when she wasn't, she took a hunk herself.

They didn't talk while they ate, they just licked their fingers and lips, enjoying every savory bite. At first Alba thought it might be because she was there, but there was such an ease to their movements that she realized this must be their norm. At her house in Rome, dinner was a much different affair. The women would make themselves up in finely embroidered gowns with headpieces to match, while the men wore rich tunics. The dishes were served by attentive slaves, and guests often joined them. The boisterous chatter was considered as enjoyable as the meal itself.

The large-boned woman stood, bid her sons good night, and hobbled into their hut. Alba wanted to know what was wrong with her legs but knew better than to ask. Max and Alex sat there silently, Alex drawing something in the dirt with his bone.

Alba cleared her throat. "I will teach you to swim and give you my necklace if you help me get back to Rome."

"We already know how to swim," Max said.

"If you swim like your brother, that stroke is not swimming."

"You can stroke my cock," Alex said, glancing at his brother with a smirk, but when Max didn't acknowledge him, he mumbled, "Sorry."

"I have no desire to go to Rome," Max said. "It's too far and too dangerous a journey."

"Will you let me stay here until they send someone to find me?" she asked.

Neither brother indicated that they'd heard her. Instead, they went into their hut and didn't come out.

Alba swept a few stones aside and lay between two roots. She had often pretended she was a village child, free from the constraints and decorum that ruled her life. Through her carriage windows, she had seen them playing in the streets, and envied how their tangled hair flew behind them as they ran. Hers was always brushed, curled, and wrapped neatly on top of her head. She tried not to think of her bed at home with its soft, velvety furs.

Lying beneath the stars, she thought of her mother with longing. She was quite sure her father was dead, and his last image, calling out to her in the massacre, tore through her. He had always been kind to her and taken time to answer her many questions. He would often be gone for long periods, returning with lavish gifts and stories that would fill their halls. Her mother would fret while he was away but within days of his return would start to anticipate his absence again. A thing that did not go unnoticed.

It was more recently that Alba felt pulled between the two as they differed, each parent trying to bestow on her their own way of doing things. Because of this, Alba too found herself looking forward to his departure, just to have peace again.

On the hard ground, she drifted in and out of sleep, the moon moving across the night sky.

She woke to a squirting noise. The big-boned woman was milking the goat, her hair hanging down over her face.

"What is your name?" Alba asked, sitting up.

The woman didn't answer. Her fingers pulled in a rhythm, the goat seemingly unperturbed. Maybe she had trouble hearing as well.

Alba spoke more clearly. "What is your name?"

"Neme," the woman finally said.

"That's a pretty name," Alba said. "I'm Alba."

"And you're still here?" Alex said with a yawn. He stretched his arms behind him as he came outside to greet the morning.

Neme passed Max the jug of milk and then hobbled over to a small garden beside the hut, poking and prodding some weeds loose with a rusty spade. Max poured the milk into a pot with some mushy, cream-colored food and mixed it up.

Alba must have made a face, as she was sometimes prone to do, because Max fixed her with a look. "Not up to your standards?"

She glanced down, embarrassed.

"Better get this to the market. It won't last long in this heat," Alex said. He climbed up the tree like a monkey and cut the boar down. As Alba made to follow, he said, "You can't come," as he slipped his knife back into its leather hold.

"Why not?" she asked.

"Because you don't know your place," he said.

"My place?"

"I don't know how things are done in Rome," Max said. "But here in Thrace, women don't speak to men unless they are related to them and they don't speak out against them in public."

"It's the same in Rome," she lied, wanting to come with them. In the noble houses, most women spoke as they pleased, but she had seen enough interactions in the city to know it was not like that among the lower classes.

"You wouldn't know that by talking to you," Max said.

"Would one know all Thracian customs by talking to you?" Alba said.

There was the sliver of a grin as Max lifted the other end of the boar. "You can come," Max called over his shoulder. "But do not speak. Observe only."

She did as she was told and stayed close to the boys. The market was a fast-paced, exciting place, where goods were moved quickly and there was constant bargaining and yelling. Max, being the older brother, was the one who did the bargaining, but it was Alex who inspected the goods, pointing out small defects in things they were getting or better goods in nearby stalls. They traded for seeds, wheat, a new spade, rope, and a cooking pot.

At one point, she lost the boys for a bit, and when she found them, they were leaving, neither one disconcerted by her absence.

———

Later that afternoon, Alba sat by the fire, her legs stretched out in front of her, and watched as the boys turned over the earth next to the hut under Neme's watchful eye. When they were done, Neme bent down, knobby-kneed, and drew lines with a stick, then planted the seeds they'd brought back from the market. With the water that Max had carried up from the river, she scrubbed the soil from her arms and hands.

Alba made a circle in the dirt with her toe and etched some letters.

"What's that?" Max asked as he poured the dirty water onto the newly planted seeds.

"Your names," Alba said, and pointed. "Max, Alex, and Neme."

When Alex started to scratch them out with his foot, Max threw the back of his hand against his brother's chest. He bent down, retracing the letters. "Teach us," he said.

"Not us," Alex said.

"Us," Max said.

Alba straightened. She'd never considered reading and writing something they'd want to learn. Excited and a bit nervous, she swept away the rocks and debris, then wrote out the symbols of the numbers and letters in two separate areas. She pointed to each one and had the boys repeat them. Max picked it up more quickly as Alex proved to be an easily distracted and agitated student.

As the sun set, the air around them dimmed, and it became harder to make out the inscriptions so they stopped for the night.

About to go into the hut, Max paused. "You can sleep in here if you want."

Alba tried to suppress her joy. Since the moment she had seen their little house she had wanted to go inside. She stopped in the doorway to take it in. It was small and cozy, with axes, spears, bows and arrows, and traps hanging from the beams and walls. Pots of dried food lined the shelves and clothing hung neatly from hooks.

Max made up a pallet for Alba, layering it with fabrics and furs at the back of the tent near Neme. His mother lowered her eyes disapprovingly but didn't say anything. The boys slept near the door like sentinels, and Alba felt quite comfortable in their home.

Four

As Julius and Alba's carriage approached the round walls of the auditorium the swell of noise washed over them. Stepping down onto the cobbled stones, she stared up at the massive amphitheater with its great archways and imposing columns. It was an architectural feat that astounded her every time she laid eyes on it.

"The wonders of Rome," Publius said, coming up behind her and following her gaze.

"Did you hear," the promagistrate's wife was saying to Publius's mother as she passed by them, "they're going to make an amphitheater that can hold fifty thousand people."

"Fifty thousand," Alba said in awe as Julius held out his arm. "Just for the games?" She glanced at him and noticed that his curls were golden in the sun.

"They're a huge draw," he said. "Especially when you have men like Spartacus fighting in them."

"Is he a gladiator?" Alba asked.

"Honestly," Pomona said, getting out of her carriage. "Everyone knows who Spartacus is."

The man accompanying Pomona had not waited for her, and realizing this, she rushed to catch him.

As they climbed the stairs, Alba said, "Why does your wife not join you for the festivities?"

"She wishes to stay at home with our daughter."

Men usually ordered their wives to stay home or to travel with them, depending on their mood or motives. That he let her choose surprised Alba.

Their group stopped, awaiting the trumpets and cornu that would announce their arrival.

"May I ask a favor?" Alba said, lowering her voice.

He tilted his head toward hers.

"You knew that Diana was a virgin?" Alba said.

"I did."

"If my aunt asks, would you mind telling her that you did not pursue Diana?"

Once the virginity of a slave had been taken, usually by a guest of honor, they were fair game for the master of the house.

He regarded her a moment. "You want me to lie to your aunt? To protect a slave."

Before Alba could respond, a flourish of sharp, clear notes pierced the air and the muffled chatter between the pairs fell silent. On the landing above them, Marcus Crassus drew his shoulders back and lifted his chest.

Alba lowered her head as she fought to conceal a smile.

It was, however, not lost on Julius, and he too had to look away.

After their introduction, they continued upward into the tiered box. Julius, Marcus Crassus, Licinius Crassus, and the promagistrate made their way to the front of the box in the most prominent and visible of spots. Liana and her uncle positioned themselves just behind them, a good place to overhear bits of conversation.

Alba sat in the farthest row back with her sight partially obstructed by a column. Nearest to her were Tertulla Crassus and the promagistrate's wife who seemed to prefer light gossip to watching the games. Once their box was comfortably seated with their slaves at their sides, the presenter in his long billowing robes made his way to the middle of the arena. Two men carried his podium between them.

"Ladies and gentlemen," he boomed out over the crowd as he stepped up onto his box and they quieted just enough to hear him. Alba was surprised to see Publius striding out onto the sand. "A thing I have never been witness to," he continued, making a great sweeping gesture with his arm toward an athletically built man with sandy blond hair. "This gladiator needs no introduction." Alba could have used one. "He has earned our respect, has entertained us numerous times, and he has won the wooden sword of freedom."

The gladiator stepped forward, and Publius ceremonially handed over the wooden sword. The gladiator inclined his head in thanks, but Publius did not acknowledge the gesture. He had already turned and was leaving the arena.

A group of dwarves took to the sands with oversize weapons in a show fight. A teaser of what was to come. Then the metal chains groaned as the gates were lifted and the first fighters came out onto the sands. They were citizens of Rome, free men who chose to fight in the games, for glory and prizes. A cage was dragged onto the sand. Two men climbed atop it and dropped the hatch. A tiger stalked out, its fur shimmering in the sun. The same tiger that had paced Alba's gardens the night before. Now it eyed those around it. Defensive and on edge.

Alba gripped the sides of her chair as the great cat let out a cry. She stared at the column in front of her, focusing her mind on the constant din. She would not watch as this gorgeous beast was slain—for the animals rarely won—not when fighting free men.

Diana fanned Alba, staring through and over her. Alba had tried to speak with her about the previous night's incident, but Diana would suddenly leave the room or redirect the conversation, so Alba let it be.

Liana leaned forward and tapped Julius on the shoulder. Alba watched as she asked the question. There was a slight pause before Julius shook his head. Liana sat back, disappointed.

Alba let out a breath, relieved. If Liana had been a man, she would've been a lethal politician. She and Alba's uncle did not share a bedroom, but Liana kept him flush with young, attractive girls to bed and she enjoyed free reign over the house. By law, Diana was to be solely under Alba's command, but her aunt was never one for following the rules. Alba tried to shield Diana by offering for her to sleep on a pallet in her room, but Diana preferred the slaves' quarters. Alba couldn't blame her as their conversations were forced and dull. With the slaves she'd have comradery and community.

Alba's attention was caught when Tertulla said to the promagistrate's wife: "A fine temple for the girl, though I don't believe her mother was happy about it."

Alba turned to her. "Of what do you speak?"

"My niece is joining the temple of Athena after the summer festivals. It's very well established, lovely structure and gardens," Tertulla said. "Do you ask for Pomona?"

"No." Alba had to be careful. "Sorry, I thought I heard something else." Not a good omen for Pomona, that she would think that way.

The temple. Becoming a priestess. That was a thought. Yes, it would be a dull, restricted life but perhaps she'd make friends. She would no longer have the worry of an unknown partner hanging over her. That was something she feared more than anything: having to live out her days in a marriage where she felt unsafe or uncomfortable.

As the sun reached its zenith, Alba's dress clung to her back. The heat was unrelenting, pounding down on them as it wrapped around the arena, not a cloud in the sky. This did not dim the crowd's spirit or oppress their cries of excitement as heads rolled and blood spurted from the necks of the slain gladiators.

The crowd chanted, stomped their feet, cried out, and oohed and aahed. Wine was spilt, food flung, and sweat poured.

Their own box observed the games with light applause and nods of approval. They did not indulge in the yelling or foot stomping of the lesser born around them. These men commanded their armies, controlled their money and most importantly their politics. It was imperative that restraint and decorum were to be observed at all times in these public areas. A quiet way of asserting themselves and showcasing their unity—the strongest way to quell any thoughts of dissension from the people.

Alba couldn't imagine how the gladiators mustered the energy on the burning sand, the piercing sun in their eyes. But then of course, they were being faced with the looming threat of death. There was an audible gasp that seized the crowd. Reticently, Alba let her gaze travel down to the sands.

A man lay on his back, blood oozing from the edges of a spear imbedded in his chest, his helmet torn off and resting beside him. The spear heaved up and down as he took his last breaths. It was harder for people to cheer a man's death when they could see his face, glistening with sweat, the life fading from his body. Unease gripped the crowd as the spear rose and fell no more.

His body was covered quickly and carried away to the pits on a stretcher. Alba hung her head, queasy from the heat. The blood and flesh caused her head to spin.

The announcer took to the podium with a gleeful glint in his eyes, ready to turn this crowd around. "Ladies and gentlemen, the man you have all been waiting for, so skilled with a sword they say Zeus himself lauds him."

The crowd quieted and those around Alba moved to the edge of their seats.

"From Capua and the House of Batiatus..."

Liana's head, which had been drooped for most of the games, perked up. She brushed away her body slave's fan. The House of Batiatus was her sister Camilla's. They had had economic difficulty over the past couple of years, and Liana had lent her sister money to start a training school for gladiators. Liana and Alba's uncle had gotten into an epic argument about it, but he conceded once he realized that a tidy profit could be made for doing next to nothing.

Thousands stood on tiptoe, taking pause from their drinks.

"Spartacus!" the announcer boomed.

The crowd erupted into an ear-deafening swell of excitement, stomping their feet and hollering. Three men stepped onto the sand.

Two were tall, broad, and muscular, the third darker, shorter, and stockier, and all were outfitted in bronze helmets and armor. They did not have the same frenetic movements as those before them. Each step was calculated as they waited for the gate to lift.

The gate did not lift. From the archway opposite them a chariot emerged and then another and another.

The man at the front of the trio picked up a broken spear that had not been cleared away from the previous fight. Letting the shaft rest in the palm of his hand, he tracked the chariots collapsing in around them. With the flick of his wrist, he brought his arm up and thrust it into the wheel. The horse reared its head as the wheel caught and it came crashing down onto the chariot, sending splints of wood bursting into the air.

Alba stood, her mouth open. It was a thing of beauty, the way the spear soared through the air and hit its mark.

It was a movement she had seen before. The deftness and precision. It was too much. The images this motion conjured. Dizzy and lightheaded, she needed to leave. With a sigh, Diana pulled Alba's chair out, disappointed to miss the main event.

Tertulla took pause from her conversation, glancing at Alba with concern.

"It's the heat," Alba said.

"I'll let your aunt know that you've left. That you are not well."

"Thank you."

As she descended the stairs, thoughts of the brothers and Neme flashed through her mind. She quickened her pace.

On the landing, she said to Diana, "You're welcome to come with me in the carriage."

"It would not look right," Diana said, and with that she started off on the long, deserted road back to the villa.

Once back, Alba had the servants draw her a cool bath. She needed to shut her mind to these thoughts. Nothing good could come from them. Too many sleepless nights had already been spent on the brothers and Neme.

Five

Two months passed and no marriage proposals came for Pomona or Alba for that matter. Though her aunt and uncle's attention had been pulled away from Alba she knew that they very much wanted to be rid of her. They'd wanted it since she'd arrived back from Thrace. Knowing her aunt, Liana would let it hang over Alba for the entire summer before casually dropping into conversation some horrendous match she'd made for her. Alba's days were filled with dread.

In late July, after Alba had already gone to bed, there was a knock on her door.

"What's wrong?" Alba asked as Liana came into the room.

"Nothing . . . nothing." Liana shifted her wig, her makeup already off for the evening. She sat on the end of Alba's bed and ran her hand over the embroidered sheets as she composed her thoughts.

Alba held her breath, bracing herself for the news. The terrible match.

"My sister and her husband have invited us to their ludus in Capua," Liana began. "Their gladiator school has been quite successful, and they're hosting a coming of age party for their girls."

Alba deflated as she let out the air. That was not at all what she was expecting. Liana turned to Alba and took her hand. "We are not friends, you and I," she said.

Though this was true, the bluntness of her statement almost made Alba laugh, except for the strain in her aunt's face.

"Would you assist me in this?" Liana said.

"In . . . you want me to go with you?"

"Yes." Liana seemed to fight back a grimace. "As your uncle cannot come. It will be the three of us."

Alba had attended only a few of the summer's festivities, and she feared she would prove an ill-informed conversationalist. "I don't know what help I can be."

"Capua is a fair ways away so there will be time to enlighten you." Her aunt lifted her hand. "Now, it appears that both Publius and Julius favor you. Perhaps we can use that to our advantage."

Alba shook her head. "I've only spoken to them the once."

"Baffling, isn't it?" Liana said, clearly perplexed that anyone would be fond of Alba. "So will you be my ally in this endeavor?"

"To help you find Pomona a husband?" Alba said, wanting to make sure that she understood what was being asked of her.

"Yes." Liana's face was so tight Alba knew the slightest thing could set her off. The woman was desperate.

"I will," Alba said. "If you offer your consent for me to become a priestess." She'd been thinking about this since the games, and it was what she wanted, to live among the priests and priestesses in the temple of Athena. To be free from the bonds of an unknown marriage.

Her aunt snorted. "You wish to take the virgin robes?"

"Yes," Alba said.

"Fine." Her aunt stood. She would finally be rid of Alba, not in the unhappy marriage she might have hoped for, but in a respectable, convenient place where she would never have to see Alba again.

"When do we leave?" Alba asked.

"First thing." Her aunt paused in the doorway, her slender fingers on the frame. "And not a word of this to Pomona."

For all her aunt's faults, in her own perverse way, she was doing what she thought was best for her daughter, and Alba had to credit her that.

Diana helped Alba into her travel robes and pulled her hair back into a quick braid as her travel chest was carried out of the room. Their departure was so early that her uncle had said his goodbyes the night before. To everyone except Alba.

Alba waited for her aunt and cousin outside of the carriage. "Alba." Liana swept over to her. "We must be careful about what is said in front of my sister and her husband. Don't let her lure you into conversation about things we must keep between ourselves."

Alba nodded. She was used to her aunt's games and false kindnesses. Was her sister similar? Alba hadn't seen her since before Thrace.

Liana's body slave and two boys climbed into the second carriage accompanying them.

"Where's Diana?" Alba asked.

"She's not coming with us," Liana said. "After you."

Alba was fearful for the girl as the carriage jolted to life. Within minutes, Pomona had fallen back asleep. Her snores were broken by the wheels against the cobblestoned streets of the city, at least until Liana launched into the latest on the houses and their current marital prospects.

The second day's journey was through the countryside on a dirt road with fine red sand. The fields were scattered with slaves working their masters' fields. People made their way toward the city with cows and cages of chickens, cloth, and barrels of wine in their carts. It was a well-traveled road, and by midday, the dust, churned beneath the wheels and feet, was making its way through every crack in the carriage, forcing them to cover their faces with their finest shawls. It was, however, Alba's saving grace as Liana had to cease talking in order to prevent coughing fits.

One man had pulled his cart off to the side and was now trying to coax his aging horse back onto the road. The wheel caught a rut, and the door swung open, sending wigs that were affixed to the wood swaying left and right.

A rich brown one caught Alba's eye.

Six

Ten Years Earlier

Days turned to weeks, and weeks turned into months, and no one came for her. Max explained to Alba how far away Rome was, and that though there were Roman soldiers in Thrace, some had been away from Rome for so long they might not even know the way back. But most importantly, Roman soldiers could not be trusted. He said this to her in the same way Romans spoke of all non-Romans. So Alba let it be.

When the river warmed, Max took Alba up on her offer to teach them how to swim. She had loved swimming in the ocean while her mother sat nearby with her toes in the sand, the sun golden across the water's surface.

Alba spotted the problem right away: they were flailers, moving their limbs about wildly in the water. She taught them first how to float on their backs, and by the third day, they were able to tread water comfortably. Alex playfully grabbed Alba's arm and pulled her toward him. Growing up she had never been allowed to play with boys, and at his touch, she went stiff. Max noticed her sudden discomfort and said, "Alex, leave her be."

She waded up the bank and straightened the dress Neme had made for her from discarded fabric. Alba loved it. She could run through the forest without it catching or weighing her down like the dresses she was used to wearing. It had also become part of their daily routine to practice reading and writing at night. Max continued to be a patient and eager student while Alex often sat on his haunches, ready to spring up at any moment. When he grew restless, Max would push him back down.

It wouldn't be long before Alba would have nothing more to teach them. The only time Alex did sit still was when hunting. For hours he would wait in the undergrowth, camouflaged by the leaves, only to rise in a flash with his spear hitting its mark. He taught Alba how to throw an ax and spear, how to set a snare, and which berries were safe to eat. She did not possess the strength for a distance shot, but her accuracy, once honed, was quite good. Her soles hardened on the forest ground, and by the end of the summer, she could catch a fish with a spear and skin a rabbit. While walking through the woods one day, she came across the alphabet neatly printed in a hand she didn't recognize. There were even a few sentences. All that time she'd thought Alex hadn't been paying any attention when in fact he'd learned it all.

Alba told Neme when she returned to the clearing.

Neme just nodded. "Alex's mind is sharp," she said.

That's when Alba understood. He hadn't wanted to show his older brother up.

Neme was a quiet woman, resilient and stubbornly independent. Alba tried to help her on many occasions, but the boys often discouraged it. When she asked Max why, he said, "Doing things keeps her strong." Her movements were slow and appeared painful but she never complained or bemoaned her crooked legs—not even when winter came. Her limbs would lock and seize in the cold, but she continued to shuffle across the earth's icy surface. The boys kept a path cleared for her and made sure there was always wood on hand for the fire.

Alba tried teaching Neme some finer sewing techniques, but Neme's thick fingers fumbled with the needle so Alba took over the sewing of their clothes. At her house in Rome, Alba had done needlepoint with a matronly woman over her shoulder, guiding her every movement. So many tedious hours were spent over drapes and tablecloths she'd never see again. But here, each piece of fabric was carefully chosen and haggled over, and the clothe was used and used again until it had fully worn out. Alba took great pride in her creations.

And though there were certain rules that she had to abide by while in town, within the family she was free to say and act as she wished. If she had an opinion, she said it without fear of being reprimanded. Over time she got to know each family member by the sounds of their feet upon the earth, their breaths at night, and their gentle smells. But Alex could evade her senses when he wished to with his silent footsteps and quick movements.

In the spring, the boys and Alba went to the market to get seeds for the garden. A man was selling wigs in all hair colors, and as Alba passed him, he eyed her hair. Though not as well kept as it used to be, it was still long, dark, and thick. She slipped away from the boys and went to his stall.

"What would you give me for my hair?" she asked.

He held up a bag of wheat.

"I want coins," she said.

He scoffed at her forwardness, but she stood there, waiting. After a short while, she turned to leave. "Fine," he called after her. He chopped her hair off, and she bought the boys each a ring. A snake with a sapphire eye for Max and a wolf for Alex. For Neme she bought a thick purple cloak.

When she found the boys, they were standing on tiptoe in the middle of the market.

"Where have you been?" Max asked, whipping around. "You can't just leave us like that—" His eyes went round. "What did you do?"

"I sold my hair." She held out the rings as way of explanation. "These are for you."

Instead of being pleased with their gifts, the brothers looked at her in dismay. Her excitement faded to shame as she realized the worry she had caused them. She lowered her head as a group of Roman soldiers passed them. "I'm sorry."

"Please, never do that again," Max said.

"I won't," she said. She followed them through the crowd clutching Neme's cloak.

Alba spread the cloak across Neme's bed. When she hobbled into the hut that evening, Neme didn't say anything, but the next morning, in the brisk air, she was wearing it. And Alba inwardly beamed. The rings were too big for the boys so they sat on a ledge near their beds.

Alba was at peace with the family. Happy and easy in their presence. Only the dreams that woke her in the night unsettled her. Barren images of dust and heat, her father yelling through the haze, and her mother searching for her in the hallways of their villa. She would wake in a damp sweat, disturbed and scared. On the worst nights she would crawl toward the boys and lie in the nook between their bodies, letting the warmth from their tanned skin wash over her. Only then did her breath slow. Only then did her mind stop racing and her thoughts quiet. Comforted by them.

Three years passed. The boys grew taller, their voices deepening. Max's arms and chest thickened, as did Alex's, though he was much leaner. They now fit into their rings and never took them off. Hair sprouted from their bodies in places it hadn't been before.

As their bodies changed so did their habits. In the evenings they would go into the village, drinking and doing other things they did not discuss with Neme or Alba. They would often take turns when going out for longer periods.

Alba's body had started to change also. Her hair grew past her shoulders, her breasts became tender, and her hips widened. One night she woke to achy cramps, her back damp with sweat, and her butt wet. What was this dark and sticky liquid? Blood. She looked over to where the boys slept. To Alex's sprawled body, deep with sleep by the door. She crawled over to Neme whose breath was a low rumble.

"Neme," Alba whispered, shaking her until she snorted awake. Alba gathered her courage. "I think . . . I'm dying."

"What?" Neme said, sitting up, startled.

"I'm covered in blood."

"Oh, Alba. You're not dying. You bleed so that one day you can bring life into this world. It is a blessing and a curse."

"Why does it hurt so much?" Alba asked.

"The unfortunate fate that we as women must bear. Come, I will show you what to do."

It was the most intimate moment they had ever shared as Neme showed Alba how to wrap herself and contain it. When they were done, Alba lay back onto her fur trying not to think of the pain pulsing through her.

"What happened to your legs?" she asked.

Neme was quiet for such a long time Alba started to drift off.

"I was beaten by Romans when I was a bit older than you," Neme said, her voice barely a whisper.

Alba opened her eyes at the thought of Neme's large body lying on the ground, bloody and broken. It made Alba's pain seem so trivial. She understood now why her presence had been so unwanted at first, why Neme had wanted her gone from their midst. Alba had never understood violence. Why people inflicted it on others.

"We are not all bad," Alba said.

"I know that now."

Alex's head moved slightly. From across the hut floor, their eyes met and Alba held his gaze until he rolled over.

Seven

Five Years Earlier

In the heat of the summer, Alba and Alex were sitting side by side on a large, flat rock eating freshly picked figs, their feet dangling lazily in the water. Alex leaned back on his forearms, his arm grazing Alba's, and as he lifted his face to the sun, the soft muscles in his arm rose and fell.

"Alex," she said.

"Hm." His eyes were shut.

"What were you and Max arguing about last night?"

He straightened. "He wants to join the Roman legion."

The boys were inseparable.

"Will you go with him?"

"I won't leave Neme."

Wanting to lift his mood, she nudged him playfully with her shoulder and jumped into the water. When he didn't follow, she splashed him as the current started to take her. He shook his head with a smile and launched himself off the rock landing next to her.

One of their favorite summer pastimes was to let the river carry them on their backs. They did it when it was just the two of them as Max was dense and had trouble floating. Alba's tunic rippled around her, and she felt a giddy sense of freedom as the rocks and trees on the bank slipped by. They let themselves be carried farther than usual to the wider part of the river where the current quickened.

"Alba," Alex called to her. He dropped his legs to anchor himself to a rock, holding out his arms to catch her. The force of her body almost dislodged him, but he planted his feet and held her steady, cradled against his chest. He smiled down at her, secure in his arms.

As they waded out of the river, beads of water dripped down their arms and legs. Alex's brown hair gleamed and his skin was golden in the late afternoon sun. His face was smooth, not blotched and marked like many of the village boys. It was the sweet scent of figs still on his lips that drew her toward him. The giddiness that filled her.

His head was angled away from hers, and just as he turned, she pressed her lips to his. After a moment of stillness, he staggered backward, his eyes wide. She pulled away, mortified by what she had done and his reaction to it.

"Alex, Alba!" Max yelled through the forest, urgency lining his voice. His chest heaved as he stood on the crest above them. "They're here," Max said to Alex. "Neme's in the village."

Alba had no idea who *they* were, but Alex must have, because he gave a quick nod and was off running.

"Who's here?" she said, scurrying up the bank to Max, trying to catch him as he made his way through the forest. "Max?"

He stopped, and when he turned, his face wore an intensity she had never seen before. "If I tell you, you have to promise not to act on it."

"Fine. I promise."

"A Roman legion is passing through these parts." On seeing her face open in hope, he shook his head. "You cannot go with them."

"Their commander will have known my father."

"I've seen how they treat the village women, without decency or respect."

"But they . . . they will not do the same to me," she said. "I heard you last night arguing with Alex. I know you're going to join the Roman legion at summer's end."

"If enough men sign up, they have promised to protect our village. With the land and money, I'll be able to build a better house for Neme." He twisted his ring, the red eye of the serpent catching the sun's last glare. It was a habit of his when he was considering something. "You still wish to go back to Rome then?"

"I have such vivid dreams of my mother," she said. "She is the only thing that draws me back there."

He stopped at the top of a ridge. Down below was a dark hovel and children clothed in rags, their skin pulled taut over angular bones, each with eggshell-colored hair. From the hovel there was a cry and the sound of a child being hit. They continued on.

"That's why you gave Saul the meat that day I first came even though he was dreadful," she said.

Max nodded. "His father's a brute. His mother's dead." He paused and lowered his head. "At the end of summer, before I join the legion, I will take you back to Rome if you still wish to go." Alba stared at him, unable to find the words to express her gratitude. It would not be as simple as Max made it out, she knew. "Until then, please stay close to home."

"I will."

As she walked along behind Max, her thoughts drifted back to Rome and the life she had lived. The halls, the meals, the people coming and going. Much of it had blurred except for the image of her parents, which were still etched in her mind.

When they got home, Neme was back.

"Did Alex find you?" Max asked.

"Yes," Neme said.

"Where is he?"

"In town. He would not come with me." Neme lowered her eyes. "He would not listen."

It was Alba's fault. She shouldn't have kissed him. She had ruined it. Ruined it all.

"I'll bring him back," Max said, turning on his heel.

But Max did not return that evening. Alba lay on her pallet, her eyes growing heavy, but she wouldn't allow herself to sleep until they returned. She heard someone come into the hut, but it wasn't the familiar sounds she was used to. As she raised her head, she was hauled to her feet and a cloth was tied over her mouth. A blade was pressed to her neck and her hands bound together. She was pushed out of the hut into the night, and a warm trickle of blood ran down her clavicle. Saul's eggshell hair shone in the moonlight.

Neme hobbled out of the hut with her cane, her legs jerking as she tried to run-walk toward them. "Leave her be, Saul."

"It's too late, Neme. I've made a deal."

"With who?" Neme came around the smoldering embers.

"The Roman general."

"He wouldn't speak with you," she said.

Saul's eyes narrowed. "One of his men."

Alba fisted her hands and hit Saul in the face. He didn't even flinch, hardened from years of abuse. Neme swung her cane and he held his arm up to defend himself, slicing his dagger through the air and catching Neme's armpit. Blood oozed out, and she pressed her hand against it, trying to stop the flow.

"Get Max!" Alba yelled through the cloth. "Get Max and I'll go with you."

"Shut up!" Saul hissed, pulling her into the forest.

Neme made to follow but stumbled to the ground. Alba planted her feet and Saul grunted under her weight. He choked her until her world faded into darkness. Her last image was of Alex's face gleaming golden in the sun.

Eight

They arrived in Capua on the third day of their journey, cramped, restless, and coated in dust. Liana stepped down from the carriage. Alba admired how she was able to walk with such grace and poise after sitting for so long. Stiff though she was, Alba pushed her limbs to do the same.

A woman with emerald earrings and bright red hair stood ready to greet them in the courtyard. "Welcome, sister." Though Camilla held her arms out wide, it was a lifeless gesture, and there was nothing natural in the movement. She clutched Liana loosely as she pecked each cheek with a kiss.

Camilla then turned to her niece. "Pomona," she said, embracing her niece with even less vigor.

"And Alba," Liana said, pulling her lips into a strained smile.

At that Camilla offered Alba a slight nod. Unlike her sister, Camilla's face and neck were lined with age, but she held her slight physique with impeccable posture. Her husband Lentulus emerged from the villa's entrance. Short and fat, his face was beaded with sweat. He greeted each of them with wet kisses on the cheek. When he reached Alba, he said, "A great beauty, like her late mother."

"My dear husband thinks every woman in their youth is a beauty," Camilla said.

Behind Camilla and Lentulus stood a wall of slaves. It was custom for the slaves to welcome guests staying overnight in their master's villa but not this many and not for immediate family members. It may have been to display their newly acquired wealth.

"I am curious to see how the money I lent you is being spent," Liana said. "Hopefully on more than just slaves."

Camilla pursed her lips.

"The gladiators have provided us with a steady income," Lentulus said, dabbing his head with a cloth and passing it to a slave. "With the arena being built in Rome, the return shall be even more bountiful."

"Is Spartacus here?" Pomona asked, her question surprising Alba. She had barely spoken the entire journey.

"I'm afraid not. He's in Rome at present," Lentulus said. "On his way home today actually—in need of a well-deserved break before we send him off again."

Lentulus led them through the entrance hall to the atrium. Set in the countryside, their house had the luxury of space, with sprawling rooms and rambling gardens. Instead of being built upward like most noble houses in Rome, it was only two levels. While their villa in Rome was elaborately decorated, each room themed with frescos, statues, and intricate floor mosaics, this one was built with one theme: elegant simplicity. The columns that lined the walls were white marble, the tables covered with linen, and the furniture strategically covered by shams to hide their use. Cut flowers were being placed in vases along the walls.

"Sister, you do not have to go to the trouble," Liana said.

"Oh, but this is not for you," Camilla said, nonchalant. "It's for the party."

Alba moved to the side as a group of slaves carried a long platform to the far wall.

"A bit early for flowers, isn't it?" Liana said.

"Did I not tell you? The party is tonight," Camilla said, a glint in her eye. Was it possible that this woman was worse than Liana?

Lentulus chuckled. "My wife insisted that we have the festivities the night of your arrival to welcome you."

"I'm sure she did." Liana's voice was light but her body rigid.

They were taken to the second level of the ludus, away from the bustling noises of preparation. As many guests were staying over, Pomona was in a shared room with Liana. The tapestries and paintings hung here were much simpler than the ones being displayed in the main entrance and atrium.

Pomona's cousins met them upstairs, full of nervous excitement at their impending debuts. Claudia had inherited her mother's height and Cilia her father's stout physique. Claudia held a mask to her face.

"Claudia," Liana said. "Is this a masked party?"

Claudia lowered her mask with an air of sultry mysteriousness and raised her eyebrows.

Liana rolled her eyes and shook her head. "For fuck's sake," she muttered.

Cilia pressed a black mask up to Alba's face. "This one was a gift to Mother from the praetor." When she pulled it away, she shoved her fingers into Alba's hair. "Where's your wig from? It's gorgeous."

Alba ducked out of her reach. "It's not a wig."

Liana left the room.

"Liana," Alba called, following her down the hall a ways.

"What?" Liana whipped around, her eyes daggers.

"Calm yourself," Alba said quietly. "Think of Pomona. There is still time to bathe and dress. Don't let her get the better of you."

Liana took a breath and nodded slowly, relaxing her shoulders. Though her mouth and eyes were still sharp, a forced calm came over her rigid body. She fixed Alba with a look and then swept off down the hall.

Pomona and her cousins were trying on dresses for the evening, sashaying about the room and holding up necklaces and earrings.

"Wait until you see our gladiators." Claudia quivered, her tall body in spasm. "Their ripples and muscles . . ." She made a motion of running her hands over something. "A shame you couldn't see Spartacus. He truly is our finest fighter and beautiful to behold."

"Careful, sister," Cilia said. "You'll make us all wet."

"But your father said he's on his way back?" Pomona said.

"Perhaps if you're lucky you'll see him before you leave," Claudia said haughtily. "Tonight, a few are being made up in the likeness of Gods."

Liana had told Alba that her evening dress was in her chest so Alba rummaged through it until she found the package. After unwrapping it, she held the thick and heavy fabric up in dismay. The layers of cloth would stifle her on this hot and humid night, but that was not her problem with it.

Cilia squealed with malicious excitement. "The virgin robes of Apollo?"

The blue trim at the bottom of the dress was fraying. "Do you have scissors?" Alba asked.

"No." Claudia cut across Cilia. "We don't."

"The dress suits you," Pomona said, joining in.

"Shut up, Pomona," Alba blurted, but because of her arrangement with Liana, followed it with an apology.

Alba balled up the dress and went down the hall. Her own room was dark and narrow, probably a converted storeroom. There was a single bed, a table with a washbasin, and a dresser. The only window was a slit many feet above her, the light it cast traveling up the wall as the sun set. She laid the dress on her bed, wondering if she could rip the inner layer out without doing too much damage. She tore at the fabric but to no avail. Yes, she did want to join the temple of Athena, but that was solely to avoid an arranged marriage. She had hoped to attend one last party as herself.

She lifted her billowing travel dress over her head. In her frustration, the fabric caught around her shoulders. She yanked it free and threw the dress into the corner.

Her door opened and Alba covered her breasts. A tall girl around

Alba's age stood in the doorway, her hair braided around her head like a golden crown. She bowed herself from the room. "My apologies," she said. "I have the wrong room."

"Wait," Alba called, popping her head out of the door. "Do you have scissors?"

"Scissors? I think so," the girl said. She returned moments later with two pairs, one large and one small. "For your hair?"

"The robe." Alba lifted one of the layers to show her.

"Oh, it's . . ." The girl searched for words.

"Hideous," Alba said, and couldn't help but smile.

"It is a bit unfortunate," the girl said. She pulled the cloth tight to the seam so that Alba could cut it loose. Even with that, the dress hung on Alba like a tent.

"I could do your hair like mine to help offset it," the girl said kindly.

"You won't be missed?"

"Not at the moment." Her fingers were fast and gentle as she wrapped the braid around Alba's head and pinned it into place. "I have an extra mask as well, a gold one that would be radiant against your olive skin. Meet me in the hall before you go down."

NINE

When the gong sounded, summoning the guests from their rooms, Alba was already leaning against a pillar. Pomona and her cousins passed by her with timid giggles, bumping into each other on their way to the stairs.

The hall filled with deep male voices and Alba straightened. The girl who had helped her was at the front of the pack, her arm woven through an older man's. Quintus, Alba believed his name was. The girl wore a pale pink gown, gold sandals, and no makeup. She was a true and natural beauty. She discreetly held the mask out to Alba without breaking her stride.

With everyone else gone down, Alba struggled to tie it, trying to make it tight enough without ruining her hair.

"Here. Let me," a familiar voice said.

With her vision obstructed, she turned her whole body. Julius's hair stuck up messily from the sides of his mask.

"It's a bit tricky," she said.

"I've had practice." He weaved the ribbons through her hair and secured it with a little tug.

"A man of many talents," she said, and couldn't help but grin. "Thank you."

He came around to face her, stooping a bit to adjust it, and resting it on her nose. "There," he said, satisfied. "Now, was that Quintus?" He nodded in the direction of the music and noise, the long beak on his mask quite comical.

"I believe it was," she said.

"So the rumors are true . . ." He lifted his beak in contemplation. "I do hope his new wife has him in good spirits."

"Wife?" Alba said, taking his arm as they leisurely made their way down the hall toward the rising din.

"The gorgeous blonde. Cloe is her name." He glanced at her. "You're surprised?"

"She is much younger than him," she said, and added, "And you should not hold our sex accountable for the happiness of yours. It is unfair to expect that of her."

"That is not at all what I meant," he said. "I have known women who have held a great deal of influence over the thoughts of others, especially men. You should not discount them."

"I don't discount them," Alba said, taken aback. She knew how hard many women worked in the background of things, trying to quell their husbands' tempers and to carefully manipulate their actions. "Who were the other younger men with Quintus?" she asked.

"His sons, products of his first wife."

Their slow walk had brought them to the top of the stairs with the room laid out before them. Alba's foot caught her robe on the first step and Julius steadied her.

"Interesting choice of garment," he observed. "When are you joining the temple?"

"End of summer."

"Shame," he said.

Near the bottom of the stairs he paused and she stopped too. His eyes swept over the crowd. She could see him calculating his path of least resistance to those he wished to speak with most. Then he wished her luck and joined a group of men from the senate. She watched as he approached Quintus with a subtle yet respectful bow of the head. His charm could rival Liana's. But was his as disingenuous? Cloe stood at Quintus's side, smiling and nodding, and Alba noticed what she had missed before. A dark and haunting void in those pale blue eyes.

"Alba!" Lentulus called, pulling her from her trance. "Are you having a merry time?" He stuffed a handful of grapes into his mouth and drank from his bronze goblet as he chewed. Bits of grape dribbled down the front of his robes.

She forced a smile. "I am."

"Good," he said. He spanked a dark slave girl's butt and took a few apple slices from her tray. "The guests are all in a tither. They were hoping to see Spartacus." A chunk of apple hit Alba's cheek.

"Lentulus," Licinius said, strolling over toward them. He really was the spitting image of his father Marcus, down to the subtle airs with which he greeted them. "Your gladiators are truly a sight to behold." As the two men turned their attention to the gladiators, Alba wiped her cheek. "You have outdone yourself. You didn't drain your pockets, I hope?"

Lentulus's chest deflated slightly. An ill-thought-out rebuke was forming in his eyes, but Camilla saved him by sweeping into the conversation.

"The Gods have favored us of late." Although well spoken, Camilla was a stiffer host than her sister, who would have come back with a clever quip or anecdote. "Have you had a chance to meet my daughters?" She waved her girls over with Pomona trailing behind them. Liana joined their circle as well, making it the last place Alba wanted to be, but she had made a deal.

Licinius scanned them. "Ah," he said, seemingly unimpressed.

"Pomona." Alba turned to her cousin. "Your hair is a vision."

"The wig makers of Rome have exceeded themselves," Camilla said.

Liana's eyes flashed toward her sister.

Lentulus chuckled. "Women . . . the things that excite them," he said before leading Licinius away from their tense circle.

With nothing to hold the circle together, the rest of the group disbanded. Liana took another glass of wine from the tray. If her aunt continued at this pace, she would eventually become glassy-eyed and relentlessly annoying with all remnants of her charm gone. Alba deliberated over whether to talk her out of excessive drink or to let her go. She let her go.

She floated to the outskirts. Dressed as she was and with her face half-covered, no one acknowledged her. It was perfect for observing the interactions between the partygoers. Events in the country villas were often more lightly attended than those in Rome, but as things went, this would be considered a success. Alba watched as Liana swayed around the room, exchanging gossip and pleasantries. She lived for gatherings such as these. At the approach of her sister, her shoulders would draw back and she would excuse herself from the conversation.

Alba knew that she would be in trouble if she didn't at least appear to help Pomona. The only problem was, her cousin didn't want anything to do with her. Where was Pomona?

She found them at the base of the platform, fawning over the five gladiators brought up for the party. As the sisters had said, they were dressed in the likeness of Gods, shimmering with gold paint and sweat from the staged fight that had offered the guests entertainment while meat, cheese, and grapes had been served around on trays. Alba wondered how they had fought in their masks. Through her holes, she could see only what was directly in front of her.

Pomona was in a fit of laughter, holding her drink out to the side as she tried to catch air. She became quite giggly when drunk. "This one is your match," she said to Alba, pointing at one of the gladiators.

The man wore the mask of Apollo, his muscular body painted in gold, with only a loincloth around his waist. Alba lowered her eyes, having trouble staring at anyone forced to do something against their will. Something blew on the nape of Alba's neck, and she swiveled around, annoyed, but her mood softened when she spotted the beak.

"Magnificent beasts, aren't they?" Julius said, popping a grape in his mouth. He stood back to take them in. When she didn't follow suit, he said, "I forgot, you don't favor the games. What was it you had in Rome? A fainting spell?" His teasing was all good-natured, but she wished he'd be more discreet.

"She has no stomach for violence," Pomona said with an air of superiority. "The sight of it makes her queasy."

"Maybe if you had it inflicted upon you, as others do, you would not find such joy in it," Alba shot back.

The gladiator dressed as Apollo tilted his chin down toward Alba.

"Ladies, ladies," Lentulus said, coming over to them. "Do they not make you swoon?" He took to the platform with unbalanced footing and clung to a statue between two of the gladiators. Camilla came over and nervously tried to wave him down as he teetered.

"Has anyone seen Publius?" Julius asked the group.

"On the terrace." Alba nodded toward the billowing curtains.

"The constant observer," he whispered while passing behind her.

"Come." Lentulus clapped his hands together and pointed across the room. "The dancing twins are coming." He stepped shakily down from the platform, holding on to a slave's shoulders.

Alba lingered, contemplating whether it was too early to retire for the evening. Ignore her while she was there, but leave too soon and she would be reprimanded. The curtains swelled in the night breeze as the red glint of a jewel caught her eye. She reached up to slide the ring off Apollo's finger and stepped behind curtain.

She knew this ring well, had sold her hair to pay for it when she was a young girl. She held it in the palm of her hand staring at it in disbelief. It could not be. The gladiator followed her behind the veil and grabbed her wrist, his grip powerful. She recoiled in pain but stood her ground. She needed to see his face. "Wait," she said urgently. She didn't want him to get into trouble.

"Guards!" Publius yelled, and Alba was knocked over as two Roman guards ran through the curtain, throttling the gladiator backward. "Take him to his cell! Are you all right?" He bent down and awkwardly helped her to her feet.

"I'm fine," she said. She shook her wrist, brushed with shimmering gold where it had been clutched. "Please," she said to the guards. "It's not his fault. I took this from him." She held out the ring, but her words fell on deaf ears. The gladiator jostled to free himself, but the guards restrained him, holding his arms behind his back. Before she could say more, the gladiator was heaved backward through the curtains and into the hallway.

Alba needed to see his face, to speak to him.

"What a spectacle!" Lentulus yelled, waving his hand in an attempt to shun it off as something comical. "He's quite new."

"And should be punished," Camilla hissed.

"He is going to Rome in the morning," Lentulus said. "Worth more when they arrive unmarked."

"If he returns, then," Camilla said.

Alba pushed past them, swatting the drapes out of her way as she dashed into the hallway. The gladiator was being taken down a dark, narrow set of stairs. With her heart beating against her chest, she followed. The light was so dim that she had to clutch the stone wall to make sure she did not miss a step.

"I wish to speak to that man," she said to the guards.

"You just did," one guard said.

"Alone, fucker," she said. She had learned a thing or two from Liana.

"To lay with him?" the guard asked.

Would that be considered normal? Did the noblewomen lay with the gladiators? "Yes," she said slowly. She needed to know if this feeling she had was true. The man could have found the ring or stolen it. Anticipation and nerves filled her. She needed to stay calm. It would be no use getting her hopes up, and yet she couldn't help it.

The guard grunted and nodded for her to follow. She had seen them watching the dancers; he would not be happy having to wait down here. The cool underbelly of the ludus would have been a nice reprieve from the sticky heat of the upstairs if not for the smell. Water trickled down the rock walls, and there were rows of cells, which caged the gladiators in for the evening. A foul odor emanated from one of the rooms where a man lay on a board. Alba couldn't tell if he was alive. Such a contrast to the festivities above her.

She waited outside the cell while the gladiator had his hands chained together by the guard.

"All yours," the guard said.

Alba started to pull the squeaky door shut, but the guard planted his foot to block it.

"If I have a problem, I'll scream," she said.

The guard raised his eyebrows to indicate that that wasn't why he wanted the door left open, but he moved his foot and she clanked it shut.

Ten

Alba took a breath to steady herself, leaving her hand for a moment resting on the latch. The gladiator sat calmly on a wooden board covered in grimy fur, his hands resting on his thighs, staring straight ahead. The room was lit by a single torch.

"May I . . . take off your mask?" she asked in nervous anticipation.

He didn't move, not one muscle. Fingers shaking, she stooped down to lift the mask from his face and gasped. She knew his face well. It was weathered from the sun, but his nose was flat like an arrow and his eyes were as blue as the sky on a cloudless day.

Her heart thumped against her chest as her fingers fumbled to untie her own mask. She bowed her head and shook it off. He glanced at her, startled by her spastic movements, and she saw in his eyes the moment he knew her.

"Alba," he whispered.

"Max," she breathed, sitting next to him. She reached across his broad shoulders and hugged him. He nuzzled his chin into her neck, the stubble from his cheeks scratching her soft skin.

"We thought you were dead," he said, lifting his head. His wild hair had been cropped close to his head.

She took a pin from her hair, and her braid drooped over her ear. "I was taken back to Rome," she said as she set to picking his lock. "What are you doing here?"

"Do you remember the discussion we had the day . . . the day you were taken."

She remembered it well. "You wanted to join the Roman legion, but Alex didn't want you to."

"We both joined. We were promised land after five years of service and the protection of our village. We got the first but not the latter so I deserted."

"Were you captured?" she said as the latch of his shackles popped and her braid came loose, falling down her back.

"Yes. Alex and I. We were forced to become gladiators."

"Is Alex here?" she said with hope rising within her.

"No." A muscle in his jaw twitched as he fought to get the words out. "He died in the arena . . . in the death pits."

She was sickened by the thought that she may have witnessed his death.

Max stood, teetering on the spot, and then he gouged his eyes with his thumbs. "Gah!" he let out, and slammed his fist into the wall over and over.

"Max, stop." She stood and grabbed his arm.

Gold glitter and blood glazed the rocks. He held his mangled fist in his hand.

"I couldn't save him," he said.

"It's not your fault."

She wanted to ask him about Neme and what had happened that night but didn't have the heart. The pain in his face was too much.

Muffled footsteps sounded on the other side of the door. Max held his finger to his lips and pushed his hips into the wooden board, rhythmically slamming it against the wall. He made a moaning, grunting noise and motioned for Alba to do the same. Not having actually lain with a man, she made the loud screeching noise her aunt sometimes made.

After a few moments, she went over to the door and peered through the crack. "He's gone," she whispered.

"What were those noises?" he asked.

She shrugged. "I've never been with a man, but that's what my aunt sounds like."

"That's unfortunate."

"Max," she said. "You cannot go to Rome. That road will lead only to death. All who enter the arena are doomed eventually."

"I do not go to fight," he said, his voice so soft she leaned in closer to hear. "There is talk of a revolt, led by the slaves."

"In Rome? It's not possible. Who would lead such a thing?"

"Spartacus."

Alba shook her head in dismay. In this wretched place, Max had lost his senses. There was no way that the slaves could escape. They were under constant watch and heavily guarded. It would be impossible to organize, especially by a man who was already captured. No one in their right mind would attempt it.

"Are you finished?" the guard yelled through the door, startling Alba. She secured the chains back onto Max's wrists.

"Tighter," he said. "He'll take them off once you leave." He glanced at her and then wiped a tear from her cheek with his thumb. "You can't let them see." He gently clutched the side of her neck, the metal chain cool on her skin. "I'm nothing to you."

She nodded. She wanted to leave him with parting words of hope but didn't know what to say. Not with so many conflicting emotions inside her. Instead, she held his ring out, but he shook his head.

"You keep it. It'll be safe with you."

The guard left her at the top of the stairs. The atrium beyond the dimly lit corridor was no longer boisterous and the drunken laughter had dwindled.

Licinius Crassus came out into the hallway, staggering while he did up his robes, his chest glistening with sweat and a childish smirk on his lips. Alba shrunk behind a column. When his footsteps vanished, she started down the hall again. The same door opened and Liana came out.

"*You*," Liana slurred, sending chills down Alba, "were of absolute no help tonight."

"There is still time," Alba said as her aunt grabbed her arm. "Many people are staying on for a couple of days."

Liana scoffed. "The fault is mine," she said. "For thinking you capable of such a simple fucking task."

Alba stared into her aunt's eyes. "Why do you dislike me so?"

"A mother only wants what is best for her daughter," she said.

What kind of answer was that?

"And now you've gone and fucked a gladiator," Liana said. "What did I do in my life to deserve you? Where did I go wrong?" She threw her hands up. "Why did you have to come back?"

"I wish I had never been brought back," Alba spat. She would not stand here and take this abuse. Alba turned, momentarily disoriented in the dark. What side of the ludus was she on? She needed to get to the balcony where there was fresh air. But before she could figure out which way it was, she was yanked back by her hair.

"You ungrateful little fuck," Liana said, fingers tangled in Alba's long locks. There was a flash of metal and a slice as her head became lighter. Liana was holding up Alba's hair as a gladiator would their sword after defeating an opponent in the arena, a triumphant smile on her face.

Eleven

When Alba woke the next morning, her dress from the night before was bunched around her waist, a bar of light across her eyes. Squinting, she sat up, and her hair fell to her ears.

So, it wasn't a dream.

Voices drifted down the hall. She followed them to the terrace that jutted out over the training courtyard where a dozen gladiators stood shoulder to shoulder as a heavyset man inspected them. Lentulus was observing the process from above, Camilla seated at his side. He had to lean on the railing for support, the task tediously early for him.

Max stared ahead as his body was poked and prodded, his hands bound in front of him. He must have sensed movement on the terrace because his eyes rose to Alba's, sharpening in concern at the sight of her hair.

He spread his legs for the portly man.

"What happened to your hair?" Camilla said, not with empathy but savage curiosity.

"Becoming, isn't it?" Liana said, joining them on the terrace, her face pale from lack of sleep.

Camilla smirked. "It's heinous."

"The Thracian is good," the man called up, moving on to the next gladiator.

"Thracian?" Liana perked up. "What is his name?"

Alba's heart dropped. As a child, she had talked in her sleep. She knew this because Pomona often asked her who Neme, Alex, and Max were.

"Max, for now," Lentulus said. "Have you heard of him?"

"I have." There was an unsettling glint in Liana's eye.

Fear and dread filled Alba. "Careful." Alba turned to her aunt, her voice low. "I know about Licinius."

Her aunt froze, recalculating.

"Don't we all," Camilla said, standing. "I could hear you screeching down the hall."

Liana's face tinged with color. Camilla brought out the very worst in her sister. This place, with its cascading flowers and lush gardens, colorful birds and vibrant mosaics was poisonous.

"Liana, we need to leave," Alba said, for her aunt's sake as much as her own.

"Don't speak to me," Liana said slowly, pushing Alba backward until she was arched uncomfortably over the railing.

"Leave her alone, you cunt." Max's voice was a deep rumble from the courtyard.

Liana twitched as though she had been slapped, and a wave of heat came over Alba as panic filled her.

"How dare you!" Camilla yelled down to him.

Liana held her hand up. "I will speak to him."

"Liana, what are you doing?" Lentulus said warily.

"Just checking on my investment," she said, slipping by him.

Alba tried to follow her, but Lentulus blocked her path.

Pomona and her cousins came out of their rooms blurry-eyed and watched with disinterest as Liana approached Max. He flexed his broad shoulders before the guards forced him to kneel. After stopping in front of him, Liana leaned down to whisper something in his ear.

"Let me pass," she said to Lentulus, her eyes on Max.

Liana reached into her pocket and there was a glint of metal.

"Liana, no!" Alba screamed.

Liana slit his throat.

Max looked up at Alba as blood cascaded down his neck. He fell forward and lay motionless in the sand.

"You can take him from the money you owe me," Liana called up to them.

Alba was light-headed and dizzy. She clutched the railing, memories of her childhood dashing through her mind. His large and patient hands teaching her how to identify plants and spear a fish, the concern on his face when he thought he'd lost her in the market. It was he who decided she could stay with the family.

Someone took her by the arm, and Alba swung around, her hand raised in anger, but on seeing them, she let it fall.

"Come," Cloe said. "Come." Her grasp was firm, but her voice was kind as she led Alba back to the converted storeroom.

Once inside, Alba convulsed and vomited into her washbasin. Her breath was short and shallow, her back and neck damp. As her heart fluttered, a pain pierced through her ribs and she pressed her hand down on it.

Cloe stood helpless, unable to understand Alba's grief. "You knew him?" she asked.

Alba nodded, a tear rolling down her cheek.

Cloe took Alba's hands in hers. "I'm sorry for your loss." Her words were sincere, and this kindness startled Alba. Coming from this girl who barely knew her.

"Cloe." Quintus opened the door without knocking. "We're leaving."

Cloe squeezed her eyes shut, keeping her back to him.

"Now," he said, holding the door open.

Twelve

Two days and nights Alba lay in bed, oblivious to everything except her own thick thoughts. A tray of plums, raspberries, nuts, and cheese was delivered each morning, but she struggled to eat or drink. The room started to smell, the sweat and stagnation becoming rancid in the summer heat.

On the third day, a slave prodded her out of the room so that they could change the sheets. As Alba staggered out into the gardens, the sunlight overpowered her, and she ducked into a shaded corner where she found refuge on a bench. The gardens were in full bloom, the bees drinking from the sweet nectar, the colors bursting and vibrant. She had not spoken to anyone since the incident, and no one had tried to bring her out of her seclusion. Many of the guests had left, although some had lingered.

A towering figure eclipsed the sun. "May I sit with you?" Publius asked.

In a daze, she nodded.

"You are in lessened spirits of late," he said. When she didn't answer, he angled toward her. "I may be able to assist you."

"Assist me?" The words were a labor, thick and heavy in her mouth.

"It's my belief that you could serve a greater purpose than that of a priestess." He cleared his throat. "I cannot make you my wife . . . but you could live with me as my ward." It took her a moment to realize what he was saying. "Your mind is sharp and you could be an asset to me. Would you consider it? My father has given his consent."

Consider it? She struggled to piece what he was saying together.

"As a mistress?" she asked, her voice raspy from lack of use. She pictured Publius on top of her, covering her with his awkward, gangly limbs and walking through Marcus Crassus's massive villa in gorgeous silk dresses. Would she get along with Publius's wife?

"More or less," he said. "It would be a very pleasant life for you, I think."

She would be at the center of it all as their house was a mecca for many great events. But what would she have to sacrifice? What would he have her do? This made little sense to her. Just a short time ago he had been unable to take her to the games. What had changed his mind and that of his fathers?

"When must I decide?" she asked.

He placed his finger on the cleft of his chin. "Spartacus arrives tonight. We leave in the morning."

With that, he left her alone with her thoughts.

Spartacus. She thought back to Max's words and how absurd they had been. Not wanting to extinguish his hope, his dream of one day being free, she had said nothing.

The sun beat down on her as the shade slanted across the garden. She didn't move until Julius plopped down beside her, causing her to start. He set a tray of bread, figs, and olives down between them, turning the cup of water so the handle faced her.

"Do you ever feel like a pawn in a game against your control?" she said. "Nothing to win, nothing to lose, because you'll never make it to the other side of the board."

"That's very serious talk for so early in the evening," he said, playfully tapping her with his shoulder. "Eat," he urged. He lifted the tray and she took an olive.

"I'm afraid I'm not at my best," she said, putting the olive in her mouth and then placing her hands on either side of her. The gold glitter was still smeared on the inside of her wrist. The dress she'd worn for days had changed texture and stuck to her skin. She patted the uneven strands of her hair down, suddenly self-conscious of her appearance.

"If you are of a mind," Julius said, "may I ask for a character assessment?"

"On who?" She didn't know many people that well.

"Pomona. Does her personality make up for what she lacks in appearance?"

Alba contemplated whether to lie. "She is a simple girl," Alba finally said. "All but devoid of intelligence, wit, and imagination."

"I see . . . it is as I thought," he said.

"What are your thoughts on Publius?" she said.

"Man to man, I have little issue with him. Though sometimes tedious in conversation, he possesses an unparalleled ability for business, like his father. However, your interests may not entirely align with the family's and that's where you'll have to decide."

"What do you mean?"

He glanced over his shoulder and paused, debating whether to share further. "They are heavily involved in the slave trade and some . . . illicit activities."

"That's why they've stayed so long?"

"Yes, to learn from Lentulus and do what he does on a grander scale."

Lentulus had been quite boastful in his successes, showing off his gladiators in training for his guests, something he might soon regret.

"Now, with that being said, I'm the one who suggested you to him."

"Why?" Alba asked, surprised by this admission.

"Because I like talking to you and I enjoy seeing you at these events." He ripped off a hunk of bread. "But to give you fair warning. He is odd. He doesn't crave the touch of women . . . nor men for that matter. He has trouble laying with his wife, needs lots of assistance to get her pregnant, but he dotes on her and she loves him for it."

"You think I should accept him?" she said.

"Do what you want, but if you join the temple, you'll never leave it. It will be a very different life. A very secluded life." He stood. "Eat."

"I will," she said, but she sat so still after he left that the birds swooped in for the taking.

When the sun had left the courtyard, Alba went inside, every step taking more energy than she was willing to exert. She caught her reflection in the hall mirror. Her eyes had darkened and the messy short strands of her hair stuck out at different lengths. The tainted outcast, in body and spirit.

That evening, while lying on her newly made bed, there was a knock at the door. She was silent, hoping the person would leave, but the knock persisted.

"What?" she grumbled, turning her head as the door opened.

Blond curls appeared as Julius poked his head in. "Come with me," he said.

"Please, leave me alone."

"I will carry you."

"Where?" She was in no mind for games. When he continued to stand there, she stood and trailed behind him down the hallway until he stopped at an ornate door. The door to the baths.

She glanced at him. If anyone saw them go in together, she could get into a lot of trouble.

"They're all at the demonstration," he said, opening the door for her.

The door clanked shut and he threw the bolt across, locking it from within. Wafts of steam rose out of the freshly drawn bath. He lifted his silver tunic over his head, and she lowered her gaze as he stepped down into the dark water. He sank down until only his green eyes rested above the ripple, watching her.

Shyly, she took off her own robes and followed him in. He held the soap out to her but she didn't take it. She had no energy. He went around behind her, tilted her head back, and gently lathered her hair. Once he was done, he waded out and said, "There's a dress hung for you there." He pointed and took her old one with him.

She shut her eyes and leaned her head against the ledge.

Long after the steam had evaporated and her fingers pruned, she lifted a lilac-colored silk dress from the hook. It was the most beautiful dress she would ever wear.

In the years to come, things would be said about Julius Caesar, aspersions cast and judgments made, and perhaps some of them were true. But when she had been in one of her darkest moments, he was the one who brought her back to the light. His empathy and compassion saved her.

Because of him, she chose life.

The next morning the halls were filled with the sounds of scraping trunks as people were loading into their carriages. Alba put on her new dress and went down to the courtyard, where she made her way to Publius.

"Your offer is very kind . . ." she started to say.

"But you have chosen the priesthood," he finished for her.

She nodded. His involvement with the gladiators was too much for her, even if it was indirect. After all she'd seen here, she knew she'd never be able to stomach it.

Julius stepped into his carriage and she went over to his window. "Thank you. For everything."

"It was only a bath," he said, a twinkle in his eyes.

"Your wife is a lucky lady."

"I tell her that all the time," he said, and the twinkle faded. "Goodbye, Alba. It was a pleasure knowing you."

Thirteen

If Alba had thought that her life before Capua was trying, it was nothing compared to the cruelty that was to come on her return. Liana made sure Alba was isolated, banned from eating with the rest of the family or leaving the villa. After weeks of speaking to no one, it was beginning to wear on her mental state. She was counting down the days until the end of August when she could leave this place, a home she had once loved when her parents were alive. Though they did not always see eye to eye with each other, they had always made Alba feel very much a part of their world. No expense had been spared in her tutelage, and she was grateful now for all that she had learned at a young age.

Even Diana ignored her, doing only the bare minimum for her. With Alba's departure she would become a house slave, which meant her days would become much more grueling. She would be at the whim of every member of the household and their guests. It was not a fate Alba wanted for the girl, but she had no choice; if she stayed here, she would go mad.

Her uncle had been called to a senate meeting that would keep him away for the rest of the summer. When he said his goodbyes to Alba, it was as if she were going to the marketplace for an errand and not leaving them forever.

Two more weeks, she thought as she watched the sun drop toward the horizon.

Liana's wails woke Alba from her sleep.

"Fucking animals!" her aunt cried.

Alba had never heard her so incensed. Concerned for the slaves' well-being, she took the stairs quickly and ran down the hall to the entrance of the villa.

The slaves had shrunk to the outer walls, their eyes on the ground, desperate to avoid her aunt's wrath. A messenger slave stood in the entrance gates, and Liana was clutching a scroll, seething.

"Liana, what is it?" Alba said.

"Get out, get out of my sight!" she yelled at them all. She grabbed her whip from its mount on the wall, wielding it at the dark-skinned slave who had delivered the message.

"No, Liana!" Alba grabbed her aunt's arm. The slave was not theirs, and they had no right to punish him for delivering a message. "Let him go."

"How could . . . it makes no sense," Liana said.

"What makes no sense?" Alba asked. She looked at the scroll. In the flicker of torchlight she caught a large *B* on the seal. The House of Batiatus. Could it be that Spartacus had acted, that he had broken free from his chains?

Liana fell to her knees, dropping the whip beside her, and Alba used the moment to wave the messenger slave away.

Her aunt lifted her head to Alba, a pleading in her eyes. Without her wig or makeup, it was with a raw beauty that she gazed up at her niece. Her sharp eyes were serene, her lips a soft pink. It was the most vulnerable she'd ever allowed herself to be in front of Alba, a side to her Alba didn't know existed. Open and fragile. Yet the image of Max with his throat slashed sat in the forefront of Alba's mind. She could not provide her aunt comfort, not after what she had done. Alba turned and walked away.

There was a crack, followed by a searing pain down Alba's back. Fire and burning. She squealed in pain as tears filled her eyes.

Had Liana just whipped her? What the fuck?

Alba blinked away the tears blurring her vision and turned, the sides of her nightgown gaping from the ripped fabric. Her aunt stared back at her, her chest heaving, grasping the whip, ready to strike again.

Alba staggered backward, down the hall as a wave of nausea overcame her. A figure emerged from the shadows and Diana took her hand. She led Alba to the back of the villa. The slaves' quarters.

"Lie on your stomach." Diana ripped the rest of Alba's dress open and made up an ointment. She dabbed at her back as Alba gripped the boards of the bed, trying to stop herself from squirming. She did not know physical pain could be so intense.

"It's her sister," Diana's roommate said, coming into the room. "The gladiators slaughtered the entire house, led by Spartacus."

"Even the girls?" Alba asked.

"Everyone."

Alba squeezed her eyes shut. "I'm glad."

"That they died?" Diana asked.

"That the slaves escaped."

"She opened you right to the bone," Diana said. "It'll leave a nasty scar, I'm afraid."

Alba thought of the twins, of Camilla and Lentulus, and the shock they must have had as their gladiators turned on them and set about their escape.

Alba woke after a restless sleep. The burning pain had subsided, but her back was tender to the touch. She waited for Liana's clicking footsteps to pass before heading down to the dining hall. The family's meal hadn't been cleared away yet so she picked the boards clean. She had no appetite but knew she must eat if she was to face her aunt's wrath. She pressed the food to her lips and forced herself to swallow.

"There you are," Pomona said, skulking into the room. She hadn't spoken to Alba since Capua. Not one to offer sympathy, Alba wondered what she wanted. "I dreamed of Spartacus last night."

"What?" Alba said only because it was such an odd statement, but Pomona took the question and carried on.

"I was wearing the dress Julius gave you." Pomona held her hands up as if envisioning it. "And taken down to his cell."

As in, the man who had just killed her cousins, the ones she had been laughing with a short time ago. This was the most candid Pomona had ever been with Alba—and the least Alba had ever wanted to hear it.

"He held me up against the wall, his muscles toned to perfection, and ravished me."

Alba gripped the arms of her chair. "Pomona, please—"

"If you'd but seen him soar through the air during the demonstration." Pomona reached for Alba's arm but she pulled it away. "When he took off his mask, his face was chiseled, yet soft, his eyes the most brilliant blue." She shuddered. "And in my dream his cock was—"

"Pomona!" Alba's sharpness broke her cousin's trance. "Please, keep your thoughts and your dreams to yourself for I do not wish to hear them."

Pomona's face dropped. "If I arrange for you to be taken to the temple today, will you give me the dress Julius gave you?"

"Yes," Alba said. Anything to get out of this house.

Liana swept into the room, and Alba straightened, careful not to rub her back against the chair. Her aunt's face was puffy, and large, dark bags were under her eyes. "You can accompany her there, darling daughter."

"But it's a day's journey," Pomona said.

"Well then, better get started," Liana said. "And Alba will wear the dress there, for I never wish to see her or it again."

. . .

Alba

The temple was a ways outside of town, built on the top of a hill. Pomona didn't speak to Alba for the entire journey. It was a funny thing, Alba's last moments with her cousin, realizing how little she cared for the girl. Five whole years they'd spent together with no kinship developed between them.

At the entrance to the temple no one greeted them but the gates were wide open. The carriage stopped just inside, and Alba waited, unsure of the usual etiquette. A toothless man opened the door with a sinister smile. "Where are the priests?" Alba asked warily.

"No priests here tonight, I'm afraid," he said, before lunging his arm in and dragging Alba from the carriage.

Another man reached for Pomona. "There must be a misunderstanding," Pomona said, trying to push him away as he bound her hands. "I'm not here to stay."

"Oh, neither are we," the man said, wrapping a cloth around her mouth, muffling Pomona's screams. "Shut up!" He pushed her so hard she fell to the ground.

More men appeared, two carrying the chest of offerings between them. "You don't think it's a bad omen, do you, taking from the Gods?"

"Our lives are bad omens," the toothless man said.

Several thoughts dashed through Alba's mind. If not for her cousin, she would have tried to run, but men were all around them now and her delay had cost her. She was blindfolded and a cloth wrapped around her mouth.

"Round up the others," a man called. "Let's go."

They were forced to walk down the hill, over roots, rocks, and dirt. Alba's feet slipped in and out of her sandals, her soles growing raw and tender. Her dress was weighed down as they trudged through water and mud, the smell of sap and pine enveloping them. Her body grew shaky with exertion and adrenaline. Pomona was crying so hard they had to take the gag out of her mouth. "Please, please," she muttered, and the smell of urine drifted toward Alba.

They were brought to a halt and a voice called from above them. "How many?"

"Eight prisoners. Tell Spartacus we have arrived."

Spartacus.

"He isn't here."

"Crixus then."

There was a groan of metal, the opening of a gate, and the texture beneath her feet changed to a soft, fine sand. Alba was pushed to the ground and her hands lifted and chained above her. Pressing her head against the wall behind her, she shimmied the blindfold and gag down to her neck. Eight of them had been chained to a stone wall on the side of a large building. Around the corner was the glow of torches and many voices.

"What are they going to do to us?" A noblewoman cradled her head in her hands. One of the rebel men unhooked her chains. "Please," she gasped. "My husband will pay you whatever you want."

The man didn't flinch. He didn't speak her language.

Tears streamed down Pomona's long face, pale with terror. "I shouldn't have had to come with you," she said to Alba.

Alba bent toward her cousin. "Can you reach my head?"

"No," Pomona said, rigid.

"Try, for God's sake." Alba held her head at an uncomfortably awkward angle until she felt Pomona's fingers in her hair. "Now, slide my pin out. Careful," Alba said. "Stick it in that little hole at the top of your lock. Do you have the strength to run?"

"Where?"

"Into the forest, follow the stream back—"

A bald man with brown teeth stood in front of them with a sneer. "Going somewhere?" he asked as he unchained them.

Alba rolled her shoulders back as they were released from their burden. She and Pomona were taken toward the glow of torches. Rebel men and women stood on the steps, overlooking a large courtyard. Alba kept her head down, not wanting to see the hatred in their eyes.

Her lilac dress shimmered in the moonlight, a stark contrast to their dull-colored clothes.

Pomona's legs quivered as the toothless man removed her necklace and bracelets. Alba wore only the ring with the serpent on her middle finger, which had swelled as the heat in her body rose. He wrenched it over her knuckle, taking with it a layer of skin.

Rusty weapons were at the base of the stairs. A sword, shield, ax, hammer, spear, and dagger. Alba was pushed toward them.

"Pick one." The man slid the ring onto his baby finger.

"For what purpose?" Alba asked.

"To fight him." He nodded at one of the rebels, a mountain of a man. Germanic by the looks of him.

Pomona picked up a tall shield. "I can't," she said, leaning on it.

Alba reached for the ax, the weight of it steadying her trembling hand.

"The first female to choose death by ax," the toothless man said, intrigued by her choice, before poking a collapsing Pomona in the ribs with the hilt of his dagger. "Stand up." He sniffed. "Did you wet yourself?" He grimaced in disgust.

Alba stepped forward and, in doing so, offered herself to go first. She knew that she represented everything they hated, the suppressor, the enemy. She was an outlet through which they could channel their aggression, vengeance, and retribution. With their lust for violence, these people had a shared passion with the Romans. But the rebels did not yell as the Roman spectators did during the games. Instead, they watched her silently, their gazes unflinching.

Alba walked to the far side of the courtyard, taking strength with every step. She pressed her finger against the blade—rusty but not dull—and a calm came over her. Everything went still. She took a breath and gripped the shaft. "Give me strength," she whispered.

"A noblewoman going up against the mountain!" the man with the brown teeth yelled to the crowd.

They let out a cheer as the gigantic man stepped down into the courtyard, an excited glint in his eye as he thumped his fist against his bare chest. Were she to somehow kill him, she knew his death would only delay her fate.

"If I win," Alba yelled, "will you let her go?" She pointed her ax at her cousin.

"When you lose, you can watch her die," a dark man in the middle of the crowd said, his voice deep and raspy. Hatred swirled in his eyes.

Alba tried to meet her cousin's eyes. She wanted to communicate some sort of final peace, but her cousin wouldn't look at her. Alba searched her mind for a fond memory of Pomona. It would not do. There was none. But she could not let her die alone, in combat, terrified.

The mountain man dashed toward her and she raised her ax over her head. She took aim and, with her whole body, sent the ax wailing through the air. There was a flicker of fear in the mountain man's eyes, but the ax landed square in Pomona's chest. Her cousin staggered backward and crumpled to the ground. She gurgled blood, her body convulsed, and then she went still. The rebels broke into a murmur, trying to comprehend what had just happened.

The dark man held his hand up. He took Pomona's shield and came toward Alba. Though not a tall man, he had a deep chest and legs like tree trunks. The energy that had pulsed through Alba upon gripping the ax seeped from her veins, and without any way to defend herself, she dropped to her knees. He stopped in front of her, raised the shield, and then brought it smashing across her face. Her body was rocked to the side, her head on fire, but she stayed upright. She hoped that he would hit her hard enough to end her life. Through black dots, she saw him raise the shield again.

"Stop!" a man roared, jumping between them, his body blocking the force of the blow.

Nauseous and dizzy, she fell onto the sand. Voices yelled from above her, but she couldn't make them out. Darkness enclosed her, and she was lifted from the ground in gentle arms, soft like leather. Clear blue eyes absorbed her.

"Max?" she whispered, and her head rolled back.

Fourteen

A damp cloth pressed against Alba's forehead as she slowly came to, fighting through the dense fog in her head. She was lying on something hard but not uncomfortable. Her tongue was heavy and her mouth dry.

She blinked the room into view. By the architecture, statues, and space between the columns, it seemed that she was in a rather large temple. A few feet away, a man was being tended to by a plump woman.

"Where?" Alba cleared her raspy throat. "Am I?"

"The medicus," the woman said, moving around to Alba. "You've been asleep for quite some time." She held Alba's head up. "Drink." The broth was warm, and as it soothed her dry mouth, flashes of memory came back to her. She'd been hit in the face with a shield, fallen back onto the sand, and lifted by strong arms while absorbing blue eyes took her in. But whose eyes were they?

Oh, and she had killed her cousin.

She was relieved to see that she was fully clothed and felt no discomfort down there. "Who brought me here?" Alba asked.

"Our glorious leader, Spartacus."

Spartacus. That didn't sound good.

"What does he want with me?"

"Didn't say, just that I was to keep you alive. Never seen him so serious and he's quite a solemn man." The woman shuffled over to a man lying a few beds over.

After putting the bowl on the table beside her, Alba sat up slowly, dizzy and sore, resting her hands on either side of her. The woman didn't say anything when Alba stood so she made her way to the stairs. Each step took a feat of strength as her legs trembled beneath her weight, and at the top, she shielded her eyes against the sunlight slicing through the columns. It was early evening. Rebels were everywhere, each preoccupied with a task, moving furniture, baskets of cloth, making the space their own. The hallway was being used to sort weapons and food. The rebels' glances were not welcoming, but they didn't stop her as she walked through them.

From the courtyard there were grunts of exertion and thwacks of wood clashing. It was a much different scene from the night when she'd stood on its sand alone. The men and women were engaged in conversation, some holding wooden swords and shields, practicing their footing and movements.

Men were perched on the outer wall keeping watch, and halfway up the wall was a platform. Skirting the trainees, Alba made her way to the ladder. She had just placed her hand on a wrung when a voice said, "You know you can't leave."

She stiffened. She knew it had all been too easy. "Why not?" she asked, turning.

"Spartacus's orders." He was a slight man, only a few inches taller than Alba. His skin was chestnut brown, his hair a gleaming black and pulled back out of his face. The sliver of a scar cut through his eyebrow. "Where did you learn how to throw an ax like that?" he asked.

"From a Thracian."

"It was a good shot."

"It was lucky."

He raised his scarred eyebrow.

"What does Spartacus intend to do with me?" she asked. "My family won't pay to take me back . . . or does he have other desires?"

"I've only known the man a short time. But I've never seen him lift his hand against a woman. He may wish to question you?" He nodded at the others. "Many of us are curious to know why he intervened. Doesn't often do that with Crixus."

Crixus. The stocky, dark man with the shield.

"Open the gate!" one of the men called from above.

The trainees stopped practicing, and people swelled into the courtyard from the inner temple. A group of powerfully built men wearing armor came in carrying weapons and a trunk bearing the Roman mark. "Gifts from Rome." One of the men dropped the chest with a clunk. His chest was splattered with blood and dirt, his hair shorn close to his head.

Alba shrunk back away from the gathering crowd.

"Alba," a deep voice called out to her, cutting through the air.

How did this person know her name? She turned as a tall man broke away from the group, muscular and broad. There was a scar across his left shoulder. His eyes were clear and blue.

It could not be. *Alex.*

"Spartacus," Crixus said, his face like thunder. He gripped his sword, eying Alba.

"If anyone, man or woman, touches her," Alex yelled into the crowd, "I will part their head from their neck." He used his sword to demonstrate the gesture.

Crixus grunted.

"Anyone, brother," Alex said. "Leave her be."

What a decree.

"Recruits from Neapolis!" a man called from the wall.

Alex glanced at the man and brought his hand up to the back of his neck. He seemed to struggle with himself for a moment. Then he said, "The women sleep through there." He nodded toward two large columns and started back toward the entrance gate.

That was it? That was all he had to say to her after all this time. "Did Neme die that day?" she asked, needing to know.

"Yes." He paused and turned. "As did Saul."

"You killed him?"

"No, the Romans did." As he spoke, his eyes would not hold hers.

And that was it. That was all he had to say to her.

She went to the edge of the corridor where swords were being sorted into piles for sharpening and watched as Alex inspected the new recruits. He had grown taller than his older brother and his voice carried in a natural bellow. "You are free to choose," he said to them. "Stand with us against the Romans or be on your way."

None of them moved, man or woman. At that, Alex was joined by Crixus and another man, and the trio disappeared up the stairs to the second floor. This was not the same boy she had known in her youth. This was not Alex. There was none of the warmth in his eyes, nor the kindness in his gestures. He had turned into this... this Spartacus. The same man she had seen calm and calculated in the arena as he cut down his opponents.

Off the side corridor, there was a room where the women slept in rows. They wore earth-colored dresses, simple braids and knots in their hair. There was a couple of dozen of them, and they seemed quite comfortable together. The male rebels might chide them and drape their arms around them in the public spaces, but they did not come into this area. It was their haven.

Alba sat at the end of one row in an empty spot.

"Natalie?" one of the women said, surprise in her voice.

Alba glanced behind her. At the far side of the room was a very pretty girl around Alba's age, wearing a rust-colored dress that complemented her dark hair and eyes. She placed a bow and a dagger beside a fur bed.

"What the fuck is she doing here?" Natalie nodded at Alba.

Alba hunched, hoping that they would ignore her. Thankfully the other woman just shrugged. Natalie spun on her heel and left the room.

That night Alba couldn't sleep, the fur beneath her too thin to act as cushion against the marble ground. She would need to find a pallet. New noises and smells washed over her, and she kept twitching awake until finally she sat up, agitated. After all these years, that was how he greeted her. No asking after her life since they'd parted, no talk of that day beside the river. And even now, once things had died down, he hadn't sought her out.

The temple was quiet, a contrast to the hustle and bustle during the day. The rebels slept clutching their weapons, some slumped against columns. She went up the stairs she'd seen Spartacus ascend earlier. A man shut the door behind him as he came out into the hallway. He stopped to look Alba up and down. He was one of the three that had joined Spartacus earlier. He was tall like Spartacus, but his muscular shoulders were rounded and he had a long face.

As she continued forward, he moved in front of her.

"I wish to speak to Spartacus."

"He's not here," he said.

"I don't believe you."

"Well, believe me when I tell you, you will not pass." He widened his stance and planted himself in a way that indicated he would restrain her if she tried.

She wanted to yell out Spartacus's name, but instead, she turned and went back down the stairs.

Fifteen

The rebels' morning started at sunrise. After finding a pallet, Alba rummaged through one of the clothing baskets and found a simple tanned dress. Porridge was scooped into bowls and milk added from two cows. Some trained in the courtyard while others cut and seasoned hunks of meat, distributed weapons, and sorted barrels of drink. Everyone in motion, everyone with a purpose except her. The gladiators came and went, craftily dressed as unassuming villagers or Roman soldiers. But there was no sign of Spartacus.

Her body was stiff and sore on the side where it had been struck. Her middle finger was purple and she was unable to bend it, and she had to sit in a certain way or her stitches pulled. To distract herself from the discomfort, she observed what went on around her, finding patterns in the flow of it all.

Those who had a *B* burned into their forearms were the gladiators from the House of Batiatus, and they oversaw the training of the new recruits. When they left the temple, they'd cover the mark with thick leather bracelets. Most of the new slaves had never held a sword, but they were strong from physical labor and eager to learn.

Alba's attention fell on the man with the rounded shoulders who had stopped her the night before. He was leaning against a column surveying the recruits. As he took a sip from his cup, Alba noticed a shiny *B* burned into his forearm.

"How do they look, Hadrian?" one of the men asked him.

"They're going to need work," he said, just as the dark-skinned man who had warned Alba from leaving the day before—Namir, she'd learned—lost his balance and slid in the sand. "A lot of work."

The women trained too, mainly with each other, except for a dark woman who trained with Crixus, swinging at him again and again with unrelenting tenacity.

"Crixus, Hadrian," one of the men called. "Spartacus craves a word."

So he was around. This only added to Alba's annoyance.

A fight broke out between a Gaul and a Syrian as the two men reached the top step. Hadrian rumbled in frustration then turned to tear them apart, slamming them both to the ground. Alba was in awe at the difference in skill between the trained gladiators and the new recruits. He said a few words of warning before leaving them coated with sand.

The woman who had been training with Crixus reached for a glass on the ledge, but it was too far in. Alba was closer and picked it up for her. The woman spat into the sand and turned away from Alba.

That night Alba woke in a sweat. If she'd been dreaming she couldn't recall it, but something had unsettled her. Her stomach and chest were damp. She sat up, holding the back of her neck for a moment before standing. The marble cooled her feet as she stepped around the women.

The training area was lit by moonlight, and on the wall Spartacus and Hadrian sat in deep discussion. Spartacus's gaze lifted over Hadrian's shoulder to Alba. She swayed on the balls of her feet. Why was she nervous? She swallowed and made her way over to the ladder. As she climbed Hadrian jumped down onto the crate beside her.

"You don't have to go," she said.

"Oh, but I want to," Hadrian said, slipping by her.

"Here." Spartacus reached down. She hesitated before raising her hand to his. He grasped her forearm and effortlessly pulled her up in one swift movement. She sat next to him and he rested his forearms on his knees. "How's your face?" he asked.

"It hurts."

He glanced at the dense forest. Was that guilt in his eyes? "It'll heal. All wounds do."

Perhaps not, she thought and said, "Some faster than others."

"Did you sell your hair again?"

"No. My aunt cut it off."

There was concern in his eyes but it was gone in a flicker. In the silence that followed, her shoulders stiffened and she felt the stitches pull. "How long must I stay here?" she asked.

His eyes drifted over her, not settling on hers. "You're not being held captive. Anyone can come and go as they please."

What a hollow answer. Where was the kindness she remembered from her childhood? Where was the boy that would chase her through the forest, swim with her for as long as she wanted, and lie next to her when she had had a nightmare? He wouldn't even look at her now. She wanted to grab him by the shoulders and shake him. She had hoped to tell him about Max, but she couldn't, not like this.

She swung her legs over the wall, and when he tried to offer her a hand, she swatted it away.

"You're mad," he said.

"Yes."

"Why?"

"Because you're an ass," she snapped. "Ever since I was taken back to Rome, all I wanted, more than anything, was to see you and Max and Neme again. Yet now that I've found you, I wish I hadn't. You are not the boy I knew."

He looked as though she'd slapped him, the hurt in his eyes palpable. She clumsily made her way down the ladder, slipping on a rung and falling to her bum. She rubbed it in frustration.

Hadrian grinned smugly as she passed him. "Fuck you," she said, anger boiling within her.

He grabbed her arm and whipped her around.

"Hadrian," Spartacus said, his voice sharp. "Let her go."

Hadrian held her for a tense moment before he released her forearm. It was white from where he had clutched it.

She went downstairs, through the medicus, and passed a room lined with tombs. At a small nook at the back, she knelt at the feet of Zeus and prayed. When her mother had been at odds with her father, she had often gone to temple, sometimes taking Alba with her. Kneeling at the feet of the Gods, she would sort through her troubles and emerge more at ease. Alba's angry chest heaved and she shut her eyes, calming herself. A wave of comfort came over her as she thought of those tender, quiet moments with her mother.

The rebels had risen when she came back up, and Spartacus and Hadrian were no longer on the wall. The sun shimmered across the temple's marbled floors as the sun broke the horizon.

It was beautiful.

"You're still here?" Namir said, not unkindly. His black hair was pulled back in a ponytail and dark scabs lined his knuckles.

"And where would I go?" she said with an edge.

"I was like you when I first came," he said. "Angry and vengeful. Tried to take the life of Spartacus."

"What?" Alba said, shocked. "Why?"

"I liked my master and had recently become the head servant," he said. "Now I realize that he was just a manipulative, salacious prick."

"What did Spartacus do when you tried to kill him?"

"He spared me and said that he understood my anger. Many disapproved of his actions." He bent down and picked up a wooden sword. "I know what it's like to be treated as an outsider. The color of my skin does not go unnoticed. I've always had to work harder." He passed the sword to her.

"I'm not much of a fighter," she said.

"I'd beg to differ." He tilted his head toward her.

The training area wasn't busy as groups prepared to hunt. Namir showed Alba how to stand and hold her sword. Natalie was at the other end with some of the rebel women. Alba found herself distracted, in awe not only of Natalie's athletic prowess and ability, but of her confidence and helpfulness to the others.

Namir noticed Alba watching her. "That's Natalie," he said. "A formidable opponent even for a woman, trained by Spartacus himself."

"Trained by Spartacus?" Alba said. "Are they close?"

"Yes, but rumors are they haven't shared a bed since the night of your arrival."

Alba wondered why that was. She wet her hair back trying to keep it out of her face, but in the midday sun it didn't stay long.

"Be mindful of your distance from your opponent," Namir said, pointing at her feet. He showed her how to hold the wooden sword and how to block an oncoming blow. After a bit her agitated back grew tender as her stitches pulled her skin with every movement.

"More later," she said as the hunting party gathered. "I really do appreciate it." What she appreciated even more was having someone to talk to. She rested the wooden sword against the wall.

"Do you fear him?" Namir asked her.

"Who?"

"Spartacus."

She was taken aback. "No."

"Then why do you avoid him?" Namir asked as they climbed the courtyard steps. "You slip away when he nears."

She did not. Namir lifted a large, flat cooking stone onto the fire's grate. The ax Alba had used to kill Pomona was leaning against nearby wall—the blood wiped clean.

"What happened the night I was brought here, after I passed out of consciousness?" Alba asked.

"Spartacus lifted you from the sand and carried you down to the medicus." He cracked a few eggs onto the stone's surface. "He said that none were to touch you."

"And my cousin?"

"The other girl? Her body was buried." He gave her a sidelong look. "You're not upset?"

"We were not close."

"Yet you killed her to spare her a torturous death."

"Out of pity, not kindness," she said.

"You should talk to Spartacus."

Easier said than done.

Sixteen

Slaves along the countryside heard whispers of the rebels' whereabouts and left their masters' fields to join them. As new slaves trickled in every day, Hadrian and Crixus divided them into groups to oversee their training. Gladiators went on raids to nearby towns and against Roman convoys. Spartacus questioned their movements and discretion on their return in order to ensure they hadn't exposed themselves or their location. Provisions were collected and inventoried and organized under Spartacus's orders. Hunters set out at dawn, returning with game for the group. Everything was done as a collective.

Guards patrolled the villa's walls night and day, and new recruits sought to prove themselves with wooden swords and shields. Every hunting party, every raid, every change of the guards was overseen by Spartacus. His decision was law with Crixus and Hadrian overseeing their execution. He often sat huddled with one or the other in deep discussion.

Crixus was never far from Junia, teaching her to fight, sharing his meals with her. Spartacus often ate with Hadrian atop the wall or leaning against columns. In Hadrian's presence he was at ease and even jovial at times. What the fuck did they laugh about together? At times

Alba felt Spartacus's eyes on her, but when she glanced at him, he'd be engaged in something else.

As the days passed, the swelling in her face subsided and the gash in her cheek closed, making it easier to eat. Her back however became so itchy and tender she couldn't move quickly in fear of agitating it.

In these long days of isolation, she found comfort in prayer. The rebels passing by on their way to the storeroom would leave her be as she knelt before statues of the Gods. After her evening meal, which she ate alone or with Namir, she would go down to the underbelly of the temple and feel the cool stone beneath her knees.

One night, as she kneeled there, lost in thought, a deep voice startled her.

"Are you praying?" Spartacus said.

She rose her head. "Yes."

"Why?" There was a hint of mockery in his voice.

She drew her shoulders back and felt the stitches pull. "Because it brings me comfort."

"All those years in Thrace I never saw you pray."

"I had no need for it then."

"In life, we choose our outcome. The path we forge cannot be altered by inanimate objects."

She stood to face him. "Here in your temple, I am all but ignored. I find solace in prayer. Do not make fun of me for it."

"I apologize." He held his hands up and made to leave. "I didn't mean to offend."

She took a breath. "I'm also here to ask for forgiveness. For I harbor both guilt and shame." For the first time since her arrival, his eyes held hers and he perched on the base of a nearby statue. "The gladiator that died a few nights before your arrival back to the House of Batiatus." She lowered her eyes. "It was Max."

His hand twitched. "What?"

She told him the story of what had happened to his brother.

"Why didn't you stop her?" he said, referring to Liana.

"I had no idea she would do that."

His nostrils flared. He paced along the tombs and then bounded up the stairs two at a time. She stood conflicted. Should she try and comfort him?

Spartacus had stormed into the trainee area, his arrival scattering the novices to the edges. He picked up an ax and started to hack at a large tree stump. As Alba slowly approached, Hadrian turned on her. "What did you do? What did you say?"

"I . . ." She had trouble speaking and so she shook her head.

Hadrian and Crixus stood back and watched their friend with pain in their eyes, knowing that they couldn't help him. Alba could not bear to watch. She'd known her aunt to be cruel but didn't think her capable of taking life. If Alba had known, if she had one inkling, she wouldn't have stepped onto that balcony.

The thought of it now made her sick, and she turned away, from this image of unbearable grief. From this man that she wished she could embrace but didn't know how to.

That night, Alba was prodded from her sleep.

"You need to fix this," Hadrian said, standing over her.

"What?" she said in a groggy daze.

"He has not been himself since you came." He lifted her to her feet and pulled her down the hall.

"Let go of me." She ripped her arm from his grip, now fully awake. "I don't have to do anything."

He held his finger up to her face. "Everything was fine until you came."

"What would you have me do?"

"I would have you gone from our midst. I wish you had died that day in the sand."

"So do I!" she spat back. "I cannot bring him comfort or clear his mind any more than you can."

He stared at her for a moment before grabbing her arm again and dragging her up the stairs. Their ruckus caused Spartacus to come out into the hall. Hadrian pushed her forward. "I've had enough," he said. "You need to speak with her."

Spartacus glared at Hadrian. Natalie came out of his room and her face was dark with anger. The four of them stood there tensely, none of them looking at the other.

"Well?" Hadrian said. "Will you speak with her?"

Spartacus stood back and Alba walked past Natalie into his room. It was large and cozy with clean, shining furs and well-made furniture carved from rich oak. It was dimly lit by a few torches. His armor was neatly laid out on a table, along with his belt, while his sword and knife were on the ledge behind his bed. The bed linens were pulled up, and Alba noted two indents where people had been sitting.

"You've met Natalie?" he said, shutting the door.

"I have," Alba said. "She doesn't like me."

Spartacus ran his hand over his face. "You must know how difficult it is for them, you being Roman."

"I know what I represent to them," Alba said.

He sat in an indent and looked up at her. "I too have guilt that has been weighing on me." This surprised her. "The night you were taken, Max came to get me to bring me home, but I would not follow him."

"Because I kissed you," she said.

His brow furrowed. "What?"

"You were not happy that I kissed you."

"No," he said. "I was surprised when you did that. Shocked really."

"Then why did you not come home?"

"I was angry with Max for deciding to join the legion."

"If you hated the Romans, why did you go with him?" she asked.

"Neme was gone," he said simply. "Max never blamed me for what happened that night, and I do not blame you for his death now."

Alba could see the pain he bore in his confession, the way it lined his eyes as he spoke and made his words heavy. She wanted to put him at ease. "Neme would be proud of you and everything you have done for these people. Her strength of will lives on through you," she said. "We cannot live with this guilt, you and I. Let us move on. Let us be friends as we once were."

"Even if there are no remnants of the boy you once knew?" he said.

"We are both different. I will get to know you as you are now," she said. "You see . . . I had thought you dead, had already mourned your loss. And upon seeing you again, I had such a rush of happiness. But you were so cool toward me and I was hurt by that."

"Alba," he said weakly. "Seeing you brought me great joy."

"Really?" she said, unable to hide the relief in her voice. "Then let us start over." She held out her hand to recognize their new friendship.

He stood and took her hand in both of his.

On her way down the stairs, her step was lighter. She was glad to have had the conversation, to put these things behind her and start anew.

Seventeen

Alba kept tucking her hair behind her ears while training with Namir. They'd just started and already her back was on fire. Not a good sign. Spartacus stood on the steps calling out the daily tasks. Alba was concentrating on her foot movement when she heard, "Natalie, Alba, hunters."

Namir knocked Alba's sword out of her hand as her mouth dropped. She turned just in time to see Natalie roll her eyes at Junia.

"Am I being punished?" Alba said under her breath.

"It's not a punishment," Namir said. "It's a tactic he uses to bond people. He must want you two to be friends."

Alba scoffed. In what world would she and Natalie be friends? The woman had given her nothing but dirty looks and scowls since the day Alba had arrived.

As Alba joined the group of people readying to leave, Natalie said, "You'll need to change into something brown."

Alba didn't argue. She went into the women's area and pulled off her rust-colored dress.

There was a gasp from behind her. "Your backs infected," Natalie said.

"It's fine," Alba said, changing quickly.

"What's it from?"

"I don't wish to discuss it."

"Care to join us?" Natalie asked Junia.

Junia shook her head, and Alba noticed a tinge of annoyance cross Natalie's face as she put some string in her pouch.

"With any luck my snares have caught and we won't need to hunt," Natalie said.

Taking her first few steps out of the villa was strangely liberating. Alba glanced back at the guards sitting atop the walls as they made their way into the forest and broke off from the other groups. Natalie was at complete ease with nature, running her hands over the bark of trees lining what must have been a familiar path. Alba soon found herself easing into her surroundings too. The singing of the birds and the trickling of the streams reminded her of Thrace. After walking for a while in silence, Alba asked, "Were you part of the rebellion at the House of Batiatus?"

Natalie gave a slight nod.

"And Junia?"

"So *you* can ask questions?" Natalie said pointedly, over her shoulder.

Alba thought back to that night she was whipped, the pleading in her aunt's eyes, the anger and resentment. "My aunt lashed me because I would not comfort her at a time she needed it most."

Natalie stopped. "Why did you turn from her?"

"She killed my friend."

Natalie nodded slowly and kept walking. "Junia had been taken to another ludus shortly before the rebellion," she said. "It was the first place we stopped as Crixus would not be parted from her."

"He's devoted to her," Alba said.

"Yes, the mighty Crixus." Natalie's voice was flat. "He was once the champion of Capua. One of his rewards was Junia, who had not yet been plucked, and they fell in love."

Natalie bent down—her snare had caught a rabbit, and after unhooking it, she set up another one. Alba knelt beside her to see how it was done, not having made one in many years. Natalie's fine fingers threaded the knot, her hands steady. Her black hair was smooth and shiny, her eyes as dark as the earth, and her limbs long and muscled. She had delicate features.

"What about you?" Natalie brushed aside some leaves and shoved a stick into the ground. "Did you lay with Spartacus last night?"

"No," Alba said, affronted by her bluntness and added with a bit of reluctance. "I've . . . never been with a man."

Natalie's face softened. "Spartacus is a gifted lover. Unlike most men, he aims to please the woman."

Alba glanced away, unsure of what to say; never having had a female friend she didn't know what was usual banter.

"When Spartacus became arena champion, I was his reward," Natalie said, tying the string to form a noose. "But he refused to take me."

"Why would he refuse?" Alba asked.

"He said that he would not lie with a woman who was forced to do so." She stood, satisfied with her contraption. "I spent the night on his cell floor to avoid punishment. As you know, one cannot disobey orders from their master."

They continued on to another trap.

"Why did you decide to join him in the rebellion?" Alba said.

"He was kind to me and the other female slaves. He didn't see us as prizes. He was different from the other gladiators, finding no joy in his triumphs, just biding his time. You could see it in his eyes. Camilla and Lentulus couldn't figure him out."

On their way back Natalie picked some dark green leaves off a low bush and shoved them into her pouch. As they approached the gates, Natalie's purposeful gait slowed. "Who was Neme?" she asked.

"She was Spartacus's mother," Alba said, and Natalie stopped, realizing that Alba had known him for quite some time.

"And Saul?"

"He was a boy that lived not far from us. He was mean—the type of mean that seeps into your bones. He was responsible for Neme's death. He's the one that brought me back to the Romans."

Their conversation stalled then, each lost in her own thoughts. When they returned to the temple courtyard, it was to find Namir standing in front of a hanging deer, looking quite pleased with himself.

"Can you help me debone it?" he asked Natalie.

Natalie stabbed her knife into its chest, flecks of blood splattering their faces. "Follow it along the seam like this," she said, passing him back the knife. Then she motioned at Alba to follow her. Alba picked up the rabbits, assuming they were going to the kitchens, but instead Natalie led her to the medicus.

"Take off your dress," Natalie said, digging into the pouch at her side for the leaves she'd just picked.

Alba shook her head. Her back was quite agitated. She was nervous for anyone to touch it.

"Let me see it," Natalie said, her voice firm.

Alba lifted her dress, wincing as the material grazed the wound. Natalie took in the fading bruises on Alba's torso and put the leaves in a mortar. With a pestle she ground them into a paste. "Whoever stitched this did a terrible job," she said. "What ointment did they put on it?"

"I don't know." Perhaps Diana had never done it before.

"It's quite inflamed," Natalie said. "I'm going to cut the stiches out, drain the pus and spread this paste over it. It should help to ease the pain."

Alba lay down on the board, and Natalie pushed down on Alba's shoulder as she tugged at the string. Alba's feet flexed at the pain as she inhaled a sharp gasp.

When Natalie finished, she left without a word. Alba lay on her stomach, her cheeks wet. It was a while before she could move again. When she did stand, it was with a wave of relief. Her back wasn't agitated and she put her dress on without wincing.

Eighteen

Spartacus was standing by the far wall with Hadrian. The rebels trained harder when he was watching, guiding them through drills, correcting their grips and stances. His own movements were as sure and steady as the earth beneath his feet. He and Hadrian paired up to show them how to evade a blow, block a shot, and cut a man down quickly. It was a wonder that neither of them got hurt, the way they brought the swords down on each other. But as Alba watched, she realized how much fun they were having, this outlet of energy, the familiarity of each other's movements.

"If you drop your shoulder back as he advances," Spartacus told the recruits, "it will give them less body to hit."

Hadrian passed Spartacus half an apple on his knife.

"How are they so close?" Alba wondered aloud.

"Hadrian and Spartacus?" Namir said. "Their bond was forged in the sands of the arena. They were often paired together." He cleaned his dagger in the dirt. "Hadrian is not that bad once you get to know him—or rather, once he decides to like you."

Crixus stood on the other side of the courtyard. In Alba's opinion he seemed the least approachable of the three yet many of the men gravitated toward him. "But Hadrian doesn't get along well with Crixus?" she said.

"Not much gets by you. They don't seek each other out, no."

"Why is Spartacus their leader?"

"He gives the best speeches," Namir said, grinning. "No, he's the one who put it all in motion. He led the gladiators' escape from the ludus and out of the city with nothing but kitchen tools. Having served in the legion, he knows the Romans' formations and tactics. They say he can spot an ambush ages out. But what caused me to follow the man is his fairness to all who join him, no matter their background."

"So long as they're not Roman," Alba said.

With a tilt of his head, he said, "He let you stay."

The rebels broke for supper, leaning their wooden sticks against the wall. Spartacus sat on the steps, swiveling the tip of his sword into a block of wood, deep in thought. As she approached, his hands went still.

"Do you have any tips for me?" she asked, sitting next to him.

"You should aim for the stomach and armpits where there is a gap in the armor, especially when your opponent is tall." So he had been watching her. He placed his sword beside him. "How was the hunt with Natalie?"

"She caught two rabbits."

"Ah," he said. And she knew that wasn't what he meant.

"I like her."

His blue eyes smiled. "Good."

"Where's she from?"

"Her mother was from Asia. Her father she never knew."

Spartacus was called away then, and Alba went down the hall to get some water. From a side hallway, she heard hushed voices, male voices. Namir's and Hadrian's.

"She's not that bad," Namir was saying, and Alba knew that they were talking about her. "If you were but to give her a chance."

"She has done nothing but disturb," Hadrian said.

"You once disliked me," Namir said.

"Do not think that my mind is so far removed from the thought," Hadrian said.

There was a soft smack and the clanking of metal as a belt hit the floor. Alba cringed at the thought of her one friend with a man who loathed her.

In the night she was awoken by rustling whispers. Natalie stepped over her, hoisting a bag onto her shoulders with a bow and shiver fastened to it. The women on either side of Alba were rolling their furs and shoving their belongings into satchels. Was this when they usually traveled? Alba followed the people out into the courtyard where the rebels spoke in low murmurs and hand gestures to organize themselves. Spartacus cut through them and pulled her aside. "The Romans are coming. You can stay here and wait for them or come with us." He held her gaze waiting for her response.

She knew that if she did stay here she'd never see him again. She'd be sent back to the temple. There was only one answer she could live with. "I'll come with you," she said.

Relief passed over his face. "Stay near the middle with Natalie."

Alba hurried back to her room and found a discarded satchel, quickly stuffing her fur and a dress into it. She caught up to Natalie as their large group left the villa. Natalie gave Alba a sidelong look, and Alba couldn't tell if she was disappointed or annoyed. Their departure was swift with very little noise as they assembled themselves.

They walked and walked, and the satchel, which at first seemed light, now weighed on Alba's every step. She stared at her feet, willing herself forward. The gladiators stayed on the edges, spaced around the group, armed and alert. After what felt like hours, Natalie stopped so abruptly that Alba almost ran into her. Looking around her, she realized everyone had stopped. She started to ask Natalie if she had missed some signal but was interrupted by a man passing her rope and fabric.

Makeshift tents were being made all around her and she was still standing there clutching her rope.

Crixus's, Hadrian's, and Spartacus's tents were grouped together, and Natalie and Namir had left to collect kindling. Spartacus was organizing the gladiators on night watch, and she wasn't going to bother him. No, she'd sleep beneath the open sky, the late August nights being warm.

"Still here?" Hadrian said, coming over to her. "I thought you'd take off."

"Take off?" Alba said.

"You know, wander off into the woods, see where the night took you." He took the rope from her hand.

"What're you doing?"

"Helping you make your tent." He lassoed a tree and strung the rope through a few branches, using his long reach to tighten it. "This should be enough room." He draped the cloth over the sides.

"Thank you," she managed.

"Oh, but this is not for you." He raised his hands. "This is for Spartacus because as fate would have it, he holds you in affection. So never thank me. I don't do it for you."

"Noted," she mumbled. Namir passed by her with an armful of sticks, headed toward Hadrian's tent. "Of all the men, you choose him?"

"He has a kind heart once he allows himself to like a person," Namir said. "His brother was killed in the escape from the ludus. The memory is still near and I fear it fuels his anger."

Nineteen

The countryside was scattered with long, teetering shanties overflowing with slaves working their masters' fields. As word spread that the rebels were near, the workers dropped their spades and baskets, slipping into the forest or traversing the plains at night. Within days, their group had swelled with strong, able-bodied men and women.

A large, affluent villa had been scouted for their next temporary home. There were no towns nearby, and as they silently approached, voices and laughter floated over them. From within was a party in full swing. Many Roman nobles summered in this area and Alba feared that she'd know people inside. Though many of the noblemen had seen battle, they'd be well into their cups and no match for this throng of slaves, let alone the honed gladiators.

It would be a slaughter.

The rebels hid in the undergrowth at the forest's edge while Spartacus surveyed the surrounding area. Staying low, Natalie made her way through the people to the front. Not wanting to be left on her own, Alba reluctantly followed.

Spartacus's movements were swift, moving like a shadow in the night. "What are your thoughts?" Hadrian asked upon his return.

"If we are to stay here," Spartacus said, crouching between Crixus and Hadrian, "we have to ensure that no one gets out. Not one."

Crixus started to stand. "Let's be done with it."

"Not us," Spartacus said. "It's a good opportunity for the new recruits to put their swordsmanship to practice."

Crixus grunted in disappointment. He enjoyed taking Roman blood.

The rebels were divided into groups. Every doorway was covered with Spartacus and Hadrian joining the initial onslaught. The drunken laughter turned to screams as the Roman nobles poured out into the night, their robes billowing behind them as they ran into a forest full of gladiators. Alba pressed her hands over her ears, unable to listen to the cries of shock and panic right before each life was taken.

Once the yelling and the grunting subsided, she lowered her hands only to realize they were shaking. The forest emptied toward the large villa, and Alba approached slowly, careful not to glance down at the bodies around her. A mass of people clustered just beyond the entrance and Alba hesitated.

"Come," Namir said. "Watch the games with us."

She shook her head. Her own horrendous evening was still etched in her mind.

"It's something we bond over. It lifts the spirits of the new recruits," he said.

"I did not enjoy the games as a Roman spectator. I did not enjoy being in them," she said. "I'll take no pleasure in watching them now." She leaned against the entrance doors to wait out the violence.

A head was thrown over the wall, startling her. Its eyes were rolled back but she recognized the face. Quintus. She ran inside, cutting through the crowd to the edge of the courtyard. Her eyes searched the few nobles still chained to the wall.

"Was there a beautiful girl among you?" she asked them. "Tall and blonde?"

Too terrified to speak, none of them answered.

"She was taken upstairs by Bacchus," Namir said, pulling the next prisoner from the wall.

Bacchus was a gladiator and a huge man. Alba swiveled around and bounded up the stairs. A stifled whimper drifted from an open doorway down the hall.

Bacchus had Cloe pinned to the bed as he thrust into her. Cloe's face was turned away, her eyes scrunched shut.

"Get off her!" Alba yelled, running toward him. She pushed his large body, but he was as solid as a bolder.

"I'm not finished yet," he spat, unflinching.

"Yes, you are." She punched his throat.

He growled and lifted himself over Cloe. "I don't give a fuck if you're Spartacus's bitch." He backhanded her, sending her stumbling into the wall. Cloe reached for the urn beside her and heaved it at him. It smashed against his face, and Alba closed her eyes as the shards pelted her also.

As Cloe rushed forward, he grabbed her first and then Alba, blood dripping down his face. "You—" Alba kneed him in the balls and he keeled over, gasping. "Fucking...cunts."

Together they forced him through the door and locked it behind him. Cloe pulled her dress down, her hair disheveled and draped around her shoulders. There was blood splattered on her arms. "I need to get it off." She tried to rub it but to no avail—it just smeared down her arm.

Alba emptied the ewer into the basin, her hands shaking so much that it spilt over the lip. "Here," Alba said, rushing over to wipe away the blood.

They stared at each other for a moment, trying to catch their breaths. Before Alba could speak, there was a bang on the door that shook them both. Hadrian burst through the door, making them both jump.

"What the fuck, Alba?" he yelled, charging at her.

It took everything Alba had to stand her ground, her face still stinging from the backhand. "She's my friend," Alba said.

"As Bacchus is mine and you just smashed his face in." He flexed his hand and she stepped farther out of reach.

"He's a pig," Alba said. "Tell him to stick his cock somewhere else."

Hadrian shook his head and turned on his heel, swinging the door shut so hard it bounced back and ricocheted off the wall.

"We thought you were dead," Cloe whispered. "You and Pomona."

"Pomona is dead," Alba said, and straightened. "Come with me." She took Cloe's hand, their palms wet with sweat. "Where are the servants' rooms?"

"They came up from over there," Cloe said, nodding at the back staircase.

After checking that the hallway was empty, they quickly made their way to the back stairs and into the servants' corridor. Alba rummaged through a trunk of female clothes. "Put these on," she said as voices boomed above them. "Quickly." The bones on Cloe's chest were visible and her limbs were quite slender. "You've not been eating."

"I've not been living," she said.

Even in the servants' clothes, Alba knew Cloe would stand out. Her hair shone and her skin was smooth and clean. Alba ruffled Cloe's hair and pulled it forward so it shielded her face.

On their way back up the stairs, Namir intercepted them.

"Spartacus craves a word," he said. "With both of you."

As they followed Namir, Alba paused at a window where a large pit was being dug for the bodies of the slain. In this heat it would not take long for them to stink.

The games were over and the drinking had begun. Rebels had congregated around a table laden with bread, cheeses, grapes, fish, and sausages. A ready-made feast.

"Alba." Spartacus beckoned her over. "Did you do this?" He motioned at Bacchus who had stuffed cloth up his nose to stop the bleeding.

She did not care for this interrogation in front of the others. "Yes," she said. For the first time since she'd been there, she felt fully at his mercy, because now she was speaking on behalf of someone else and she did not like it. "This girl is my friend."

"And what would you have us do with her?" Spartacus asked.

This question and his tone angered her even more. "I would have you leave her be." Annoyance fueled her words and gave her strength. "She is as helpless as you were when you stood upon the sands in the arena. She has had no transgressions against you." Alba spoke loudly, so her argument was heard not just by him, but the others as well.

"Her presence among us is a transgression," Hadrian said, and Alba knew he wanted to add "as is yours."

"You would have us leave her be, would you?" Crixus said. "Did this girl never own a slave?"

"They were the property of her husband," Alba said, and then spoke to the group. "I know that many of you have been called savages all your lives, that you resent that word. You are human beings. Can you not see her as one?"

Spartacus studied her a moment. "We can," he said. "And we will."

Alba let out a breath.

There were mutters edged in anger and annoyance.

"Spartacus!" one of the rebels yelled.

Spartacus glanced around and nodded to show that he was coming, but before he left, he said to Alba, "There's a side room off the master. You can both sleep there."

Once he had gone, Crixus said, "You do not thank him?"

"For having compassion?" Alba said.

"For allowing you both to live."

"Did you thank your master for such a thing?"

He growled under his breath.

Cloe and Alba took their leave quickly, making their way up to the master bedroom. Blood smeared the walls of the room, and a boy approaching manhood lay dead next to the bed.

"Did you know him?" Alba asked, going around to the boy's shoulders.

"He was the host's son," Cloe said.

Together they dragged him over to the window, hoisted him onto the ledge, and pushed him through. There was a loud crack as the body hit the ground, sending a quiver down Alba's spine. They went into the side room meant for changing, and Alba arranged some clothes made from fine fabrics onto the floor for bedding. Cloe's shoulders trembled as she sat and pulled her knees into to her chest.

"I wish you'd let them kill me," she said.

"I wished for the same when I first joined them," Alba said, remembering her early days of isolation and anger.

"Joined them?" Cloe said.

The door opened and they both jumped. It was Namir with cheese, fish, and a few figs. "Here." He passed the plate to Alba.

"What's happening down there?" Alba asked.

"Usual speeches," he said tersely.

He turned to leave without looking at her. She hoped he wasn't in trouble for telling her Bacchus was upstairs with Cloe.

The sounds of laughing and drinking from down below were similar to those they had heard while waiting in bushes. Alba wanted to know what was going on but knew better than to leave Cloe unattended.

"Your husband is dead," Alba said, ready to offer comfort, but Cloe's face didn't change.

"You're not sad?"

"No." She hugged her knees. "For I was never happy with him."

Twenty

In the night Alba twitched awake. Through the gap in the sliding door she saw Spartacus's tanned, muscular legs as he emptied the bronze ewer into the wash basin. She stepped over Cloe, trying not to disturb her, and shut the door. As he washed the blood and dirt from his neck, he caught her shadow and lifted his head. His eyes were clear.

"You do not drink?"

"I leave that to the others." He took his wrist guards off and placed them beside the bed.

"I don't appreciate being reprimanded by you in front of the others," she said. "You don't humiliate them so."

His expression softened. "It's not my wish to humiliate you," he said. "If I make the discussion public, it will help them to understand and to accept your presence among them. I grew up with a Roman. They did not." He undid his sandals and slipped them off. "Had I not known you in my youth, I doubt I ever would have thought kindred spirit toward a Roman possible."

"And yet of you three you spoke to me the least."

"Only because I did not know what to say."

She thought of him now, making speeches in front of large groups. "Gone is that quiet boy," she said.

"Forced out of me when I had to take up arms in battle." He glanced at the closet door and thumbed his knife. "Your friend is very pretty. I fear she may attract attention from the men. Roman or not, they might not try to quell their desires."

"What would you have me do?" Alba said, glancing warily at the knife. "Disfigure her?"

"No... but perhaps you could cut her hair."

She pulled at her own short hair.

He scrunched his face, realizing his blunder. "Long hair is feminine, becoming." He set the knife on the table.

Alba took it, rejoined Cloe, and lay down beside her. It was strangely familiar to be sleeping near him again. She thought back to her last summer in Thrace and of the brothers growing into their manhood. She'd been so safe and happy with them all. As she shut her eyes and drifted off, she remembered the nightmares she'd had in Thrace, thrashing in her sleep, and waking to find Alex lying next to her, the heat radiating off his body, his hand resting on her stomach, and the great comfort he had brought her.

It was late morning when the rebels staggered to their feet, shielding their eyes from the sun. They flinched at the sound of the ladles against the cauldrons and groaned when they were called to train.

Cloe was upstairs, having wanted to cut her own hair, and Alba made her way toward a pot of porridge. One of the new female recruits waddled by Alba, balancing a heavy basket on her hips. "Let me help you with that," Alba said, reaching for one side.

"She doesn't need your help," Natalie said coolly, organizing the bows and arrows.

Was she angry at Alba for saving Cloe? "Don't let us go back to how we were before." Alba turned to face her. "I thought you were made of stronger stuff than that."

"You do not know what stuff I am made of," Natalie said.

"I never thought you'd remind me of my aunt who could be quite petty," Alba said, scooping herself out a bowl when Natalie shoved her. Alba twisted around and grabbed Natalie's hair. Natalie quickly overpowered her, pushed her down to the ground, and sat on her torso. "Me helping Cloe," Alba said, her breath laboring from Natalie's weight, "would be like you helping Junia."

Natalie rose her head and flexed her shoulders. With a grunt, she got off Alba and sat next to her.

"I would like to be your friend," Alba said.

"Why?" Natalie asked.

"Because I am not those who raised me. I do not share their mindset or their views. I never liked their treatment of the slaves," she said and added, "I like you, Natalie."

"You don't even know me," Natalie said, getting to her feet. "You should not say such things."

Alba returned to the dimly lit closet with two bowls of porridge and a plum in her pocket. Cloe had cut her shiny blonde locks unevenly and wore a baggy, frumpy frock. "What do you think?"

"It's perfectly hideous," Alba said.

"You knew Spartacus in your youth?" Cloe said, taking a bowl.

"I lived with his family for a time in Thrace."

"The savage family?" Cloe said, and added, "That's what Quintus called them."

Alba nodded and settled in next to her, slicing the plum. It was odd eating while surrounded by such fine clothes and fabrics.

"That's why you were spared," Cloe said. "He's very sweet with you."

"Sweet?" Alba said. Had they not been at the same interrogation?

"He let you plead your case. Not all are so lucky. And he let me stay." She ran her finger over the gold trim of a dress. "Do you remember Claudius Glaber?" she asked.

"Vaguely," Alba said. "He's a praetor?"

"Just became one," Cloe said. "He's leading a few thousand men to quell the 'Spartacus situation' they're calling it in Rome."

"When?"

"I don't know. Quintus was talking about it with a magistrate last night," she said. "But they're not proper soldiers as most of the legions are fighting in Spain under Pompey."

"You wish to go back to Rome before they arrive?" Alba said, understanding this to be Cloe's reason for telling her.

"And be at the mercy of Quintus's sons?" Cloe grimaced and shook her head. "It's better they think I'm dead."

Spartacus came into the room, sweaty and covered in sand. Alba slid the closet door fully open. "We should not linger here," she told him as he wiped the sand from his throat and face with a wet cloth. "Her husband's absence will not go unnoticed. Nor will many others."

"It would take them two days to make the journey if they left now," he said. "The festivities were to end tomorrow. We have some time." He glanced at Cloe, taking in her new appearance.

Alba told him about Glaber.

"We do question the men before we kill them," he said.

"Spartacus." Hadrian came into the room with his hands resting on his belt. "The new recruits have assembled for the demonstration."

Spartacus tossed the cloth back into the basin and left the room. Hadrian cleared his throat and with a pained expression tilted his head to indicate that Alba should follow him. She thought about ignoring his request, but wanting to keep things as peaceful as possible at the moment, she got to her feet and followed him to the room next door.

"This is my room," he said, standing in the center of it.

"Very nice," she said.

He rolled his eyes. "No." He placed his hands together to show that he was using every ounce of patience he possessed. "I'm assuming you're a prude."

Where was he going with this?

"So," he continued, "you can send that blonde girl—"

"Cloe—"

"Here for the evening, so that you may grace Spartacus with your presence." He forced a grin.

"My presence?"

"In his bed," he said quickly, seemingly exasperated by this long-winded conversation he was having to have with her. "Namir and I would house the girl for the night."

His words left her speechless. She had no idea what to say to that. "You're very kind to offer such an arrangement," she mustered. "But . . ."

He raised his eyebrows, waiting for her to continue. When she didn't, he wrung his hands. "Useless," he muttered, and pushed past her out of the room.

"Maybe you could try Natalie?" Alba offered to his back. "I think they had—"

"What the fuck are you talking about?" He paused in the doorway. "He doesn't want Natalie. He wants you."

She hurried behind him. "What?"

He stopped on the top step, whipping around. "I told him to pursue you, like a man, but he refuses, so you must go to him."

"He told you"—she swallowed—"that he wants to be with me?"

"Don't pretend the feelings are not mutual. I've seen the way you look at him."

The way she looked at him? "Wait," she called as he descended the steps.

"I'm done with you," he yelled over his shoulder. "This is why I prefer men. You don't have to deal with this bullshit."

She went back to the room and told Cloe what had transpired.

"Is that something you want?" Cloe asked.

"I'm not sure," Alba said.

Cloe placed her hand on Alba's arm and then took a blanket from the shelf and left the room. Alba went over to the window and rested her forearms on the ledge. The body beneath had been cleared away. Hadrian joined Spartacus atop the wall, and they sat together while they ate their dinners. As usual, in Hadrian's presence Spartacus was open and at ease, but it didn't bother her as much as it did before.

Alba knew that if she had met Spartacus today, he would have watched her slain in the rebel games. It was their common history that saved her. She thought back to the boy of her childhood, to the kindness and warmth, and now to the man he had become with his physical prowess and ability to bring people together. They believed in him and the words he said. He gave them hope. So much had changed for them both in these five years. She tried to imagine the things he had gone through, the ordeals and mistreatment he had endured, but how could she ever really know? Just as he would never understand the dynamics she'd had to navigate in her own villa.

The tufts of clouds were illuminated a radiant pink and she raised her face to it. It was a wonder how life had brought her here to the master suite of a villa, taken with the blood and sweat of those who had spent most of their lives in servitude.

She lay down on the bed with great relief that her wound no longer bothered her. Oh, how she'd missed the comfort of a bed. She didn't know for how long she slept but she was roused by a gentle dip. Spartacus's eyes met hers as he lay down next to her and he cupped her cheek with his hand.

"What do you want from me?"

His brow furrowed. "To be with you."

"But we don't really know each other. Not anymore."

He pulled his hand away. "What kind of a thing is that to say? You are the same inquisitive girl that I met on the banks of the river who followed me home and became a part of our family. I've never known someone to adapt to an environment as you do. You embrace everything around you and fear nothing."

"I fear a great many things," she said. "You see, I've never been with a man."

He studied her closely. "Is that something you want?"

"I do. Very much. I'm just nervous."

He leaned in and kissed her softly, then pressed his lips to her neck, her shoulder, her breast.

The skin between her thighs was taut. When he hesitated, she squeezed his shoulder, urging him on. As the skin gave way, she let out a gasp of pain. He kissed her, giving her time to adjust, before coming into her farther. She closed her eyes to this new sensation building inside her.

Afterward he lifted himself over her and intertwined his fingers behind his head, watching her in the darkness.

"How can one feel both pain and pleasure at the same time?" she asked.

He grinned. "I'm glad you did feel pleasure. Not many do the first time."

She could barely look at him as she asked, "Did you enjoy it?"

"I did."

Caught in this moment of happiness, she forgot about her back and turned to put her dress on.

"Alba," he exclaimed, horrified. "Did we do that?"

"No," she said, quickly pulling her dress over her head. "It was my aunt."

"The one who killed Max?"

She nodded.

His face hardened. "I shall pray to your Gods that we shall one day meet."

"That is not what they are there for," she said. "If you let your anger consume you, you will be the lesser for it."

In her sleep she startled as her foot brushed up against something unfamiliar, a warm mass. Her heart slowed realizing that it was Alex—Spartacus, she reminded herself. He slept much like he had when they were children, sprawled out, heavy with sleep, his breath a low rumble. Except now he was naked.

The moon cast a soft glow over them and she took him in. The curves of his body, his smooth stomach and strong shoulders. She had seen him use sandalwood and pomegranate oil on his calloused hands and feet to sooth the cracked skin, and she breathed it in.

He had been so gentle with her. So tender.

Lying next to him now was so familiar, it made her ache with nostalgia. Spartacus, a man who drew glances and turned heads when he walked into a room, who could silence a boisterous crowd with a stern look. The rebels were witness to his intensity, standing under his watchful gaze. She was witness to his early years, to the family who raised and cherished him. She had seen all sides to him and loved them all.

Twenty-One

Alba put some smoked fish, cheese, and fruit on her plate. Turning, she almost collided with Natalie.

"And?" She stared at Alba. "How was it?" She slid a few arrows into her quiver, restocking it.

"Fine," Alba said.

"Fine?" Natalie repeated, incredulous. "It'll get better with time especially with that man, trust me. How's your back?"

"Much better," Alba said quickly. The searing pain at Natalie's hands was etched in her memory. She carried the food up the narrow stairway to the master bedroom. Halfway up, she met Hadrian who hesitated and then stood up against the wall to let her pass.

Once by him, she turned, careful with her plate of food. "I just wanted to say—"

"No!" was all he yelled as he continued to make his way down the stairs.

Cloe set a small table by the window to eat while Spartacus organized his weapons. The gladiators were going on an evening raid. As Spartacus was lacing his sandals, there was a knock at the door. Other than Hadrian and Namir, none had been allowed into the room, not even Crixus. Spartacus glanced at the girls before cracking it open. "Natalie," he said, unable to hide his surprise.

"I'm not here for you." She stood in the doorway holding a mortar and pestle.

Spartacus stepped back to let her in and slid his dagger into the sheath on his thigh. He nodded at her and left the room. That morning Alba had overheard Natalie and Hadrian arguing. Only bits of conversation, but from what she gathered, Natalie had wanted to go on the evening raid and they had said no.

"Take off your dress," Natalie said.

Alba swallowed and took her dress off, her whole body tensing.

"I still can't believe that Liana did that," Cloe said as Alba lay down.

"She was adept at hiding her psychotic tendencies," Alba said.

As Natalie was finishing, there was a quick knock on the door and Namir came into the room. Alba had not interacted with him much since the night they had arrived.

"We'll be leaving soon. Pack your things," he said, and turned on his heel to leave.

Pulling on her dress, Alba rushed out after him. "Namir, wait. I'm sorry if I got you into trouble for telling me where Cloe was."

"They were not pleased," he said, but then lowered his voice, "Though you know what Natalie said to me after?"

"What?"

"That she thought you quite brave for standing your ground before those three."

"Did she? I was very nervous."

"You didn't look as nervous as you felt." He shook his head with a sly grin. "And to take on Bacchus like that. Most men would cower. Now, pack, quickly. We are leaving soon."

In the courtyard the gladiators were organizing the rebels, their weapons, and some light provisions. Alba made sure to stay well clear of Bacchus as everyone assembled.

"Where are we headed?" Alba asked as Spartacus strode by her.

"Toward Vesuvius," Spartacus said without breaking stride. "Stay in—"

"The middle, near Natalie," Alba said.

He swiveled and nodded at her.

It was going to be a long, warm night. For such a large group they moved quickly and quietly, the moonlight their only light. Alba grazed Cloe's arm as they stumbled up a ravine. It was slick with sweat.

"Are you all right?" she whispered.

Cloe nodded.

Hadrian snaked through them to pass messages from Spartacus in the back to Crixus in the front.

"What's happening?" Natalie asked him.

"They're in pursuit."

"Then why are we headed toward Vesuvius?" Natalie asked.

"Spartacus says we'll make camp at the top of the mountain," Hadrian said.

Natalie lowered her voice. "The men who've been there say there's only one way up, one way down, that we should continue on around it."

"That's what has been decided," Hadrian said.

It wasn't questioned further. The faith they had in that man.

Soon they started to climb the mountain, their feet slipping in the dewy morning grass. Alba and Cloe linked arms, helping to push each other up the large rocks. Their bodies were not used to this kind of prolonged physical exertion. The pitch grew steeper, their steps bigger, and as they went higher, the slippery grass turned to jagged boulders. Alba clutched a stitch in her side, panting, while the rebels jumped from one rock to the next like mountain goats. When she and Cloe started to fall behind, Hadrian bore down on them from the back. "You know I can't pass you," he said.

Alba slipped on a patch of moist moss.

"Move!" he yelled.

"I'm trying!" she yelled back.

"Grab the vines," he said. "Use them to pull yourself up."

Using the vines was much easier. Hadrian hopped from rock to rock, waiting for them with a pained expression. When they finally got to the top, Alba and Cloe sat on the ground, their limbs shaky and marked by dirt and scrapes.

"Out of shape?" Natalie said, her hands on her hips, standing over them.

Alba had a myriad of untoward comebacks dash through her mind, but she held her tongue.

"We're trapped," Crixus's gruff voice yelled. "It's a drop off a cliff."

Spartacus shook his head. "They won't attack us up here."

"And if we stay up here for any length of time we'll starve," one of the other gladiators said.

"How many?" Spartacus asked one of the scouts.

"Three thousand. They're setting up camp in the foothold at the bottom of the mountain and have stationed guards along the path."

"Natalie," Spartacus called her over. "Can you teach a handful of men how to braid?"

Puzzled, she nodded.

"I was *wondering* how we would pass the time," Hadrian said, clapping his hands together.

"This is how we'll get off the mountain," Spartacus said. He turned to the group and yelled, "Collect as many vines off the mountainside as you can!"

"Probably best if we do the braiding," Natalie said, nodding at the women. "Years of practice. We'll be quicker. Bring the vines to us."

The vines were peeled off the rocks, and the women braided them into long, tight ropes. Men who had worked on fishing boats were tasked with tying the vines securely around large rocks close to the cliff's edge.

The edge was a straight drop, the rocks sheer. Alba's stomach rolled as she leaned over it slowly.

"Not afraid of heights, are you?" Hadrian said, coming to stand beside her.

"I didn't think I was," she said.

"What's that girl's name again?" he said.

"Cloe."

"Cloe!" Hadrian called, startling Alba. "When you go over the ledge, concentrate on your footing, then look straight ahead and"—he showed them how to do hand over hand with the vine—"move quickly. You don't need me to tell you that neither of you has the strength to dawdle."

"Right," Alba said, thinking about his words. "Thank you."

He nodded. "And this way if we find you smooshed at the bottom, it won't be on my conscience."

"That must be a relief," Alba said.

He placed his hand on her shoulder. "You have no idea."

Once everything was prepared, Spartacus gathered six gladiators around him. With a stick, he drew the mountain, Glaber's encampment, and the surrounding area in the dirt. "We'll assemble here once we reach the bottom." He pointed with the stick. "Then take your groups and drop down here behind the Roman camp. On my order, we attack." He dragged the stick through the dirt toward the camp. "We'll make our descent once darkness falls."

When it was time to set off, Natalie joined the first group. She was the only woman in the initial barrage.

"Be careful," Alba said to her.

Natalie just gripped the vine, no snappy comeback this time. Alba and Cloe sat apart from the others as the groups went over the ledge. Namir was one of the last to go over. It was a still, dark night, the moon buried beneath the clouds. From down below two balls of fire soared up into the sky. Alba and Cloe went to the mountain's edge. In the stillness, the sound carried, metal on metal, grunts and shrieks from below. Then it all went quiet and a flame was shot directly upward into the night sky, the signal that all was clear.

"Ready?" Alba said.

Cloe gave a small nod, pure dread in her face.

They gripped the vines and lowered themselves over the cliff's edge just as the moon peered out from behind the clouds. Alba shuffled down as quickly as she could, not wanting to hold her body weight any longer than she needed to. By the bottom her palms had been rubbed raw and her arms were shaking under the stress. Her landing was wobbly but there was no time to catch their breath. When Cloe landed beside her, she took her hand and they set off to find the others.

A man ran toward them, the metal on his helmet catching in the moonlight. Alba pulled Cloe behind a tree and they crouched down until his footsteps faded.

Twenty-Two

The Roman encampment was strewn with mangled bodies being turned over for weapons.

"What happened?" Alba asked Namir.

"We killed them," Namir said, turning toward her with a torch in his hand. "We killed them all."

"Not all," Spartacus said. The tip of his spear dripped with blood. "A few got away."

"Tell me," Crixus said, coming up to Alba. "Are all Roman leaders this inept, to leave their encampment so poorly fortified? Two scouts and no men on watch. Do they believe themselves to be invincible?"

"They saw no other way off the mountain," Namir said. "You said so yourself, it drops right off. They didn't expect an attack from behind."

"Is this the best Rome has to offer?" Crixus roared, eliciting a cheer from the crowd.

"Glaber is not Rome's best," Alba said under her breath.

"Speak up," Crixus said.

"Rome's legions are away in Spain fighting under Pompey. These soldiers are not even fully trained," Alba said.

"How would you know that?" Crixus said.

"I have ears, don't I? Much was discussed in the villa where I lived," she said.

"She's right," a man said as he came through the darkness toward them.

"Gannicus," Crixus said in surprise. He took the man by the arm and pulled him into a hug. Alba noticed a shiny *B* etched into his forearm. "Where did you come from?"

"You didn't think I'd miss all the fun?" He turned to Spartacus. "You're not disappointed to see me, I hope?"

"Not at all," Spartacus said.

"Who's he?" Alba asked Namir on the side.

"No idea," Namir said.

As the gladiators assembled for a meeting, Alba glanced around for a good place for her and Cloe to spend the night. The rebels were claiming the ready-made tents for the evening.

"Natalie," Alba said, catching her as she ducked into one. "Can we share with you?"

"We?" Natalie said, and she glanced passed Alba's shoulder to Spartacus, who Alba hadn't realized was standing behind her. "Fine."

"You don't have to if—"

"I said fine."

Everything went quiet as the rebels were finally able to get some proper rest. Alba had just started to drift off when Namir gently shook her awake. "Sorry to wake you. Spartacus craves a word," he said.

She pulled herself from her slumber and went into the large tent. His knuckles were resting on Glaber's map.

"Your hands are like Neme's," Alba said.

He looked up at her. "Rough and calloused?"

"Large and powerful."

"Crixus has taught Junia to defend herself," he said. "I wish for you to learn as well."

"I am learning to fight. Namir is training me."

"Not with a sword for battle but regular, everyday defense so that you can protect yourself. I need someone who is not afraid of being firm with you." Why couldn't it be him? "Someone with a particularly honed skill set."

"You asked to see me?" Hadrian ducked into the tent.

"No," Alba said.

"You must consider it. He's the best there is," Spartacus said.

"Best at what?" Hadrian asked apprehensively.

"Will you teach Alba to defend herself?" Spartacus said.

"Why me?" Hadrian said.

"Because I trust you, as I would no one else, with this task," he said.

Hadrian lifted his chest and unhooked his belt that held his weapons, placing them with a thud on the map and toppling the little men and horses.

"Right now?" Alba said.

"Is there somewhere else you need to be?" Hadrian asked, holding out his hands.

Spartacus clapped Hadrian's arm in thanks and left them. Alba's limbs were still quivering from the climb. How did these people have the energy to be so physical all the time? Hadrian was already squaring his shoulders and getting into position. Until then, Alba had never fully appreciated how large he was.

"Right. So, go for the weak spots: throat, groin, nose. And with force." He made fast jabbing motions. "But keep your own limbs tucked in tight, nothing for them to grab onto. Make each movement count. You have to be quick but strong."

He was taking this task much more seriously than she had expected. He showed her how to throw a punch, how to protect her face, and how to roll her shoulder back. He was much stronger and quicker than Namir.

"Now, say I come at you from behind." He stood behind her and placed his hand on her shoulder. "What can you do?"

She rolled her shoulder back and jabbed her elbow toward his groin.

"Good." He grabbed her arm before she made contact. "But faster and throw the force of your whole body into it." He showed her.

"Let's try the other move I showed you." He lunged at her and she tried to block his hand, but he grabbed her throat and pushed her into the wall. "The problem is," he said, releasing her, "you're not fit. You have no stamina. And you're tired and lazy."

"You have all spent years honing your muscles through labor," she said. "I will get stronger."

He raised his eyebrows. "Right. Enough for today."

As she handed him his belt, she thought of him patiently teaching Namir, jovial and joking, adjusting his stance and grip. "When did you first know that you liked men?"

"I have for as long as I can remember," he said, cinching the strap. "Alba, do not misinterpret these sessions. We both have a job here. I teach." He placed his hands on his chest. "You learn. No need for pleasantries. Don't confuse this with friendship."

"Wouldn't dream of it," she said, but he'd already left.

Natalie was awake when Alba came back into the tent. "I envy you," Alba whispered as she crawled back onto her bed.

"Me?" Natalie said quietly.

"I'm being trained to defend myself by Hadrian," Alba said.

"Ah," she said. "That is unfortunate."

"I don't understand it. He has such a strong dislike for me, yet he helps me, even when Spartacus does not ask it of him."

"He has seen what I have seen. How Spartacus's eyes brighten when you are near," she said, resting her head on her hand. "You bring out a softer side in him, a side we had not known."

Alba glanced at Natalie. "Do you miss him? Being with him?"

"I miss reaching for him in the night and the shared glances we used to exchange. I never had anyone in my life treat me as he did, with such kindness and as an equal. Spartacus and I grew to rely on each other for comfort in the cells of that ludus. Together we would be as much of ourselves as we dared. But in the end, I never deserved him."

"Why do you say that?"

She shook her head. "That is a long story," she said, and rolled over.

Twenty-Three

It was here that the rebels decided to stay for the time being. Their number had become so large that their camp naturally divided into sections as groups settled into their routines. Each was their own entity, cooking and looking after their space, but the hierarchy around them was clear and unquestioned. The gladiators oversaw everything and Spartacus was at the top. Communal training areas were scattered throughout, and the gladiators constantly moved between them, organizing the men and women, the food and hunting parties.

Their own camp was in the nook of a steep ridge and comprised of five tents—Hadrian and Namir's; Cloe, Natalie, and Alba's; Crixus and Junia's; and Spartacus's, which was the largest tent where many of the meetings were held and Alba sometimes slept. The fifth tent was currently empty but had been reserved for the fleeting Gannicus who Alba had yet to meet.

Inside their own communal area, Alba and Cloe were able to find a place. Namir and Natalie started teaching them how to prepare meat, cut vegetables, start a fire, and keep it going while they cooked. Crixus and Junia ignored them, but that was fine because they mostly kept to themselves anyway. Alba continued to train with Hadrian and her body became stronger.

· · ·

In early autumn Alba was sitting next to Namir as he showed her the motions of kneading dough, massaging it with his knuckles. In the distance Natalie was speaking to Spartacus. He was angled in toward her, staring at the ground, nodding at what she was saying.

"Do you know what happened with Spartacus and Natalie? What their story is?" Alba asked as she leaned over her dough, flipping it over.

"They say that she brought him back from the dead. He almost died in the arena, but she nursed him through a fever that would've killed most men. Three days and nights she stayed with him until it broke."

"She was steadfastly devoted."

"She still is." Namir took Alba's dough, wrapped it up, and carefully placed it in the hot ashes.

Alba was collecting kindling when she spotted Spartacus standing on his own. A rare occurrence. His stance was alert but she could tell his thoughts were elsewhere. As she approached, he glanced over his shoulder and she wrapped her arms around his torso. She rested her forehead on his back and for a long moment let herself be at complete ease. She released her grip and he turned to face her. His bright blue eyes were contrasted by his tanned face.

"How is the training going with Hadrian?" he asked.

"Fine. Though I'm not sure I'm ready to fight alongside you just yet."

His brow furrowed. "That's not what the sessions are for," he said. "I'm having Hadrian train you so that you know how to defend yourself, that is all."

"Oh." It was a bit of a relief but she was thrown by his statement. "Because you do not think me capable?"

"Because I could not focus with you out there."

"And we couldn't have that," Hadrian said, approaching them with a bowl in each hand. "He is right. Defense is very important. You stick to that."

There was no use in talking to Spartacus with Hadrian there. She turned to leave, not wanting to disrupt the meal they always shared together.

"Alba, you stay," Hadrian said, passing one of the bowls to Spartacus.

"Would you both stay?" Spartacus asked.

Hadrian stared at Alba for a moment, as if sizing her up, and then glanced at his bowl.

"I've eaten," she said quickly.

They sat together at the base of a tree, Hadrian hunched over his food, Spartacus sitting up straighter than usual. Hadrian ate his meal quickly, his spoon clinking against the bowl, and then he shot up. As he walked away, Alba said, "I'm really growing on him."

Spartacus lowered his eyes. "He and his siblings were taken from their mother when he was a boy. All he has known is mistreatment at the hands of Romans. His sister was separated from them. His brother was killed. A man can only take so much."

"It haunts him."

"As it would any man with a heart as large as his," Spartacus said. "It is no small feat that he can sit here and share a meal with you."

"I appreciate you trying to endear me to him, but I think it best you leave it," she said. Some things could not be changed, no matter how much one willed them. "Namir told me that Natalie brought you back from the dead."

He nodded.

"Do you hold her in affection?"

"I care for her, yes."

"You should make that known to her. I fear that she feels cast aside."

"That was not my intention . . . I shall make amends." His eyes wandered toward the camp. "Did you find such kinship while living in Rome?"

"No."

"Not with all your festivals and celebrations?"

"In everything we do there is a structure, unsaid rules of who you can and cannot talk with. It's not like here where you have people of all different backgrounds working side by side with common purpose." Then she thought of her brief time with Julius. "There were some I grew to be found of."

"What of your family? Your mother?"

"She had taken her life. My aunt and uncle were living in my childhood villa, and neither of them were very kind to me. Because of that I dreamed of raising a family in a home filled with warmth. A safe space where one could do and say as they pleased."

A look of longing passed over Spartacus's face. Perhaps he too dreamed of a world where he could set aside the fighting, the scheming, and the plotting. The constant reorganization of people.

"Now," Hadrian said, reappearing and startling them both. "That's the one snag about my lifestyle, not being able to have children of my own."

"Is that something you'd like?" Alba asked.

"It would be nice to have the option," he said, and then to Spartacus, "Crixus craves a word, with both of us."

Like water through a sieve, the look of longing faded from Spartacus's eyes. He got to his feet and started back to their camp.

"Alba," Hadrian said, gesturing with an upward nod. "Let's go. You shouldn't be this far out alone."

In the early evening dim, Alba went down to the river with Natalie and Cloe. They found a spot away from the other rebels and took off their dresses to wash. Alba cleaned the short strands of her hair and scrubbed between her fingers and toes. She put on a clean tunic and hung her washed dress, pinning it in place next to Cloe's.

The camp was quiet except for the crackling fire and the wheeze of a damp log. She walked over to Spartacus's tent with the swell of excitement and yearning that came with her newfound desire. At the tent opening, she took a breath and clutched the cloth of the flap.

"I'm behind you," Spartacus said, giving her a start.

His silent footsteps. He offered her an apologetic grin as he reached over her and held the flap open.

The air inside the tent was musky and sweet with the faint smell of sandalwood oil. Taking his hand, she led him to the bed and ran her fingers over his broad chest. He swelled at her touch. *Her* touch. This man. Slayer of giants.

Natalie was right. Their kiss broke as he came into her and her legs wrapped around him. Her body ripened, tingling as he found her place of truest pleasure. A sensation unlike any she had ever known gathered inside her and her back arched. It seemed that he was listening for her breaths, for a rhythm she liked. He held her wrists, pinning her down, and she pushed against his grip until her body erupted and she let out a gasp.

His damp chest pressed against hers and she felt the soft flutter of his heart. She melted beneath him, her bones hollowed out. She ran her hand through his cropped hair as he pressed his forehead to hers. Drifting off, she held him close, this great peace he brought her.

The early morning light stole through tent. Spartacus lay naked next to her, his body warm and heavy with sleep. She traced her finger along the shiny scar beneath his shoulder and then slid the linen from his body to take him in. His tanned skin, which had been so smooth and untouched as a boy, was now littered with scars and what appeared to be burn marks. Her own skin only bore two blemishes. The scar that traveled the length of her back and the other at the side of her temple where the shield had hit, leaving a bone-colored web that crept toward her hairline.

Alba pulled the linen back over him and shut her eyes.

Twenty-Four

"May I have a word," a solid voice said, stirring Alba from her sleep. A man came into the tent and plopped down at the end of the bed. Spartacus was dressed and leaning over a map.

Alba held the covers to her chest as she sat up.

"Apologies." Gannicus shot up. "I didn't realize you had company."

"Alba, this is Gannicus," Spartacus said, tossing her dress to her.

"Nice to meet you," she said.

"And you." He offered her a small but polite nod and then turned away while she pulled her dress over her head. He seemed vaguely familiar, not from the other night but before that. He had a cleft chin, thick eyebrows, and sandy blond hair that almost touched his shoulders. Not short hair like the other gladiators, yet he had the *B* etched into his arm.

"Gannicus here won his freedom on the sands of the arena shortly after I arrived at the ludus," Spartacus said.

Gannicus. Publius had awarded him the wooden sword at the opening of the games.

"Spartacus would've done the same . . . if he hadn't broken out." Gannicus casually swiveled his dagger into the wood table. "You've got quite the entourage of followers. Not just here but in the city as well. Slaves are being crucified for merely speaking your name." He held the dagger still.

Spartacus turned away from them, sliding his wrist pads on.

"That is not his fault," Alba said.

"I'm not here to place fault," Gannicus said. "Only to make him aware of the power that his name alone wields. Some are calling this the War of Spartacus, and Rome is not happy with you, not at all. This upheaval you've created—the fear, in the very city itself."

"I hope you didn't come back just to tell me this," Spartacus said. "I know it all already. Or have you come to join us?"

"Join you?" Gannicus said. "I thought you knew me better than that."

"We could use your sword and your mind."

Gannicus shook his head. "I'm no longer a pawn, fighting at will for others. I'm a free man. I'll not be seduced by your flattery or your games."

"I am not playing games, Gannicus. You're welcome here, whether you fight alongside us or not," Spartacus said.

An outbreak of voices drew them from the tent. Angry words were being thrown about in a language Alba did not understand but recognized. It was Germanic. Their last swell of recruits had brought them a considerable amount of people from the tribes east of the Rhine. A group of rebels were huddled around a deer. Some were still drunk from the night before with bare chests and glazed eyes.

Hadrian was attempting to reason with them in their mother tongue. One of the women, with hair like a lion, hoisted the deer up onto a thick tree branch. She was tall and muscular with two daggers and a slave collar around her neck. Hadrian approached her and she jeered at him, licking the skin of the deer and then smiling widely. Hadrian, who did not like this mockery from one of his own, charged toward her.

"What is their quarrel?" Spartacus asked.

Hadrian stopped. "They don't want to share the food they've caught."

"Tell them we share everything."

Gannicus leaned against a tree, amused.

In an undertone, Spartacus said to Hadrian, "The next time they hunt we will divide them into groups with the others so that they do not form a pack. And tell those who can speak in common tongue to do so and we can share in their thoughts."

Spartacus went up to the woman with the lion's mane and took the slave collar off her neck. "What is your name?" Spartacus asked.

"Ava," Hadrian said.

"Welcome, Ava." He held up her chain and threw it into the forest.

Hadrian went over to speak with his fellow countrymen and Crixus came up to Spartacus. "I think we need to reassess how we distribute food. Those who go into battle, those who defend, they should receive it first," Crixus said. "These people have only been here a few days."

"They shall receive food as we all do. Equally divided among us," Spartacus said. "They could be of great asset to us."

"Absolutely," Hadrian said, rejoining them. "Look at them. They're built like rocks and they can run like cheetahs."

"What a description," Gannicus said.

The men were thick and barrel-chested, their legs like tree trunks. The few women among them were tall and strong as well.

Ava eyed them cheekily as she passed by them.

On the edge of the group, Natalie slung two traps over her shoulder. As their numbers had grown, Alba and Cloe had to be more careful. They could not leave their campsite unattended. Alba hurried after her, wanting to stretch her legs.

They walked toward the stream, and as Alba glanced at her friend, she decided to broach the topic that she'd been thinking about for a while. "Namir told me that you brought Spartacus back from the dead."

"That is what they say." Natalie's voice was flat.

"Is it not true?"

"You ask more questions than anyone I have ever known."

"Because I wish to understand what happened before."

"Sometimes it is best to forget." Natalie sat on a rock and bent to fill her cup with the fresh water trickling down the stream. After taking a sip, she passed it to Alba. "Camilla's body slave was sick, and I was asked to accompany her to the games. It was my first time in the arena and we were seated front and center." From her tone, Alba could tell that she too did not enjoy the games. "Spartacus staggered out onto the sands. No one knew who he was and it was clear that something was wrong with him. He couldn't walk straight. There was another man with him who kept trying to protect him but they were both overtaken. Spartacus was speared and taken to the pits." She paused and then forced herself to continue. "When the games were over, I was sent to retrieve the armor from one of our own gladiators. It was horrible: the smell, the bodies, twitching and gargling. In that moment I knew that Camilla was truly evil and I hardened to her in a way that I fought to mask. I pulled the armor off as fast as I could, ripping it from his chest and arms, needing to get out. Then I felt a hand on my arm, slick with heat. The gash beneath Spartacus's shoulder still bled."

"He was alive," Alba said.

"Yes." Natalie lowered her head, deep regret crossing her face. "And I left him in the pit. Only later did I find out Crixus had brought him to our villa's medicus. Once in the pit, any person is considered fair game. I was *assigned* the task of caring for him, a piece they do not mention in the story. I was devoted to his recovery only because it was a reprieve from my other duties." The guilt in her confession now filled her whole face and made her words thick.

"You did not know him then," Alba said. "Don't dwell on this memory. Many people would have done the same."

"He would not have," Natalie said, her voice taut. "The first time he requested me, after his first big win for Camilla and Lentulus, Camilla refused, saying someone of his caliber deserved someone pure. They offered him a fine bed, silks, their best meat and wine, any virgin slave he desired, but he refused them all. Again and again they asked him what he wanted after his wins. 'Natalie' was all he said."

She stood and slowly they started to walk.

"Lentulus and Camilla basked in his wins and the praise that came with it. His name alone caused his opponents to cower and he became their greatest source of their income, their biggest bargaining chip. Then one day he stepped out into the arena and just stood there, did not raise his sword, did not turn his head. He had been known for his theatrics before but never this. Camilla and Lentulus were forced to intervene. 'What is it?' Lentulus said, stepping out onto the sand, 'What is it you want?'"

A tear rolled down Natalie's cheek. "'Natalie,' he said."

"That night I was washed and dressed in the finest fabric and taken down to his cell. I hadn't spoken to him other than the broken words of comfort I offered when I nursed him through his fever. The last time we had been close he had been wet with sweat, delirious. Now he stood upright, strong and powerful. The men I had been forced to lay with were crude pigs—ones I could shut my mind to. Not a man like this."

It took everything Alba had to hold her friend's gaze. She fought to steady her emotions knowing that if she faltered now she may never hear the story.

"'Bed him well,' Camilla said to me as I descended the stairs. When I entered his cell, he didn't move, not one muscle, so I reached for the strap of my dress. He placed his hand on mine. It was the only time I have ever been nervous with him. 'Natalie,' he said, 'you are safe here. I won't touch you.' I sat on his bed and told him that I wanted to be with him. He gave me a small, sad smile. Then he went to sleep."

Natalie lifted her head. "So you see me for what I am. They call me a kind and gentle healer when I was nothing but a . . ."

"A survivor," Alba said. "You did nothing wrong."

They continued through the forest, falling silent as they passed a few men on patrol. Once out of earshot, Alba said, "What happened after that night?"

"We became friends, and this enraged Camilla." A darkness fell over Natalie's eyes. "So one night when Spartacus was away, they lied to an esteemed guest and told him that I was a virgin. I was dressed and taken to his room, but just as the door shut, Camilla came in, extending her apologies, tight and brisk. Hadrian had requested me for the night."

"Hadrian?"

Natalie nodded. "Camilla thought they were sharing me."

"I'm glad she is dead," Alba said.

"You know, I was one of the slaves who greeted you on your arrival to their ludus."

Natalie had been part of the wall of slaves.

"You were there with Max?" Alba said.

"Who do you think turned him into the God Apollo?" she asked.

"Was Hadrian there that night?"

"No. He, Crixus, and Spartacus had been sent to Rome together. It made Camilla and Lentulus very anxious to have their three best gladiators gone. Funny to think of now."

One of her traps had caught a small hare. Its legs were wounded and she broke its neck.

"Thank you for sharing that with me," Alba said.

Twenty-Five

It was a training day in the camp with each of the gladiators taking large groups of differing skill levels. Hadrian's group was nearest to their encampment so Alba and Cloe were able to watch on the edges. A tall blond boy around their age had sweat through his tunic. He lifted it over his head and there was a guttural reaction from those behind him. Hadrian's expression however did not change as he passed him a fresh tunic and Alba and Cloe glimpsed his back. It was broad and muscular and layered with long scars in his flesh.

"Alba," Hadrian called over to her. "You and I, later."

She nodded.

Ava took her turn with the wooden sword. She was fast and feisty, taking on her male opponent with aggressive movements. Her hair whipped around as she moved from side to side throwing him off balance. He toppled to the ground and she planted a foot on his chest.

"She's quite good," Alba said.

"She isn't bad," Natalie said, rejoining them with Spartacus. They had been doing rounds of the camp. "For a barbarian."

"Got that right," Gannicus said, watching her in admiration.

Crixus was training a group of Gauls in the valley beside them, his tactics much different from Hadrian's, with a lot of yelling and grunting coming from their area.

"How are they doing?" Spartacus asked Hadrian, nodding toward Crixus's men.

"Crixus's group? They leave much to be desired," Hadrian said.

"Didn't we all when starting out," Spartacus said.

"Not all," Hadrian said pointedly.

"Tomorrow you will train Crixus's men and he will train yours," Spartacus said.

Hadrian's jaw tightened.

"He has some natural ability," Spartacus said, approaching the boy with the scars. "What's your name?"

"Gus."

"Have you ever held a real sword?"

Gus shook his head. He stood at the same height as Spartacus and his shoulders were just as broad, but as Spartacus approached, he hunched as if trying to make himself seem smaller.

"It's heavy," Gus said with a thick accent, gripping it. "You make it look so light," he said to Hadrian.

"As will you," Spartacus said, "once you get used to the weight."

"When you have us fight Romans?"

"The choice to fight is yours." Spartacus took his sword back and Gus rejoined the others.

"Do you remember the day," Hadrian said, "when you and I were forced to train without food or water in the scorching sun? We were swatting at flies and that night our hands were chained to the pole beneath the open sky in the middle of the courtyard."

"What of it?" Spartacus said.

"You shouldn't spoil them with kind words. It will not serve them well on the field of battle."

"I will not mirror that wretched place here," Spartacus said.

"Fear is what drives you," Hadrian said. "It makes you stronger."

"They will not fear us," Spartacus said.

Hadrian didn't respond. Instead, he went over to watch another pair of men.

"Crixus told me of his brother," Gannicus said.

Spartacus nodded. "A great loss to him."

"The greatest pain that one can feel is the absence of another. Isn't that how the saying goes?" Gannicus shrugged. "Not that I would know anything about it."

"Would you care to train a few men, Gannicus?" Spartacus asked, turning to him. "A man of your caliber would have a lot to bestow."

"That I would," Gannicus said. "However, I'm going to go see if one of these German girls will fuck me." He nudged Spartacus with his shoulder. "What do you think my odds are?"

Cloe leaned over a large, thick cauldron and started to drag it with her whole body into their camp. Alba moved to help her but Gus reached her first. As he bent down and moved it for her, his hair caught the sun and gleamed like summer wheat. Cloe directed him to the spot where she wanted it, thanking him. He gave her a shy, polite nod, only then glancing at her. His large, gray eyes rounded, taken aback by her beauty. Then he inclined his head and went back to the Germanic camp.

"Who was that?" Cloe asked Alba.

"He came in with the Germanic tribe," Alba said.

"The one causing all the ruckus?" Cloe tipped a bucket of water into the cauldron.

Natalie passed by them in the other direction, her face set in a scowl.

"What is it?" Alba asked, following her into their tent.

"We, we, we," Natalie said. "That's all Junia ever talks in anymore. Does she not remember that she is still an I?" Natalie paced between the beds, which had been neatly made by Cloe. "And she refers to Crixus as a God. She is her old self less and less."

"What is it that you cling to?" Alba asked.

"When she and I were at the House of Batiatus, we shared a room.

I found such comfort in her during some of my darkest nights." She stopped pacing and sat on her bed. "I don't know what to do."

"There might not be anything you can do. Just accept her as she is now."

"I feel as though I have lost a friend, yet she is right there."

"Alba," Hadrian called through the tent fabric.

She gave Natalie's shoulder a squeeze before leaving.

Alba found her training with Hadrian to be quite frustrating. Every time she improved or got into a rhythm he'd elevate his level, throwing her newfound skills off course. As Hadrian held her down on the bed for the third time, his eyes momentarily fell on the slit in her dress.

"Are your breasts bigger?" he asked.

"What?" Alba pushed herself up and adjusted her straps as Hadrian left the tent. "Are we done?" she called after him.

He came back moments later with Natalie. "Does she look different to you?" He held his hand out toward Alba. "Her breasts."

Natalie's eyes swept over Alba, taking in her appearance. "Have you felt nauseous?" she asked. "Do you have an aversion to smells? Are you more tired than usual?"

Of course she was more tired; she was much more physical than her body was used to and some of the odors around the rebel camp had made her nauseous.

"We shouldn't tell Spartacus until we know for sure," Natalie said. "He doesn't need more on his mind."

"Agreed," Hadrian said, and they both turned toward Alba.

"Tell him what?" Alba asked.

"That you might be pregnant," Natalie said.

"Pregnant?" Alba said in disbelief.

The shock must have shown on her face because Natalie started to rub her back. "I've seen many women through their pregnancies."

Alba clutched her chest as it began to tighten, her breath deepening. "I don't know how to be a mother." Her body convulsed, and Natalie grabbed a jug for Alba to vomit into.

"Be happy that you can bring life into this world," Natalie said. "Not all are so lucky." She took the jug and left the tent.

Over the years, some of the slaves in Alba's villa had become pregnant by her uncle or guests to the villa. Some masters allowed their slaves to keep the child with them through infancy; others took them from the breast and sold them. Liana didn't even allow it to get that far. Once the slave was showing, they were sold.

"Has Natalie ever had a child?" Alba asked Hadrian as he cinched his belt.

"No and I doubt she ever will."

"Why do you say that?"

"Too much damage done, I'm afraid," he said.

"She told me of the kindness you showed her while at the ludus, taking her in some nights," Alba said.

He nodded. "We didn't even like each other all that much at the time."

"But you did it for Spartacus," Alba said. She wondered if there was anyone that Hadrian did like upon meeting. "You're a loyal friend."

"To those who are deserving." He slid his sword into its sheath. "We'll take a break from training, just in case. We won't want to bring harm to the child."

"You have taught me so much already," she said.

He grunted to indicate otherwise.

"Spartacus," Alba said through the tent. "May I come in?"

He lifted the flap and stood in the doorway with beads of water dripping down his limbs, freshly back from swimming in the river. "Alba, you do not need to ask permission. You can just come."

"The others ask permission," she said, brushing past him.

"You are not the others." He lowered the flap.

"I know you have a lot on your mind." She gestured toward the map and scrolls. "I don't wish to disturb you."

"You're not a disturbance. Far from it." He leaned down and kissed her, easing her back against the tent's pole. She rolled her hip against his, and he slid his hand through the slit of her dress, cupping her breast. At his touch she winced. Her breast was tender and sore.

"I'm sorry." He pulled back. "My hands are rough."

"No, it's not that . . ." He stood over her, waiting. To tell him or not to tell him? Perhaps she should take Natalie and Hadrian's words to heart. What if the seed didn't take? What if it was a false alarm? He had so much on his mind already.

He watched her patiently, waiting.

"It's not you," she said finally, and turned away, unable to say more. There was a town on the map, the closest one to them, circled in a thick black. She traced her finger over it. "What's this?"

"We do not touch this town. No plundering, no women. We trade with them and have made good relations. Gotten to know its streets and buildings."

"The Romans are trained to fight on open fields, not in towns."

He nodded. "Exactly."

Twenty-Six

Cloe was standing at the edge of the camp talking with Gus. He listened to her intently and watched her closely as she spoke, grappling with this new language. Cloe's face was lit in a way Alba had never seen, and as she spoke, it seemed that she was trying to contain a smile.

"Gus," Alba called over to them. "Would you care to join us for dinner?" She gestured toward their camp. It was common knowledge that you could not enter Spartacus's camp unless invited.

"I don't... I'm not... sure," he said finally.

Gannicus came out of his tent with Ava, both glistening with sweat and drinks in their hands staggering slightly as they walked. Ava playfully bit his arm and then went back to the Germanic camp. Gannicus came to stand next to Alba. "In all my years and all my travels. I have never seen someone so beautiful as that girl," Gannicus said, staring at Cloe.

Alba tried to hand him a bowl of the rabbit stew, but he wouldn't take it. She had seen this before, too many times, the darkness that took some when they drank. Gannicus stumbled over to Cloe. Gus shifted, uncomfortable.

"Gannicus," Alba said, "leave her be."

He held his hands up. "I've not touched her."

Keeping her head bowed, Cloe slipped past him and into her tent.

"Where're you going? I just want to talk to you." Gannicus made to go in after her.

"No, Gannicus." Natalie came out of the tent, holding her hand up.

Gannicus grunted and stalked off into the forest as Gus went back to his camp. Alba and Natalie glanced at each other before going into the tent.

"Don't mind Gannicus," Natalie said to Cloe. "He goes into a state sometimes. He's harmless."

Was he, though?

As Natalie sat next to Cloe, Alba was filled a sudden and intense gratitude for these two women. Their kindness and dependability. For the first time in her life, she had female friendship. Women she could laugh with and confide in. Oh, how she cherished them and the warmth they had toward each other.

The next morning Spartacus greeted the dewy dawn with his arms stretched over his head, his wrist guards dangling from his fingers. Alba and Natalie were cooking eggs on a large flat stone while Cloe cut the bread. The air was brisk and their breaths rose above them as they spoke. Crixus came out of his tent, followed by Junia, and he too was dressed in his warrior garb.

"Where are you going?" Natalie asked as Hadrian came toward them sliding his dagger into his thigh sheath.

"To explore the area," Gannicus said, coming from the direction of the Germanic camp.

Hadrian leaned down and ran his thumb over the ridge Namir's cheek before kissing his head. Crixus wrapped his arm around Junia's neck and kissed her. Neither Alba nor Spartacus moved toward the other. She was not affectionate toward him in front of the others.

"Let's go hunt some fucking Romans," Gannicus bellowed. "Don't worry"—he turned toward Alba and Cloe—"you two are safe."

Alba shook her head, baffled by his constant state of insouciance.

"A little more discretion would be nice," Hadrian said, and the four of them took off into the forest.

Gus came to the edge of their camp, holding a string of silver-backed fish.

"Come," Natalie said. "Join us."

He nodded appreciatively, setting down his catch, and taking a seat next to Cloe.

"Imagine none of them came back," Namir said.

"We would all be fine," Natalie said, which made everyone laugh except Junia. "Will you not join us?" Her voice was edged with annoyance.

Junia just shook her head and went back into her tent.

"I hope you don't mind me asking." Alba turned to Gus. "Who gave you those scars on your back?"

His shoulders straightened. "My father," he said.

"Is he still alive?" Natalie asked.

He shook his head.

"Pity," Natalie said.

Twenty-Seven

By late autumn, the rebels had amassed to over ten thousand people. The gladiators went on daily patrols and worked to quell any disputes between the different nationalities before they broke out. Hadrian and Alba continued their sessions, but he would show her moves instead of having her do them.

Natalie stoked the embers of the fire so that the flames licked the grate and placed a large metal skillet on top of it. Hadrian rubbed his hands together. "What's for dinner?" He leaned over her placing a hand on her shoulder.

She glanced up at him. "That's for tomorrow. Tonight it's fish, figs, and bread."

"Ah," he said. "Will you save me some? I'm going on rounds."

She nodded.

"Can I come with you?" Alba asked. She hadn't been too far from their own encampment now that they'd grown so much.

Hadrian rolled his eyes, adjusting his belt so that his sword was at his side. She took his lack of a response as a yes.

It was the time of night when everyone was settling in. Alba stayed near Hadrian but trailed back a bit while he approached the groups and chatted with them as the light faded to gray. People gathered around their fires cooking hares, birds, and fish. Some used the last light to patch fishing nets, fashion a pallet for their tent, or sew pieces of fabric together. One woman was kneading dough in a way that reminded Alba of Neme.

Crixus passed by them, having just spoken with a group of men. He tilted his head in their direction, and Hadrian nodded, then held his hand up for Alba to stop. They stood within earshot of the group but out of sight. There were a half-dozen middle-aged men sitting around a fire.

"Tend to the fucking horses?" one of them said. "As if we would take orders from a Gaul and what kind of a job is that?"

"Bring those olives back out," another man said.

One of the men reached beneath him and pulled out a large bag, stashed under his seat.

"Evening," Hadrian said. He stepped forward but stayed out of the fire's light and was draped in darkness.

"We're not interested."

"Interested?" Hadrian said.

"In training. We hear it's brutal work for those becoming gladiators."

"First of all, there is no world in which you would ever be capable of becoming a gladiator," Hadrian said. "And second, I hope that your feet are swift for when Rome does bear down on us, there will be no prisoners."

The men didn't respond, unmoved by Hadrian's words.

"Are you not sharing those?" Alba asked, stepping into the light and pointing at their large sack of olives.

"I'd share a few with you," a man said. "In my tent."

Hadrian planted his foot on the log next to the man and angled into the light, gripping his shoulder pad.

The man choked on his drink and the others bowed their heads. "I meant no offense," the man stammered. "I did not know that it was you . . . that she was with you."

"She's not," Hadrian said.

The man wheezed a sigh of relief.

"She's with Spartacus."

In what little light was left, Alba noticed the color drain from his face.

"Worry not," Hadrian said, taking a handful of olives, "as long as the horses are well tended to and that your food is shared."

They all nodded.

"Poor man," Alba said as they walked away. "He looked as though he was going to shit himself."

"So long as he does it once we're well clear of the area," Hadrian said.

Alba thought of the man's proposal. "Hadrian, do you find me attractive?"

He glanced at her. "You know that I like men, right?" He popped some olives into his mouth and passed her the rest.

"Yes, of course." After years of Liana's ridicule, she sometimes wondered what others thought of her appearance. Spartacus had known her since childhood so he held her dear for other reasons.

He shrugged. "Yeah, you're pretty . . . normal."

"Pretty normal?" she repeated. Now she felt stupid for even asking the question.

"No. I'm saying that you're pretty and normal looking, which is good, no?"

"What's good?" Spartacus said, appearing in the darkness with Gannicus. They had also been making rounds.

Alba's face grew warm and she was thankful that it was dark. "Nothing." She glared at Hadrian.

Hadrian raised his eyebrows, clearly taken aback by her reaction.

"Alba was just wondering—" he started to say.

"Hadrian, leave it." She swatted him with the back of her hand and took off toward their camp.

"Alba." Hadrian caught up to her.

"Why do you need to embarrass me?" She rounded on him.

"I'm not trying to embarrass you," he said. "I'm not used to such . . . to these sorts of conversations."

"Oh." Conversations. Something he wouldn't even have considered having with her before.

He went over to Natalie and Namir, who were sitting together in front of the crackling fire. "Here." Natalie held a plate out for him.

"You have outdone yourself," he said, taking it from her.

"It's just some seasoned fish," she said.

As Hadrian settled in beside Namir, Spartacus came into the clearing. At his approach, a determined look crossed over Natalie's face.

"Spartacus, may I have a word?" she said. "And with you, Hadrian."

"Certainly," Spartacus said.

"Do you think me a good fighter?" she said matter-of-factly.

"You're one of our best," Hadrian said, scooping fish into his mouth.

Spartacus's expression however did not change. He was waiting.

"Let me come on your raids," she said.

Spartacus shifted.

"Why?" she demanded, standing. "Why will you not let me?"

There was a flicker of a glance between the two men.

"Do you not think me capable of holding my own? Of keeping up?"

"It's not that." Spartacus struggled for words. "As a woman it would seem odd, you with four men. It would raise suspicion."

Hadrian lowered his voice. "And then Crixus may wish to bring Junia."

"Since when have you ever given a fuck about what Crixus wants," she said, keeping her voice down too.

The three of them quarreling was one thing, but to bring Crixus in would tilt the entire conversation. Natalie, Spartacus, and Hadrian not only respected one another but were good friends.

"The answer is no," Spartacus said, the finality in his voice bringing the conversation to an end.

Her nostrils flared in frustration, and Alba felt Natalie's disappointment. The gladiators held her in high esteem and everyone knew it. She was considered an equal and quite capable, so why deny her this? Why not let her join them? They had already broken so many boundaries already.

Alba pulled a shawl over her shoulders and joined Gannicus on the other side of the fire. Though the days were mild, the nights had cooled considerably.

"Did you know that I was Roman when we first met?" she asked, sitting next to him.

He nodded and took a sip of his drink.

"Yet you didn't dislike me?"

"Why would I dislike a person I didn't know?"

"Ask the camp," she said. "Most people here can't stand the Romans."

"I've had my fair share of bad dealings with them." He stretched his legs out in front of him. "But Spartacus holds you dear so . . ." He tilted his head to indicate that that was enough for him.

"You don't mind Cloe either."

"Look, most Romans are pompous shits, but you are not and your friend is not. I'm glad Spartacus *has* found someone he holds dear, someone he has chosen to be with and devote himself to."

She smiled.

"What? You don't believe me?" he said.

"No, I do. It's just a contrast to his youth when he laid with a fair few."

"Until he found one that he holds close to his heart."

This statement surprised her, coming from Gannicus.

"Why do the men fear him so?" Alba asked. From what she had seen Spartacus was kind and fair to all who joined them, welcoming them, guiding their swords and movements to make them better warriors.

"Have you ever seen him in arm to arm combat?"

She shook her head.

"Once the beast within him is unleased, there is no reckoning for those who stand before him except death."

Namir, Natalie, and Hadrian burst into laughter as Namir regaled them with a story. Gus passed Cloe a bow he was having trouble restringing.

"Leave her be," Alba said as Gannicus stood.

Ignoring Alba, he went over to the pair. At his approach Gus's broad shoulders hunched, Cloe's hands going still. She set the bow down and went into her tent. When Gannicus sauntered back over to sit with Alba, she stood. "If you turn out to be a bully, Gannicus, I'll have no love lost for you," she said. "I've lived under one too many in my life."

"A bully?" he exclaimed. "What're you talking about?"

"You know full well. You won't leave them alone."

He held his arm out toward Gus. "What does she see in him?"

"He does not value her for her looks," Alba said. "When they're together he is timid and sweet. Not crude and crass. He does not stare."

Gannicus threw a hunk of wood in the fire, sending sparks flying. He went toward the German camp and came back with Ava, taking her into his tent. Alba was annoyed with Gannicus and angry at how Spartacus and Hadrian had treated Natalie. She strode toward Spartacus's tent only to run into Crixus as he came out, his face set in a scowl. He shouldered by her, knocking her off balance, the same hatred in his eyes for her as he had the night of her arrival. But now, it didn't bother her.

Spartacus and Hadrian were leaning over maps.

"Why will you not let Natalie go with you on your raids?" Alba said.

"This is not a good time," Spartacus said, glancing up at her.

"Then tell me your reason and I shall be gone," she said.

"There are many reasons," Hadrian said, "many of which you would not understand."

"Try me," she said.

"Crixus has ideas . . . and we are trying to keep things together."

Together? "Does he wish to leave?"

"We are hoping to avoid such a thing," Spartacus said. "But he is proving to be a bit..." He looked to Hadrian.

"Small-minded, difficult, stubborn—"

"He has not been blessed with patience," Spartacus cut across him.

"You're not as fond of him as you once were," Alba said to Spartacus. He lowered his eyes in response. "Natalie is tall. She could disguise herself as a man, perhaps she is a bit slight—"

"Alba," Spartacus said, his tone uncharacteristically sharp with her. "We will not change our minds."

She looked at Hadrian to see if he balked at being part of this all-encompassing 'we,' but he just stood there, his hands resting on his belt.

"You fear Crixus will wish to bring Junia or perhaps Gannicus would want to bring Ava." She shrugged to show how ridiculous the whole thing was.

"It's not that," Spartacus said quietly.

"Then what?" she demanded.

"It's because we love her," Hadrian said simply.

This was not a response she'd expected.

"She has been separated from us in the past." There was pain in Spartacus's voice. "By force."

"It's not something we wish to endure again," Hadrian said darkly.

Alba understood. She was like a sister to them and they wanted to protect her. "I see. Was she the one who killed Camilla?"

Hadrian glanced at Spartacus. "That one was a bit of a team effort."

"Spartacus," Namir called urgently through the tent's fabric. He came in, his face was taut. "A scout has just reported there are men approaching us from Rome. Six thousand."

"Gannicus!" Spartacus bellowed. After several moments, Gannicus appeared, adjusting his tunic. "Is your mind fit?"

"Fuck. Fit enough," he said.

"Alba, tell Gus to ready the horses," Spartacus said.

Twenty-Eight

The men and women who were able to fight were outfitted with the armor and weapons collected from their raids and those taken from soldiers after the slaughter at Mount Vesuvius. Spartacus gave Natalie a sword from Glaber's private inventory. It was well made and lighter than the one she usually carried, but she didn't want it as she was not used to it. Their camp was readying themselves with haste, all hunting parties called home, everyone congregating.

Ava broke away from the Germania camp and came over to Natalie, who was sharpening her sword. "You go to fight?" Ava asked.

Natalie gave a curt nod as she continued to run the stone over the blade.

"I see you in training," Ava continued. "You are good."

Natalie paused and said, "So are you."

"In battle we stay together, watch back of other woman?" Ava said.

Natalie reached for the sword Spartacus had given her and held it for a moment before passing it to Ava.

Ava took it from her. "Good."

. . .

Alba woke to him sitting on the edge of the bed. She watched him as he sat there staring at the wall. So calm and still, his hands resting on his thighs. Then he pushed off and stood. He lifted his armor over his head, clipped his wrist guards, pulled his greaves up his calves, and cinched them into place.

Alba sat up and pulled her knees to her chest, trying to hide the dread taking hold of her. He came over and pressed his forehead against hers. She gripped his arm, and they stayed like that for a moment before he was called from the tent.

The gladiators had gathered, outfitted in their armor, their weapons secured to their sides and on their backs. Hadrian stood with his hand resting on his sword, watching and waiting as the men congregated. He glanced at Namir and then bent down, adjusting his belt so that his dagger was at his side and easier to reach for. Natalie's long, dark hair was braided in the same style as Alba's had been at the mask party only much tighter. Cloe came to stand beside Alba as the others prepared themselves.

Gus wasn't dressed for battle.

"Are you not going?" Alba said.

"Spartacus has asked me to stay behind," he said.

Alba had been wondering if there was a plan in place if they didn't return.

Spartacus called Hadrian, Crixus, and Gannicus together, giving them quick instructions, the others listening, focused and sharp. Even Gannicus. There was a ripple of movement, each having been set a particular task, and the four made off in separate directions. Natalie went with Spartacus and Namir with Hadrian.

"Collect your things," Gus said to Cloe and Alba. "We are leaving." He pulled a bag onto his shoulders.

"Where are we going?" Alba asked.

"A ways from here, bring only what is essential," he said to them.

"Just us?" Alba asked.

He nodded. A few hundred women and children would be left behind at the camp.

. . .

Cloe, Gus, and Alba walked for a long while. As they climbed the side of a valley, a misty rain fell over them, seeping into their clothes. They stopped in a nook that was carved into the hill and protected by a jut of earth above. The rain clung to their skin, dripping from their hair and clothes. They changed out of their tunics and sat huddled together in the cool autumn air, unable to start a fire. They were to remain as inconspicuous as possible.

Gus slept between them, his sword resting on his stomach.

Three days the rebels were gone, each one grating on Alba more and more. She did not like it, the not knowing. Being so far away from it all.

In the night she would toss and turn, her body pressing into the uneven and hard ground. The nightmares she had had in her youth returned and every so often she was shaken awake. What noises had she been making? Sinister thoughts dashed through her restless mind and she fought to quiet them. What if Spartacus never knew of his unborn child and that he was going to be a father?

She was quite sure she was pregnant.

Earlier that morning Cloe had said something to Gus. He hadn't heard her so he placed his hand on her back and tilted his head down, asking her to repeat it. Cloe dropped her shoulder back away from his touch, just slightly, but at that Gus lowered his hand and stepped back, suddenly awkward and uncertain. For the rest of the day she was not the light woman they had grown accustomed to but reserved and withdrawn.

Their dinner was hard bread, nuts, and fruit.

"I am . . ." Cloe started, and they both turned their attention on her. They had gone a long while without speaking, and her words cut through the air. "Pregnant," she said quietly, and covered her face with her hands.

Both of them, Alba thought.

After a moment, Gus leaned forward and pulled her hands away, holding them tenderly in his.

"I have always wanted to be a mother," she said in a small voice. A confession. She turned to Alba waiting for her reaction, what she thought of this.

"I too am pregnant," Alba said.

"No," Cloe said.

"But the thought of it scares me." The image of her own mother had faded and then there was this. The life they lived. The waiting, praying that each day was the day that the people she had grown so fond of would return. And even if they did win this battle, Rome would send more soldiers. Who would want to bring a child into this life of uncertainty? When Alba herself could not even walk safely through the camp.

"Have you told Spartacus?" Cloe asked.

Alba shook her head.

"He is the father," Gus said. "He should know."

On the fourth night, two hands roused her from her sleep.

"Alba," Spartacus said, pulling her awake.

Relieved to hear his voice, she sat up and held him against her. His skin was rough to the touch and leaning back, her eyes widened in panic. His body was covered in grime and crusted blood.

"It's Roman blood," he said quickly. "We're all fine. There were casualties but none... none from our group."

He shouldered her bag, and they made their way down the ridge, cutting through the morning mist that floated above the meadow. Alba and Spartacus trailed a few paces behind Cloe and Gus. The outer patrol had already been reestablished, men nodding at them as they passed.

Alba slowed as they crested the hill, their campsite nestled at the bottom, spaced apart from the hundreds of others.

"Spartacus."

He stopped and turned to face her.

She took his arm and slid her hand down to his, oblivious of the blood and grime. "I am pregnant."

He stared at her for a moment and then turned slowly.

"Gus," he yelled, making her jump. "Prepare that horse."

"For what purpose?" Alba asked as they descended the ridge to their tents. He was pulling her forward, still holding on to her hand.

"To take you north," he said. "You will be safer there."

"North?" she said, taking her hand back. "I am not going anywhere."

Spartacus's quick movements unsettled the horse causing it to whinny as he looped the bridle around its neck.

"Stop," she said. "Be reasonable." She hadn't seen him in such a state since she had told him about Max. "This news wasn't meant to cause panic. It was meant . . ." *To bring joy*, she wanted to say, but he was no longer listening to her.

The thought of having a child made her breath catch and her palms clammy when she let her mind linger on it for too long. She hadn't realized until this moment that she had been hoping that Spartacus, who was ever calm in the face of hardship, would have taken her hands at the news, as Gus had Cloe's, and assured her it would all be fine.

"What's going on?" Natalie asked, coming out of her tent. She too was covered in blood and dirt.

"Alba's going into the mountains," Spartacus said.

"I told him," Alba said.

"Spartacus," Hadrian said, "she is safer here with us. Our numbers have grown, continue to grow, we can protect her."

"I agree," Gannicus said. "Let her stay."

"It's not your decision," Spartacus said.

"Nor is it yours," Alba said.

Spartacus shook his head and went into his tent.

Hadrian gently stroked the horse's neck, steadying its agitated hooves. He lifted the bridle off and turned to Alba. "Go and make it right," he said.

Alba stepped into the tent slowly, deflated.

Spartacus had stripped out of his clothes and emptied his ewer into his basin as he wiped away the remnants of battle.

"Neither of us chose this life," Alba said to his back as he scrubbed his arms. "But we have chosen each other and I'd like to spend my time with you for as long as I can. I can't guarantee that our child will be safe, but I've never known such comfort as I do in your arms. Please do not force me from them."

The cloth stilled in his hand. "My arms bring you comfort?" he said.

"You bring me comfort, Alex," she said quietly. "Ever since we were children."

"It's been a long time since I've heard that name." He rested his hands on the lip of the basin. "If that is your wish, you will stay with us."

Twenty-Nine

Once the rebels had washed the blood, dirt, and sweat from their bodies, they tended to their wounds. By the afternoon, those who could took up their usual daily tasks. Namir and Natalie sat on a log bench that had been planed by Gus, chopping and peeling vegetables at a makeshift table.

"What happened in the battle?" Alba asked, joining them. She pulled a basket of carrots toward her and picked up a knife.

"The man is a genius," Namir said. "As the Romans approached." He used the vegetables to show Alba, laying out the scene. "We assembled on the field in their formation. In straight, neat lines. The scouts rode toward us, saw us in rectangles, and went to report back. When their army approached we were gone, having run into the city, luring them in."

"It was as Spartacus had predicted," Natalie said. "The Romans are so disciplined and unyielding in their organization that they entered the city as a unit. They didn't know what to do. They are trained for field battle."

"We attacked them from all angles," Namir said. "The rooftops and alleyways, picking them off."

It was the town that the rebels were quite familiar with, trading and bartering with the citizens for several weeks now. Under strict orders not to bother the town, they had developed a relationship with the citizens who welcomed their presence and the abundance of business it brought them.

"We almost got their commander but he escaped," Namir added, clutching his knife. He lifted the basket of peeled vegetables and tipped them into the boiling water. They cascaded over each other, plunking into the cauldron with small splashes.

"You've spoken with Spartacus?" Natalie asked Alba.

"Yes," Alba said. "All is good. I'm staying."

"I am happy for you, Alba," Namir said. His gaze fell on Hadrian, who was striding back into the camp.

"What was it that first attracted you to Hadrian?" Alba asked.

"His thighs," Namir said.

"What?" Natalie said, losing her grip on the potato she was peeling.

"Those little balls of muscle right above his knees."

"How's the stew coming along?" Hadrian asked. He leaned over the pot and prodded at the raw vegetables.

His thighs were long, muscular, and thick.

"What are you two looking at?" he said to Natalie and Alba, following their gaze to his legs.

"Nothing," Natalie said.

She and Alba stood, lifting the heavy pot and placing it carefully over the fire, neither daring to glance at the other.

When they approached their tent, Cloe said, "What?"

They told her and the three burst into quiet laughter.

It was decided that the group would splinter off into two factions for the winter. The fall had seen their numbers grow to seventy thousand and it would be too difficult to sustain enough food and provisions for such a mass of people. Crixus would take close to half of the people south to Lucania while Spartacus and Hadrian would stay in the Campania region to raid Nola and Nuceria. The one big problem was that Crixus's group comprised mostly of the trained warriors whereas the young families, women, and elders were staying with Spartacus and Hadrian. Spartacus tried to convince Gannicus to accompany Crixus, but he refused to commit to either camp.

The rebels fortified their shelters as the winter winds enveloped them. The hunters had to expand their territory and the food provisions were closely monitored. Many shepherds, herdsmen, and farmers had joined them, and the gladiators that remained with Spartacus used this time to train them with weapons won from their battles. Their bodies were fit. Now they just had to be honed into a new purpose.

On a midwinter's morning Alba stepped out of Spartacus's tent, the wisps of her hair blowing against the sides of her face. She had layered against the biting air, and the snow clung to the trees and bushes, lying like a blanket over their tents.

Something was amiss but she couldn't place it. She rested her hand for a moment on her rounded stomach, then turned toward Gannicus's tent.

"He's gone," Hadrian said.

A wave of sadness she did not expect fell over her. She'd become so acquainted to his greetings in the morning, their shared grins of amusement, and the chats she had with him. Though the others didn't mention him, there was a melancholy in their camp that day, his loss felt keenly by them all. It was unlike when Crixus and Junia had left as their absence made the atmosphere easy and light.

Cloe's and Alba's bellies grew, Cloe's body staying mostly the same while Alba's became plumper, her arms and legs thickening. She found herself watching Cloe, envious of her. "She still walks as though she's floating," Alba said to Natalie. "I cannot walk without waddling."

"Most women do in the end."

"But do they all get this big?" Alba asked, holding her arms out. The dresses she wore were now tents.

"Alba," Natalie scolded. "Embrace the glow of pregnancy."

"I'm not glowing!" Alba said.

Alba slept with Spartacus now except on nights when he was away on raids. Against the winter winds, he protected himself with a purple cloak, similar to the one Neme had worn, and had grown a beard. It was coarse and rough on her cheeks, but it shielded him from the bitter air, and so she scrunched her face to its bristle saying nothing. One night he caught her making a face and the next day it was trimmed back.

One morning Natalie emerged from her tent, blurry eyed from a sleepless night.

"Natalie?" Alba said, standing.

"Cloe had a daughter in the night," Natalie said.

"Why did you not get me?"

"She's fine," Natalie said. "You need your rest."

"She was so quiet."

Hadrian stumbled out of his tent, his face puffy with lack of sleep.

"Did you hear her?" Alba asked.

He grunted as he leaned down to prod the fire back to life.

"He and Gus stayed with us throughout, assisting and getting me what I needed," Natalie said.

"Not Namir?"

"He fainted early on so Hadrian had to remove him," she said. "Gus did a marvelous job cutting the cord."

"Gus did . . ." Hadrian said, indignant. "Who was the one bringing you the warm water, the clean cloths . . . oil! Gus makes one little snip."

Eight days after the birth she was given a name, Aleni. Alba meanwhile wondered how large someone could become. She was so uncomfortable she struggled to find a position on the bed she could stay in without moving. Instead she knelt and shut her eyes. She did not hear Spartacus's silent footsteps as he came into the tent.

"You're praying?" he said, concern lining his voice.

"For the safe delivery of the child," Alba said. It wasn't uncommon for complications to occur during a birth. She placed her hands on the bed and lifted herself back up.

"Natalie has seen many women safely through," he said. "As she will see you."

"But how much longer must I wait?" Alba said, opening her arms. She was suddenly overcome with emotion. "Have you ever seen someone get this big?"

He pulled her into an embrace with a grin. "You are not that big."

She appreciated his tender lie.

Thirty

The early spring brought the vibrant greens of new life sprouting from the earth and the noisy nesting of birds in the branches.

Alba and Cloe had gone down to the river, and Natalie was warming herself by the fire. She had been training a group of females with Ava for most of the day. Many of the rebels were taking the day to enjoy the warm rays of sun, cutting through the trees. Spartacus sat next to Natalie, stretching his legs out in front of him.

"I heard there was a messenger from Crixus's camp," she said. "Will they join us now that winter's ended?"

"That was my hope but—"

A scream pierced the air, shrill and electric. A current shooting through them all. Hadrian threw his tent flap open. Cloe ran toward them, panting, clutching her baby to her chest.

"Alba," she breathed. "The river."

Spartacus stood. He and Hadrian took off through the forest.

Alba tried to climb the muddy ridge, but a pain pulsed through her that was so great it hindered her every movement. A warmth grew inside her like the embers of a fire ready to ignite, and her whole body broke into a slick sweat. On her bum she edged her way backward up the ravine until she came to a shaded patch and, unable to go farther, lay back against the forest floor. The cool ground sent a shiver through her. Leaves and bits of bark clung to her wet arms and neck, scratching her.

There were quick footsteps thudding down the hill, and Hadrian boomed, "Out of the way," to someone.

How good it was to hear his voice. He and Spartacus slid to a halt and squatted on either side of her. They gently eased her up to a seated position, but with her head hung, she said, "I can't . . ." She squeezed her eyes shut to the pain as her whole body clenched. "I can't stand."

"Lay back," Spartacus said.

She shook her head, planting her palms in the dirt beside her. He slid his arm beneath her legs and Hadrian did the same. They lifted her like she was seated in a chair. Their arms held her steady even as she squirmed to the pain passing through her like a spasm of growing discomfort. She pressed her wet forehead to Spartacus's shoulder.

"Oh, Alex," she said as they approached their camp.

"In here!" Natalie called through the tent fabric. They lowered Alba down and got out of Natalie's way. Natalie sat between Alba's legs, massaging her thighs. "I need warm water, oil, sponges, bandages, clean clothes, and a sharp knife," she yelled as they left the tent.

Alba lay her head back against the pillow, the strands of her hair sticking to the back of her neck. She squealed as waves of discomfort washed over her and moved her head from side to side. "I can't, I can't, I can't." She pressed her palms to her temples. The pain was too much.

"You can and you will," Natalie said firmly.

As she faded in and out, her whole body wet, Natalie encouraged her throughout. Spartacus and Hadrian sat outside the tent, bringing things as Natalie called for them.

"You feel that ebb and flow passing through your body like waves in the ocean," Natalie said. "When you feel the flow, you push . . . good. And again, push."

The baby slid out and Alba raised her head.

"It's a boy," Natalie said to Alba, smiling down at her. "You have a son."

Spartacus threw the tent flap aside and, kneeling next to Alba, cut his son's cord. With the baby in the nook of his arm, he leaned forward to show Alba and kissed her wet forehead. "Well done, my love," he said.

Happiness rushed through her at the sight of her son in his arms.

"A bit slimier than Cloe's, no?" Hadrian said to Natalie. She responded by smacking his chest.

"Thank you," Alba said to her.

"I was thinking . . ." Spartacus lifted his blues eyes to Alba. "We could name him Max."

"Yes." Alba smiled and looked down at her son. "Max."

The three of them sat crouched around Alba for a long while savoring the moment.

Alba had drifted off and was gently woken by Natalie. "Alba," Natalie said softly. "It's time to feed him."

Alba sat up and pulled her strap down as Natalie passed her the baby. Alba cradled his head and held him to her breast. She glanced at Natalie, unsure of what to do.

"Guide him," Natalie said.

When he latched, Alba said, "How often do I do this?"

"Often. Whenever he fusses, assume he's hungry."

"Cloe makes this seem so easy," Alba said.

"As you will once you get used to it."

Natalie scooped Aleni into her arms and swayed her from side to side. "Have you ever seen two babies so beautiful?" she said.

Alba was feeding Max, her breasts sore and tender to the touch. As Max latched, it stung and she winced, clenching her teeth to the pain. Cloe was so peaceful and serene when feeding Aleni, almost like she was enjoying it, the way she gazed down at the child. Alba spent some nights fighting tears as she fed. Worst of all, she now had an aversion to being touched by anyone, including Spartacus. She spent most nights with Natalie and Cloe, unable to explain this unknown sensation she was experiencing to him.

"Do you ever miss the life you had before?" Natalie asked Cloe.

"No. Except my hair perhaps." She had just trimmed it back again. "But it is a small price to pay."

"What of your villa? Of being waited on and the fine clothes?"

Cloe shook her head. "I was suffocating in that place, screaming from within. Every move I made, every word I said was scrutinized. I would hide behind pillars when my in-laws would pass, drift in and out of rooms just often enough so that my presence was not questioned."

Alba shook her head in amazement. "I did the exact same in my house," she said. "You always seemed so calm and composed."

"Because I had to be. If I was not, things were less pleasant," she said. "Watching you wander around the parties, speaking to whomever you wanted. I envied your banter with Julius. I even envied the slaves their friendships."

"I wish I'd known you better then," Alba said. "You would've been a welcome companion during the summer festivities."

"I'm afraid not," Cloe said. "I was not to leave Quintus's side during the parties."

"I come in?" a woman's voice called through the tent. The flap was pulled back and Ava appeared. "Gannicus? He come back?"

"We're not sure," Alba said as Max finished and she pulled her strap up. "We don't know why he left or where he went."

"He no say goodbye," Ava said.

"He does that," Natalie said.

Ava sat on the bed. "Man."

"*Men* is right," Natalie said.

Thirty-One

Crixus and his camp of followers came back to join them on a cool spring day. Alba was putting Max to sleep when she heard the commotion outside, the greetings and stilted pleasantries. Natalie went over to greet Junia, but their embrace was stiff. Junia's body was more muscular than when they had left and her hair shaved on both sides. Cloth was wrapped around her knuckles.

In the evening, voices raised in frustration and anger came from Spartacus's tent.

"Don't," Natalie said in warning as Alba stood.

She went anyway. Too many times in her life she had stood aside when she wished she hadn't. She paused next to the tent to listen.

"If we go north across the Alps, we can get out from under Rome," Spartacus pled with Crixus. "You can go home to Gaulia."

"You once said that you wished to stop the very heartbeat of Rome, to free all from chains," Crixus said.

"That was before we had grown to such a number," Spartacus said. "We have many among us now who are unable to fight."

"So we turn our backs on the rest? All of those who are still in chains."

"And put everyone here at risk?" Spartacus said.

"We are so close," Crixus said. "Nowhere in history has there been a rebellion like ours with such success. We must finish what we started."

Finish what they started. He was unwavering and stubborn. Agitated by his ignorant comments, she swatted the tent flap open.

"What is she doing here?" Crixus said. "I don't ask Junia to meetings among men."

"I've spoken to Roman generals, taken dinner with members of the Senate and men currently on the consul who make decisions about the army," she said.

"Your point?" Crixus said.

"My point is that I know things," she said. "The soldiers you have come up against are led by the praetors. They are nothing to Pompey who is in Spain at present with most of Rome's legions. Their elite and highest trained."

"Which is why we strike Rome now," Crixus growled.

"Do you not think that if Rome itself was threatened that they would not call back every legion at their disposal?" she said.

"We have cut Rome down at every turn," Crixus said. "We will do so again."

"You are blinded by a single thought. Your naivete will be your downfall," Alba said.

"My naivete," Crixus scoffed. He took a step toward her. "Every time I see that mark"—he held his finger to the spider-webbed scar on her temple—"I wish I'd hit you harder."

Spartacus placed his hand on Crixus's shoulder. "Enough," he said.

Hadrian met her eyes and made a slight motion with his head. She understood. Her presence was not welcome. It would only aggravate Crixus further.

This was one thing she missed about living in a Roman household. There, a woman's opinion would not be so easily discarded. They often gave good insight and their words were not dismissed but appreciated and held weight.

. . .

Hours later, she slid from between Natalie and Cloe and went quietly into Spartacus' tent. His long body was straight—he was awake.

"What is the decision?" she asked.

"Crixus will not be bent," he said, sitting up. He rested his forearms on his knees. "Our forces shall be divided. Those who wish will follow Crixus toward Rome while I take the rest toward the Alps."

"He has never led an army without you. He does not have your knowledge, your discipline. Rome will not let us pass peacefully to the Alps, not after all that has been done, all they have lost," she said. "We stand a greater chance united as one."

"I know. I know," he said. "It was once my only desire to take Rome. While standing there in the arenas, that was my single thought, the vision of their deaths, releasing all who were chained against their will."

"Is it the women and children among us that have swayed you?"

"Yes. But also you and Max. The thought of us living out the life you described in peace."

Natalie came into the tent then. "What of your responsibility to us, to the people who have followed you?" she said. "You would leave us to fend for ourselves?"

"Natalie, all of these people will need to fend for themselves eventually," Alba said.

Natalie's face darkened. "I see," she said.

"I speak of the others," Spartacus said. "You would always have a home with me."

Natalie scoffed and shook her head.

"It's true," Alba said. "We could all live together."

"Don't be absurd," she said. "You would not want me once you made a house of your own."

"Of course we would," Alba said. "And never think differently."

Natalie looked from Alba and then to Spartacus, emotion taking hold of her face as she shook her head.

Thirty-Two

Word was sent through the camp that there would be two courses of action. After much discussion and back-and-forths, some thirty thousand rebels decided to join Crixus. Much to Alba's surprise, this included many warriors from the Germania camp, but Ava remained seated by the fire.

"You're not going with them?" Natalie said.

"No," Ava said, and nodded at Spartacus. "This one knows better."

If only she could convey that to her fellow countrymen. When Hadrian came out of Spartacus's tent, his face somber, Alba's stomach dropped.

"Are you going to stay with Spartacus?" Hadrian asked Namir.

"Of course," Namir said. "Are you not?"

Hadrian shook his head. "War is the only life I know."

"It wasn't always," Namir said.

Hadrian leaned down to kiss him farewell, but Namir ducked out of reach.

"Hadrian," Natalie said, a pleading in her voice. "Don't leave us."

"My mind is made."

"You can unmake it," Alba said.

Hadrian rounded on her. "Do not comment on a decision that you could not even begin to fathom."

So they truly were being divided. Gannicus gone, and now Hadrian and Crixus. As Hadrian prepared his belongings, he looked to Namir, who usually helped him, but today Namir's hands remained still. Hadrian pulled Natalie into a short embrace and kissed her on the head.

"Junia's over there," Alba said to Natalie.

"I said goodbye to her a long time ago," Natalie said.

The tension in the air was palpable. Crixus and Spartacus gripped forearms, and Crixus made a joke about Spartacus missing out on the spoils and the lives his army would take. Ill-timed, it fell flat and punctured the air, drawing Spartacus's chest tighter. As they shouldered their weapons, a dread filled her, constricting her. It all seemed surreal. So quick. Gus's eyes were on his countrymen, solemn and grave, as he stood next to Cloe.

In their wake was left a huge void. Whole swaths of the camp gone, leaving patches of trampled earth, the smoky remains of campfires were soon out for good.

In the days after, the tension did not ease.

Weeks later, when the dreaded message came, Namir looked as though he was going to be sick. It had been a slaughter, the army being overtaken and cut down at Mount Garganus. Crixus had fought valiantly to his death. Spartacus questioned the few who returned about the fate of Hadrian, but no one could give a definitive answer.

"I should have gone with them," he said, his face hard.

"They made their choice," Natalie said just as hard. "And we have made ours."

A dark shadow fell over Spartacus, one that Alba could not lift. Her own spirits were dampened too. Left with half the camp, what would they do now? They could not stay here, living this way forever, hiding in a forest.

Spartacus had taken to pacing. A restlessness Alba had never seen in him before coursed through his veins. Agitated, uncertain. It was Natalie who spoke to him. Stern words. Trying to redirect his energy.

Later than night, a rebel hobbled toward their encampment, his leg was gashed and turning purple. "Six hundred. The Romans have captured six hundred," he said through labored breaths.

"Prisoners?" Natalie said.

"It was announced. They are being taken to Rome to be crucified," the man said before collapsing to the ground.

As he was taken to the medical tent, Alba glanced at Spartacus's grim face. The Romans would use the crucifixions to instill fear, to dissuade others from joining them and quell the uprising. An example of what would happen if you chose to follow Spartacus.

The next night a scout burst into Spartacus's tent. A Roman legion was bearing down on them.

"Get Natalie," he said to Alba.

Only twenty gladiators were left from the House of Batiatus, and as they assembled, diagrams were drawn and weapons prepared for battle.

Alba, Cloe, Gus, and the babies were high up on a ridge, able to hear the yells, grunts, and clashes of metal. Alba covered her ears to it.

The Romans were again defeated. As Alba trudged back to the camp with Cloe, Gus, and the babies, she didn't know how much longer she could take this. The cycle of fighting.

At dusk the rebels started to congregate in a massive semicircle. Spartacus hadn't sought her out as he usually did after returning, but she knew that he was back by the way the swarm moved, with purpose, preparing for something.

"What's happening?" Alba asked Namir.

People passed by them to join the crowd.

"Death by games, gladiator style," Namir said, and stopped. "I don't think you should watch."

She had not been planning on watching, but this was the first time Namir had said that to her.

"Why?" Alba asked.

He hesitated.

"Namir, tell me."

"The Romans, they're fighting each other."

The statement hung between. Namir must be confused. It was one thing to have the prisoners fight the rebels but to have them fight themselves to the death. That was another thing altogether.

"I'll speak to Spartacus. There must be a mistake."

"Alba." Namir took her arm.

It took her a moment to process his unsaid words. She felt as though she were falling off the cliff at Vesuvius. It couldn't be. She stumbled through the crowd, her feet carrying her in as if in a drunken stupor, thoughts slipping through her mind.

The prisoners were being forced into lines, and the glow of a torch lit on Spartacus's purple cape.

"Spartacus!" she yelled.

He shouldered past the crowd to come over to her. She knew that he was hurting, that without Crixus, Hadrian, and Gannicus, he stood before them as the last of the rebels' leaders. She wished that Hadrian or Gannicus were here now, for he had that glint in his eye, the same one he had had the night she told him about Max. Fevered and wild.

"Who are they fighting?" she asked. She would not believe it until she heard it from his lips.

He adjusted his wrist guard, his lack of response sending a wave of panic over her.

"I know that you are grieving your friends' deaths," she said. "Their losses weigh down on us all, but this is not the way."

"You need not watch," he said. His eyes were dark and dilated, absorbing his face. The bright blue that shone from them extinguished.

"As you force them to kill each other?" she said in horror. "That is barbaric."

The first set of men were being prodded and dragged by their chains through the rebels toward the inner circle.

"What would you have me say?" he growled, a muscle twitching in his jaw. "What response would you have me give you?"

"A human one," she said.

He came right into her face, his nostrils flared, and his jaw clenched. There was anger in his eyes. Anger like she had never seen before, directed at her. She had made him question his moral compass, but was it enough to realign it?

"You have not seen what I have seen." His voice was a deep, low rumble. "You have not witnessed the mistreatment and the torture that we as slaves have been subjected to and endured. You have been shielded from it."

"Thank the Gods I have if it means that one of us has an ounce of humanity left," she spat back. "Though they stand before you Roman, they are still people."

He did not respond.

"You are not yourself," she said, a pleading in her voice.

"Haven't I only ever been what others want me to be?" he said, his face hard.

There was a shift in him then from anger to resolve, and she knew that he would not be moved. He slipped back through the rebels.

"Alba," Namir said. He wore the grief of Hadrian's death in his face, yet he did not seem to hold the same need for vengeance as the others who had lost dear ones. "Perhaps it's best if you wait out the night on the other side of the camp." He said it kindly, which made it all the harder to bear.

"You are fine with this?" she asked as he took the next prisoner from the wall.

"Unforgivable atrocities have been committed on both sides," he said.

Alba lowered her head, her chest heaving in anger. In a trance her eyes floated over the prisoners nearest her. At the end of the line was a young man. His face was chiseled as if from stone, and his muscles were more defined than when she'd last seen him. His coiffed wig was gone.

Marcus Crassus's son. Licinius.

An idea came over her then and began to take hold, urgency coursing through her. Elbowing her way through the spectators, she kept an eye out for Spartacus as she looked for Cloe and Gus. Spotting them on the other side of the semicircle, she caught Gus's eye and motioned him over.

Once they broke through the crowd, Cloe said, "Alba, you must speak to him."

"I've tried. He won't listen to me." Alba lowered her voice and Cloe leaned in closer. "That boy over there is Marcus Crassus's son." She tilted her head in his direction. "We may yet have rebels who are alive in their camp."

"Are you thinking of a trade?" Cloe said.

Alba nodded. "Yes."

"You must tell him quickly," Cloe said.

Alba shook her head.

"No," Cloe said, realizing Alba's intentions. "It's too dangerous."

"Spartacus cannot go," Alba said. This, they all knew. "And they wouldn't pay heed to anyone other than a rebel leader, someone with authority. You know how their minds are. I'm their best chance at a negotiation."

"A woman?" Gus questioned.

"In the Roman houses," Cloe explained, "women are skilled negotiators in their own right. They're allowed to speak on behalf of their husbands when they are away or unable to attend an event. They'll hear her out."

Gus's eyebrows rose, skeptical.

"Alba." Cloe turned to her friend. "They're clever. They'll see that you're unharmed, that you're healthy. They might ask questions. What if..." Cloe could not voice the thought.

"I must try, Cloe," Alba said. "It's one life against hundreds."

"What of your son?" Cloe asked.

This was the one thing Alba could not explain away. Only a few months old and already with a little personality. The way he would light up as she lifted him from the ground or smile at her from the laps of the others. His dark hair was as dark as hers, his eyes the same shade of blue as his fathers. Oh, she could not think of him.

"He's among those who love him," Alba said finally.

The man next to Licinius was being taken from the wall.

Alba turned to Gus. "Will you help me?"

Many of Gus's countrymen and women had gone with Crixus. He nodded and strode over to his tent.

"Not a word to anyone," Alba said to Cloe. "Especially Spartacus. If he intervenes, it will all be in vain."

Cloe shut her eyes and nodded. A tear rolled down her cheek. "You have been the most wonderful friend," she said.

Alba took her arm. "I won't let Gus get anywhere near the Roman camp, I promise. But you must be careful not to give us away." Cloe's tear glistened in the light of a passing torch, and Alba thought of Max. "You can't let them see." She wiped the tear from Cloe's cheek.

Cloe nodded.

There was a burst of cheers and Alba knew she would have to be quick. She picked at Licinius's lock with her hair pin. His eyes were on her, trying to place her. "Alba of the Junii," she said in a low whisper. "You're coming with us." She tilted her head toward Gus. "He's a gladiator." Gus pushed his shoulders back at the lie. "If you try to escape, he will kill you."

It was a dark, cloudy night, lit only by the torch she carried, and once out of familiar terrain, her step faltered. Thankfully Gus had vast knowledge of the area, having been able to explore the freely and taking it upon himself to do so. After walking a long while, they approached the dark shapes of the Romans' tents. Gus chained Licinius to a tree, double-checking that he was securely bound, and Alba made note of her surroundings.

They moved out Licinius's earshot. "When Spartacus finds out that I am gone, he will try to come for me," Alba said. "But you remind him that if he leaves they will have no one. He is their last leader."

Gus scratched the back of his neck, not relishing the idea that he would have to bear this message. She lit Gus's torch and he placed his hand on her shoulder.

Thirty-Three

It was the time of morning when everything was completely dark, right before the sun broke over the horizon and spilled its light into the world. A faint glow lit the Roman camp, and she rolled her torch in the dirt, extinguishing it.

"Give me strength," she said under her breath. She needed to find the largest tent.

The guards were pacing the aisles of tents, and she crouched down, darting through them, keeping to the shadows.

"He says nothing but curse words in German," a man said, causing her to stop.

"Well then," another man said. "Let us make an example of him and help to draw the words from his mouth."

There was a fist on flesh and a grunt, sounds of a struggle. A man was raised up on a cross, his feet dangling, his face puffy and purple.

Alba gasped and her stomach turned to bile. A guttural pain surged through her as she stood in shock. Hadrian's chest heaved beneath his drooped head. To look at him was unbearable. His body hanging there, covered in his blood, bruised and battered.

Strong, unbreakable Hadrian.

"What the—" one of the Roman guards said, noticing Alba.

"I am a Roman noble," she said as strongly as she could, trying to be brave. "My name is Alba of the Junii. I wish to speak with your commander."

"My commander?"

"Yes, who is in charge of your legion?"

"That would be me," a familiar voice said from behind her.

She turned to see the silhouette of a tall, lanky figure. "Publius," she said.

"Yes?"

"It's me, Alba."

His torch lit her face, and his long body swayed back in disbelief. His shimmering blue tunic was a contrast to the bronze and red of the Roman soldiers' uniforms. Composing himself, he jerked his torch toward a tent and she followed him. The tent was large, with two long tables and a few chairs.

"Where did you come from?" He placed the torch in a sconce.

"I've been living with the rebels," she said.

"The savages?"

"They're not savages," she said. "Publius, I'm here to make a trade."

"What could you possibly have that we would want?" The good-mannered tone he'd once directed at her was gone.

"Your brother."

The concern that flashed across his face gave him away. So they were close. Thank the Gods. "You have hundreds of rebels held prisoner here. Return them to us and you shall be reunited with him," she said.

"You think I would trade one man for hundreds?" he said.

"I do. I know how close your family is. And as you said, they are savages. What is one man to a few hundred?" she said. "Not many in the grand scheme of things."

He shifted. "I cannot approve this."

He was thinking of his father, of the chain of command and layers of their politics. "You can. We both know that, and I know it's what your father would want as well," she said, and paused, looking him in the eye. "Once you release them—all of them, including the one on the cross—I will tell you where Licinius is. And it must be done now."

"I cannot send back a rebel leader," Publius said, lifting the flap. "And he would not last the journey."

"Than his release should not matter to you," Alba said.

Publius dropped the flap and turned to her. "There is a rumor I have heard that is most unsettling to me," he said. "That rebel women fight alongside the rebel men."

She nodded. "It is true."

"What kind of a man has women fight alongside him?" he asked.

"He doesn't have them. They volunteer," she said. "No one is forced to stand with Spartacus. He sees them in equal standing upon the field of battle, and they can choose to fight if they wish."

"Women choose this?" Publius said, unable to comprehend the notion. Having spent his life surrounded by the noblewomen, Alba could see how this would be a difficult concept for him to grasp. "And you stand with him, Spartacus?"

She nodded.

"Do you know what it is they do to the Roman women in the towns they plunder?" he asked.

He was trying to bait her. "Why is it that they are able to gain entry so quickly into those towns?" Alba said. "Why is it that the citizens turn their eyes?"

"The existence of the slaves is paramount to our social structure, one which is built on levels. Progress and forward movement are driven from the bottom up. We are the minds. They are the bodies. The very structures of our cities, the architecture you so greatly admire, has been built on the backs of the slaves. You think your rebellion will be remembered as something heroic? It will be a blight, a blunder in history, a small disruption in our daily routine," he said. "When you plunder and steal for your cause, you do not take from Rome's elite—you steal from everyone, yourselves included."

Alba would not indulge him in this conversation. "Licinius is waiting," she said. "Will you make the trade?"

He ran his hand over the fine silk of his tunic, annoyed that she was unmoved by his words. This feeling was foreign to him. Of not being in control. "I will make a trade," he said, and left the tent.

Alba could hear the men outside, taking their morning meals, their voices gruff and tight. Not like the rebel camp where people rose with greetings and plans of the day ahead. People of different nationalities and languages. She sat on the floor and her stomach grumbled.

Publius returned with a sparsely bearded man, his long hair clipped with feathers and toggles. His arms were sinewy and covered in shiny scars. He was some sort of pirate. She had seen men like him bartering in the markets.

"She's better looking than you let on," he said to Publius.

"Every man has his tastes," Publius said.

"I owe Horatio some money so he has agreed to take you in order to offset part of the debt," Publius said—the son of the richest man in Rome. "Now, tell me where my brother is and I'll let the prisoners go."

"Every single one of them?" she said.

He nodded.

"Even the one on the cross?"

"Yes, even the one on the cross," he said.

"Once the rebels have left, I'll tell you," she said.

"I'll make the arrangements." He exited, his robes sweeping behind him.

Horatio came over to Alba and bent down so that his face was inches from hers. He thumbed her lip up and nodded at the state of her teeth, though she had no idea why as his own were short, brown stumps. He started to pull the strap of her dress from her shoulder, but she swatted him away. He grabbed her shoulder blade, digging his thumb into her flesh. He pressed so hard she thought the bone would pop through her skin.

"I'm going to have to teach you some manners," he said as she recoiled in pain. His breath made her eyes water. He took out a knife, the handle curved like a hook.

"Out!" Publius barked from the mouth of the tent. "You can take her when you leave, once the rest of our business has been taken care of."

Horatio snarled and left the tent.

Publius clasped his hands together. "It pains me to do this, you know. You having been one of us. But you have brought this upon yourself," he said with a hopeless shrug.

Alba had to be careful of what she said now, not to undo what she had done.

"Do you miss your life among us?" he asked.

"No," she said. "For I was never really one of you."

"But you were. You were born into one of Rome's finest families," he said. "Though you may have been damaged, your blood line is pure."

Damaged.

"Yet you yourself would not escort me to the games," she said, looking up at him. "And no one of merit would have me as a wife."

His body swayed. "I know a handful of men that would have had you," he said. There was truth in his eyes.

This admission stunned Alba. She opened her mouth to question him further, but a guard called his name.

"You can watch as they are set free," Publius said, and ducked through the tent.

The prisoners were unchained and released. By the state of some of them, Alba prayed that they would make the journey back.

"I am not damaged," she said softly. "No more than the rest of you."

THIRTY-FOUR

Time passed slowly, gnawing at her belly, and pressing heavily on her eyelids. She waited on the floor of the tent, her only comfort in knowing that as the day passed the rebels drew closer to safety. She leaned her head against the fabric.

"So it is true," a familiar voice said.

She forced her eyes open and her chin lifted up toward the voice. Julius Caesar stood before her with his golden curl, his tanned skin, smooth and clean. He wore a pale green tunic and his hands were clasped in front of him but not in the annoying, pretentious way Publius had. Instead, contemplative, taking her in.

Having Publius lord over her with his all-knowing superiority did not affect her. It might have once, before she had found strength through her friendships among the rebels. But Julius, he was someone she had been fond of. Someone who had seen her and spoken to her when no one else would.

"Your skin." He bent and gently rolled her forearm. "Is unmarked. You were accepted as one of them." His eyes narrowed as he touched the spider-webbed scar at her temple. "But there was a struggle." His ability to read her was uncanny. Impressive and unnerving. "Why were you spared?"

He was too clever. There was no use in lying. "One of the rebels was a childhood friend."

"From your time in Thrace?"

She nodded.

"He's quite important, this childhood friend. Or you would not be sitting here before me now."

She needed to change the topic before she revealed something that could undo all she had done. The rebels would still be within the Romans' reach, just barely, but it would be those who were weakest. "Why did you let me believe that the priesthood was my only option other than Publius?" she asked.

"I didn't," he said. "You chose to believe that. I merely suggested the idea of you to him."

She thought of that day in the garden. "Why did you warn me away from Publius's family if you wanted me to be part of his household?"

"My words were not meant as a warning," he said. "I had gained your favor and so you confided in me. I told you that information to assess your adaptability, having determined that you did not confide to anyone in your own house. From the moment I met you, I knew you had a good mind, but your morals were strong so I needed to see if you would waver." He paused. "I never put you in harm's way. Publius would've provided you a good life affording you every luxury, save sexual pleasure."

"So I was merely a vessel through which you would extract information from their family?" she said.

A girl with dark hair came into the tent.

"You remember Diana?" Julius said.

Diana kept her head down so that Alba could not see her face.

"Few female slaves wanted to accompany our legion but she volunteered," Julius said.

Publius came into the tent with two guards behind him. He didn't acknowledge Julius, not even a glance—in fact his shoulders tightened.

Julius's shoulders remained relaxed. What had caused this shift between them?

Julius bowed himself out and left with Diana.

"The rebels are out of our reach," Publius said. "Where is my brother?"

Alba told him where he would find Licinius, and with that, her bargaining power was gone. He nodded at the guards.

"You did not do the rebels a service by coming here," Publius said. "We will catch up to them, perhaps not today or tomorrow, but sooner or later, and your act here will have been in vain." He chained her hands and feet together. "Goodbye, Alba," he said.

In the early evening, she shut her eyes and rested her head against the side of the tent. She was dreading the return of the pirate. She knew that she was not strong enough to withstand a life of rape and servitude. She had already decided, the moment she was taken onto his boat, she would jump over the side and let the weight of the chains take her swiftly to the bottom.

"Are you familiar with Spartacus?" Julius's voice made her twitch. He was standing in the tent opening.

"Of course," she said, her voice cracking, her throat parched. "He is our leader."

"Would you give me a character assessment of the man?" He knelt down in front of her.

"You have seen him," she said. "You know what he is capable of."

"In the arena, yes. But you live among him, spend every day in his presence."

"To what end do you wish to know?" she asked.

There was a slight crease in his brow. "You betrayed your own cousin's flaws to me more candidly."

"Lives did not hang in the balance than," she said.

"There is only one life you need be concerned about now," he said. "Tell me something worth knowing."

He was an intuitive man and clever. He would know if she was not telling him the truth. Her mind was dull from hunger and fatigue. She didn't trust herself to speak.

After a lengthy silence, he said, "I told my wife about you. Your story fascinated her."

"Cornelia."

He nodded, the green glimmer in his eye revealing surprise at Alba knowing her name. "The thing Publius doesn't realize about people like you, people like me, is our enduring fortitude when faced with pain and discomfort," he said. "You have been here almost a whole day without food or drink and said nothing. He has never missed a meal in his life, never known hardship or adversity."

"It's the only life he has ever known," she said. "Which is why he does not understand the rebels' plight. He would never consider a man like Spartacus as an equal."

"That is where he and I differ," he said. "You are fond of him? Of Spartacus?"

A sinking feeling spread through her stomach. She needed to be careful. "Yes."

"Why?"

She thought back to Namir's words. "Because he is kind and fair to all. He does not play games. He does not try to manipulate people," she said pointedly.

"I am not the monster you think me to be," he said.

"I do not think you are a monster, Julius," she said. "People get caught up in how they think things should be. Publius believes I have betrayed Roman ideals, and so his punishment for me is that I am to go with the pirate Horatio. You are angry that I did not agree to live with Publius and that I will not speak of Spartacus now. Or maybe I think too much of myself and you've dismissed my life completely."

A shimmer of disappointment crossed Julius's face. "After all our time together, all our banter and serious discussion, that is what you have distilled me down to?" Julius reached for the chains on her feet and then on her wrists, unlatching them. "I am not people. I do not get caught up in things." He set them beside her. "Find this friend of yours, this Thracian, and desert the rebels," he said. "For we will catch up to you and we will kill every last one." He placed his hand on hers. "Make sure that we do not meet again."

Then he was gone.

Thirty-Five

She sat crouched by the edge of the tent, her body loose with adrenaline. Her senses were heightened, alert, the fall of footsteps and voices through the tent fabric amplified. She collected her limbs and steadied her hands as the sky dimmed to gray. She slipped out the side and started to run toward the forest when something caught her eye.

"No," she whispered, paralyzed with horror.

Hadrian's large body still hung on the cross.

There was an eruption of whinnying and the stomping of horses' hooves. In the distance there was a great plume of smoke and the orange blaze of a fire. Men dashed from their tents, yelling for water, trying to corral the frantic horses. Alba stayed low, making her way cautiously toward Hadrian. There was a hooded figure, hacking at the bottom of Hadrian's cross with an ax.

He swiveled around at Alba's approach.

"Gannicus?" she said, stunned.

"Help me," he said urgently.

The cross fell to the ground with a thump. Alba placed her ear to Hadrian's chest and felt a faint heartbeat while Gannicus slid his knife through the ropes that bound his arms.

"Cover his mouth," Gannicus said to Alba.

He crouched over one hand, prying the nail out of his flesh and the wood. The eye that was not swollen shut bulged open.

"It's me, Alba," Alba said. She cupped his cheek in her hand. "Don't cry out."

Hadrian blinked to show he understood. He clenched his teeth, his chest rising and falling on the cross as Gannicus pried the second nail loose.

They lifted Hadrian to his feet, and he leaned on them as they stumbled together into the woods. There was a rustle, and Gannicus whipped around with his sword raised.

It was Diana.

"She's a slave," Alba said.

"I'm coming with you," she said.

The moon was bright, and they followed the footprints of the released rebels. Hadrian's breath labored, his chest heaving as he lumbered between.

He collapsed to his knees. "Go. Leave me," he said, and then roared out in pain when Gannicus tried to pull him back to his feet.

It would not do, Hadrian could not stand on his own. Gannicus searched the ground for two long, strong pieces of wood. He, Diana, and Alba took off their clothes, tying them to the logs to create a sling that Hadrian could lie on. Diana quickly knotted the clothes, and Gannicus dragged Hadrian onto the fabric between the wood. "Fuck, he's heavy."

Gannicus lifted the back, and Diana and Alba each took a side at the front. They started to walk, jostling a bit until they settled into a pace and rhythm.

In the cool night air, Alba started to sweat and shiver. "Gannicus, what were you doing there?" Alba panted, gripping her feet into the earth as they went up a slippery ridge.

"I had dealings with the pirate Horatio," he said, pausing to catch his breath. "I heard there was a trade made, but when Hadrian wasn't among the rebels going back, I lit their stable on fire."

"Was it not Publius who awarded you the wooden sword of freedom?" Alba gritted out, her arms shaking.

"Thing is, pompous shits like him don't look you in the eye," Gannicus grunted as they crested the ridge. "Didn't even recognize me."

"You're insane," Alba said.

A tinge of deliriousness was coming over her. She no longer felt hunger. Her mind was light as though disconnected from her body. She was in dire need of respite but she kept walking, knowing that if she stopped she would not be able to start again. Her hands chafed on the wood, the sting of it helping to keep her awake and connected to her senses.

"Hadrian," Gannicus would say sharply every now and again and Hadrian would moan in reply.

They climbed another ridge and Alba's legs shook. Her knees dropped beneath her. She stood, knowing that Diana could not carry the front alone. Once they were at the top, Alba's legs wobbled with every step she took and she fell to the ground. She tried to lift her side but her arms had nothing left.

"How much farther is it?" Gannicus asked. He slid his clothes from the makeshift sling.

"It's still a ways," she said.

Gannicus propped Hadrian's limp body up at the base of a large tree and turned to Alba. "Come with me," he said to Alba.

She shook her head. "I am spent."

"I'll carry you."

"No, I'll stay with Hadrian."

"Then take this." He gave her his dagger.

Diana glanced at Alba, pulling her clothes on.

"Follow the path of footprints," Gannicus said to Diana. He would not wait for her.

Diana nodded and Gannicus took off through the forest. Alba pulled her ripped dress off the pole and draped it over her body. It was spotted with shiny, crusted stains of blood.

Hadrian's head drooped to the side.

"Hadrian," Alba said, wrapping her arm around his. "Stay with me. We're almost there. They won't be long."

Her cheek warmed as a tear rolled down it. Shivering, she leaned her head against the prickly bark of the tree, her eyes growing heavy. She fought to keep them open, the dagger resting in the palm of her hand.

Through the darkness there was the quick crunching of leaves and the snapping of branches. Alba jolted, hitting her head on the tree. Her stiff fingers clawed at the cold, hard ground for the dagger.

"Over here," she heard Gannicus yell, and the tension across her mind and body eased.

Dark figures swarmed out of the trees. Spartacus reached them first. She knew him by the soft thumps of his footsteps swift across the forest floor.

He dropped to his knees, his breath rising above him as he cupped her icy hands in his. He whipped his cloak off and wrapped it around her shoulders. She could feel the heat from his body, cocooning her in warmth.

Gus and Gannicus lifted Hadrian onto a stretcher while Namir covered him with his cloak.

Spartacus's arms were sweat-slick beneath her, his chest heaving as he lifted her from the ground. He had been running hard and fast.

"Alex," she said into those blue eyes, and then everything went dark.

She was placed on soft furs and wrapped in blankets. In their faces she could see their worry. Familiar voices washed over her and gentle hands wiped the grime and sweat from her body. Their words grew firm and firmer still as they instructed her to drink warm broth, tilting her head up.

. . .

She broke into a fevered sweat and the blankets were removed. Her body trembled, her teeth chattered. Spartacus's deep voice washed over her, calling her back to him, the soft smell of pomegranate and sandalwood oil floated around her. His face came in and out of a haze, in and out of focus. Her head was thick as lava, heavy as an anvil, her body dried over and over. "Drink . . . drink." Cool cloths dabbed on her neck and forehead.

Thirty-Six

A bird chirped and she twitched awake. Her arms were resting on a soft, clean fur. The sun illuminated the side of the rust-colored tent. It was early evening.

She turned her head to the side and was overcome with joy to see Hadrian lying a few feet away from her. The swelling in his face had subsided and the purple bruise had faded to a light green. She reached out and touched his arm.

Relief filled his face. "Alba," he said thickly, reaching a heavily bandaged hand toward her.

"Hi," she said back.

His eyes misted over. "I was wrong. Blinded by my hatred for anyone Roman. I was unyielding, unfair, and unjust . . . I know that it is too much to ask, that I do not deserve it, but I beg you for forgiveness."

For the briefest of moments, she wanted to chastise him. For following Crixus. For ignoring them all and their pleas. But he was studying her face so closely with so much regret and hurt in his eyes that she did not have the heart.

"There is nothing to forgive," she said, her voice a rasp.

"Alba."

"It's fine," she said, her voice a bit stronger.

His face was unwaveringly solemn. He would not be at ease until she had said the words.

"I forgive you."

His eyes misted over.

"Alba," Namir cried in delight as he lifted the flap of the tent. "Thank the Gods you're awake."

The utter joy that filled his face worried her. "How long have I been out?"

"Five days," he said.

"Five," Alba breathed in disbelief. "What happened after I left?"

"It wasn't until morning that we realized you were gone. Spartacus thought you were with Natalie and Cloe, and Natalie thought you were with Spartacus." Namir paused. "It took everything we had to keep him from going after you."

Alba hadn't thought of this, the stress it would have caused the others, the upheaval it would have caused.

"I'm very grateful to you," Namir said, his eyes falling on Hadrian.

She smiled at him and shut her eyes. A few moments later, there was a weight next to her.

Spartacus gazed down at her, his blue eyes absorbing her. "Your fever has broken," he said.

"So it seems," she said. "How is Max?"

"Well cared for. Cloe took him to her breast."

"I'm sorry that my absence caused you worry."

"Worry?" he repeated as if this word could in no way capture the magnitude of what he had been through. "I was beside myself. Do you think my moral compass so rigid that you could not have enlightened me to your plan?"

"You would have stopped me."

"Of course I would have. You are my life," he said. "Alba, please never again, no matter what quarrel we have, do something like that."

"I can't promise you that," she said.

"Why not?"

"Because you would not see reason. You were too narrow and unbending," she said, her voice breaking from the strain of talking. Forming these thoughts and sentences took more energy than she had.

"Spartacus," Hadrian said. "She's just woken."

Spartacus nodded. He was annoyed with her of course but he didn't press it further. More than anything he wished to see her well and wouldn't do anything to hinder her recovery.

The flap of the tent was lifted, and Natalie and Cloe came in carrying herbs, cloth, and a pestle and mortar. Spartacus got to his feet, moving so that they could sit between Alba and Hadrian.

"It's so good to see you awake," Cloe said to Alba.

"Thank you for taking Max to your breast."

Natalie ground herbs, yarrow, and honey together while Cloe unraveled a stack of cloth bandages. Spartacus watched for a moment and then took his leave.

Natalie and Cloe sat on either side of Hadrian, each unwrapping one of his hands. At the end of the ravel, Alba clenched her teeth so that she didn't let out a gasp. Hadrian's palms had large gouges and his fingers were coiled like claws. As Natalie dabbed ointment around the edges of the wound, he took a sharp intake of breath and squeezed his eyes shut. She was thorough, folding back the fur and checking the gash down the far side of his chest.

Cloe gathered the used cloth and left them. Natalie moved around so that she was sitting between Alba and Hadrian. "Now that you have both regained some strength, I wish to have a word with you," she said, looking from one to the other. "You are both idiots."

"Nat," Hadrian said, raising his head.

"You, for following Crixus when you should have known better, and you"—she set her eyes on Alba—"for leaving us like that. Have you no thought? For your son, for Spartacus, for those who care for you? It was no small task keeping him from going after you."

"There was no one else who could have gone," Alba said.

"Do you think your lives replaceable?" she said, taking her mortar and pestle and getting to her feet.

"Honestly," Hadrian said as the tent flap swung shut behind Natalie. "You'd think they would've been a bit happier to see us." He lifted his head, glancing at the opening of the tent. "Alba, what did they do with you? In the camp."

"Nothing, really," she said. "I was once friends with Julius and Publius."

"You had a mark." He patted a spot near his neck.

Oh, right. She'd forgotten about that.

"Alba," he said, and the concern in his voice drew the words from her.

"Publius sold me to the pirate Horatio. He came in to inspect me."

"Did he . . ."

"No," she said.

"Good," he said. "Always made me feel sick, the nights Nat had to . . ."

"Were you gladiators ever forced?"

"Rarely. We were usually the ones requesting if we had a big win—though the tall twin did request Spartacus one night."

Spartacus came in then with two bowls of steaming broth. Hadrian gave Alba a stern look to try and quell her brimming curiosity.

"Thank you," Hadrian said, propping himself up and cupping the bowl in his bandaged hands. "Will you eat with us?"

Spartacus didn't answer. He just set the other bowl next to Alba and left the tent. A short while later, he came back in with a plate of meat, potatoes, and carrots. He sat between them, his hands on his knees.

"I made a mistake going with Crixus. He is both brash and bold," Hadrian said. "You were right, both of you. Though skilled with a sword, he is nothing to you when it comes to commanding. On the field of battle, you see all. He only saw what was in front of him. From here on out, I stand with you only."

"First you must recover your strength," Spartacus said, picking at his meat.

"Are you to hold this against me?" Hadrian asked.

Spartacus put his plate down. "You are a brother to me," he said. "There is no grudge I can hold against you."

A wave of emotion came over Hadrian then. He looked away for a moment before lifting his bowl to his mouth.

"What happened with you and Claudia?" Alba asked Spartacus.

Hadrian choked on his soup.

"Claudia?" Spartacus said as if trying to recall a distant, insignificant memory. "It was the night before our planned escape so I had to be careful. Camilla and Lentulus were away for the night and the guards brought me to her room. They left me chained and waited outside. She lay down on the bed and beckoned me over."

Alba regretted having asked. "I'm sorry—"

"I stayed where I was," he continued. "I knew she wouldn't tell her parents so I didn't move."

"What'd she do?"

"She asked me to touch her. I said no and then she touched herself."

"Did you kill her?" Alba asked. "During the escape?"

"They both climbed onto the roof when the slaughter began. We had already killed Camilla and Lentulus. I followed them up there, and they stood at the edge, terrified," he said. "It wasn't my intention to kill them. I offered my hand, and Cilia reached for it, but the slat beneath their feet came loose."

"Not very graceful girls," Hadrian said. "Somehow they both managed to land right on their necks, the loudest cracks you've ever heard." He glanced at Alba. "They weren't friends of yours, were they?"

"No," she said.

"Didn't think so."

In the days that followed, after all the initial interactions, Alba realized that there was a stiffness between Hadrian and Namir. Hadrian didn't reciprocate Namir's tenderness as he once did.

"What's your quarrel with Namir?" Alba asked Hadrian when it was just the two of them.

"I have none," Hadrian said. Seeing that she wasn't satisfied, he continued. "He's the first person I have ever truly loved and I left him."

She had thought he was being hard on Namir. "You have to forgive yourself."

"How can I?" Hadrian said. "I don't deserve him. Not after . . ." His voice trailed off.

"What?" She studied his face. "Tell me what happened." The forcefulness with which she said it surprised her, and in that moment, she realized that their relationship had forever changed. Before she had been so careful with her words, not wanting to draw his ire or irritate him. Now she could push him and know that he wouldn't resent her. Looking into his face, she saw that he welcomed it. He was open to her thoughts, whatever they may be.

"We defeated the Romans or so we thought," he said, his voice low. "They retreated into the woods where the rest of their army was waiting. We began our celebration. The barrels were emptied and we fell into a drunken stupor. In the early hours of the morning, they came back to slaughter and capture us. We didn't even put up a fight."

Alba was quiet a long moment. "Don't tell Spartacus," Alba said. "It would kill him."

"I almost killed you with my stupidity," Hadrian said. "By following Crixus."

"We have all made decisions we're not proud of," she said.

"Spartacus won't be himself, not until you promise that you won't leave like that again. He'll be agitated and restless."

"I can't promise something like that. Not if there's a chance I could break it."

"Then don't break it."

"You say that to me, yet you will not allow yourself to find comfort in Namir's arms."

"Because I am undeserving."

"You are not," she said. "Allow yourself to love and be loved."

THIRTY-SEVEN

Cloe brought Max to Alba, but her milk had dried up so Natalie made her up a bottle of goat's milk.

Alba relayed the story of Cilia's and Claudia's deaths to Cloe while Natalie changed Hadrian's bandages. His legs had started to grow sores from lack of movement so Cloe was bending them to help ease their stiffness.

"Does it matter?" Natalie asked, holding one of Hadrian's large hands in both of her own. "To know how they met their end?"

"They were only girls," Cloe said.

Natalie raised her eyebrows, her dislike for the twins clear. Despite Natalie's annoyance with Alba, she brought Max to see her every day as well as diligently checked on the progress of her recovery. Her words and huffs were often harsh, but her hands were always skilled and gentle.

"Perhaps Max could sleep with me tonight," Alba said, passing him to Natalie so that she could change him.

"I will make a little bed beside you," Natalie said.

"If you don't mind?" Alba said to Hadrian. "Babies can be loud sleepers."

"Course not," he grunted, his face scrunched as Cloe pressed his thigh to his chest.

Alba felt stronger today than she had any other. She craved the feel of fresh air on her face, the sounds of nature, and the smells of the earth. Slowly she got to her feet.

Natalie glanced up at her warily, wrapping new cloth around Max's bum.

"I'm all right," Alba said, taking a few wobbly steps around the large tent. Then she held out her hands.

Natalie handed him over. "Got him?"

Alba nodded.

Max's dark, curly hair had thickened. It was so soft through her fingers. Holding him against her, she paced the length of the tent. She took in his round, content face, his tiny fingernails, and the pudge of his arms and legs. He stared back at her with his large, clear blue eyes. Spartacus's eyes.

She stepped around Hadrian and went outside.

Spartacus was in bed. She couldn't see his face but guessed by his sprawled, relaxed body that he was asleep. Not wanting to wake him, she turned to leave, but Max let out a small sound. Spartacus's head came up.

"I'm sorry," she whispered. "I didn't mean to wake you."

"I'm glad you did," he said, moving so that she could sit beside him. "You look well."

She laid Max between them and Spartacus put his finger in Max's fist. "He's strong," he said.

"Like his papa," she said.

"He will make a good warrior."

"No. He won't," Alba said more sharply than intended.

"I didn't mean he will be a warrior. I only meant if he were to become one."

He hadn't been this stiff with her since the first days of her arrival.

They needed to put this behind them, to move forward. "What you said earlier, about being for others. Do you feel that way, that your life is not your own?" she said.

"I'm ashamed to think of those words now. Please do not hold me to them for they are not representative of my true thoughts. In my grief I had left myself. My deepest regret is that I turned from you when you tried to speak sense to me. I have chosen this life. Nothing holds me to it."

"And yet everything does," she said.

Spartacus rose his head. "You know me better than anyone I've ever known."

She held his gaze. "I don't regret what I did but I won't leave you like that again. You have my word."

He pulled her into a hug so tight she could feel his heart beating against his chest. Max cried out and Spartacus scooped him up with one hand.

"You've gotten quite good at that," Alba said.

"Gus taught me," Spartacus said.

"Gus?"

"It's how he picks up Aleni."

The next morning Alba awoke to a bah, reminding her of Neme and the goat she had milked when Alba was a child. She picked Max up from his bed and stepped out of the tent. The morning air ruffled pleasantly on her face.

Gus was placing sticks on the fire, building up the flame so that they could place the cauldron over it. Natalie was peeling carrots and Cloe chopping onions and parsnips.

Cloe smiled warmly at Alba while Natalie offered her a curt nod. She laid Max down next to Aleni, his olive skin and dark curly hair a contrast against her fair complexion and vibrant blonde hair. Her eyes were a pale blue like her mother's. She looked nothing like her father.

Gannicus was a few yards away, standing over a wooden table with a large hunk of meat, a cleaver in hand, his face speckled with blood. He nodded at her in greeting.

"I'm glad you're back," she said, going over to him.

"You know, you're the first one to say that," he said.

"Have you spoken to Ava since your return?" Alba asked.

"Ava?" Gannicus swung the cleaver.

"She was sad to see you go."

"I never know what to say to women," he said, pulling the meat apart and passing it to Cloe.

"You find words easily enough with me," she said.

"You seek me out. You're easy to talk to," he said. She liked this side of Gannicus. Honest, vulnerable, and kind. "I've spent much of my life separated from women. Speaking to them does not come naturally to me."

"The more you do it, the easier it will get," Alba said.

Gannicus grunted and picked the cleaver back up as Gus set off into the forest for more kindling.

"Gus," Alba said, following him in a ways, wanting to speak with him alone. "Thank you for coming with me."

He nodded in acknowledgment. "It's not something I would do again."

Namir cut through the brush toward them, a quail in each hand, and Gus continued on in search of sticks. A pretty girl waddled by them carrying a heavy basket, her figure full, and her flushed face shining from the exertion. She met Alba's eye and let out a small, yet audible gasp, her waddle quickening.

Alba glanced questioningly at Namir.

He made a face, debating with himself.

"Tell me," Alba said.

"When you were gone, word spread quickly throughout the camp," he said. "A few women found themselves wandering into Spartacus's tent."

"What happened?"

"Have you ever seen a catapult?"

"Poor girl," Alba said.

There was a squirting sound behind her. The bah that drew her out. Diana was milking a goat, a dark braid hanging down her back. This was the first time Alba had seen her since they had carried Hadrian together.

"Diana," Alba said, going over to her. "Cloe told me that you helped care for Max while she and Natalie saw me back to health. Thank you for that."

Diana nodded but did not look up.

"Is that for Max?" Alba asked.

Diana made a noncommittal head tilt.

Alba mustered her courage to ask, "How was it that you came to serve in Julius's house?"

"I became pregnant by your uncle." Diana did not raise her head as she spoke. "Your aunt sold me as a house slave to Julius."

Alba dreaded her next question and forced herself to ask it with a steady voice. "And the baby?"

"He died, shortly after he was born."

"I'm so sorry to hear that," Alba said. "And that you had to serve in Julius's house."

Diana stood with her jug. "It was much more pleasant than yours. He never touched me . . . not after that night. That's why I came with him." She turned and swiftly went back into the camp.

Never touched her. The words went through Alba. After all that time, he had honored Alba's wish.

Though Alba was only moments behind, Diana had already cradled Max in her arms and held the bottle to his mouth.

"I can do that," Alba said, reaching down.

Diana angled her body away. "We're fine," she said. "He's comfortable with me."

Alba was torn. She didn't want to offend Diana after she had gone to the trouble of preparing the milk, but she wanted to feed her son. This child she was getting to know better and better every day, her love for him growing.

"Diana," Natalie said, coming to stand behind Alba. "Give Alba her son."

Diana kept her eyes down as she stood slowly and passed him to Alba. She retreated to the tent she had made in the narrow stretch of land between Natalie and Cloe's, and Hadrian and Namir's. Alba was debating whether to try and speak with Diana or to leave it for now when Gus limped toward them, carrying a pile of sticks.

"What happened?" Cloe stood.

"Stepped in a trap," he said.

Natalie glowered. "I have told them not to set the traps so close to the path. Let me look at it," she said, patting a stump.

Natalie knelt and took his foot in her lap. With gentle hands, she brushed away the dirt, picked out some small stones, and dabbed at the edges of his gash with clean water.

"The cut is shallow." She reached for some cloth and tore a strip, wrapping it around his foot. "But it'll need a few days to heal."

Gus nodded.

"If the wound doesn't close by tomorrow, have it sewn shut. I'll be on a hunt, but Diana has skilled hands," she said.

"Diana?" Alba said, lowering Max onto a soft fur.

Natalie gave a quick nod, her back to Alba. Then she straightened and turned.

"Did she do your back?" Natalie said.

Alba did her best to remain inscrutable, but Natalie knew her too well.

"Diana!" Natalie's voice rang out, sharp and harsh.

"Nat," Alba whispered. "She may not have known."

"She knew," Natalie said darkly. "That infection would have killed you."

Diana emerged from her tent, those dark eyes, wide in feigned innocence. She'd heard their interaction transpire.

"You're no longer welcome here," Natalie said. "Take your things elsewhere in the camp."

Spartacus came to stand in the entrance of his tent. Diana turned to him, a pleading in her dark eyes. She was waiting for him to decide.

"Did you not hear her?" Gannicus said, holding the cleaver at his side as he came to stand by Natalie.

When she realized that no one would intervene, anger took hold of Diana's face. She packed her things quickly and was gone.

Thirty-Eight

The sun hung low in the horizon, casting a blue light through the trees. Alba sat at the fire wrapped in furs. After her first full day outside, she was tired and content.

"We can take him for the night," Natalie said, nodding at Max.

"Thank you." Alba kissed his little forehead and passed him to Natalie. She started toward the tent she had been sharing with Hadrian, but on hearing voices raised in banter, she went into Spartacus's. He and Gannicus were leaned over maps and scrolls.

"Planning the next raid?"

Gannicus rolled up a sheet. "I'm going out on rounds."

"You're doing rounds?" Alba said.

"With Gus and Namir," he said. "You know, just around the whole fucking camp."

"And it's very much appreciated," Spartacus said. With Crixus gone and Hadrian unable, it was an important task Spartacus entrusted to few men. There was a certain art to it.

"I know," Gannicus said, tapping Spartacus on the shoulder with the scroll. He pulled the string and dropped the flap on his way out.

Alba went over to Spartacus and clutched his cloak. She pressed him up against the pole.

"Alba," he said. His blue eyes were smiling but there was reluctance in them. "You're not fit."

She reached for his belt and slid it loose from his waist, then unclipped the clasp of his cloak and tugged it from his shoulders. Last she lifted his tunic over his head. When it bunched, he helped her.

She slipped her dress from her shoulders and let it fall in a cascading pile to her feet. With him before her tall, muscular, and robust, she was suddenly conscious of the weight she had lost.

He didn't move.

"Will you not have me?" she asked.

He pushed off the pole and pressed his forehead to hers. "I am yours," he said.

As he lifted himself over her, she felt her skin tingle with yearning. Every part of her body heightened and relaxed at the same time.

When they were finished, he lowered himself down beside her and she curled into him. He wrapped his arm around her and they fell asleep.

Alba woke with a gasp, a great weight pressing on her chest, as if something had stopped her from breathing. In a wave of panic, uneasy and unsettled, she sat up. Someone was not right.

Spartacus stirred as she pulled on her dress and went barefoot into the night.

Beside the burning embers of the fire she stopped, listening. Silence throbbed against her ears. Then she ran into Natalie and Cloe's tent. Aleni was awake. Max was gone.

"Natalie," Alba said, taking her friend by the shoulder and shaking her. "Natalie, where is Max?"

"What?" Natalie said in a groggy daze.

Alba glanced once more at the basket before dashing out of the tent. She scanned the area, the shadows through the trees, but there was nothing, not a soul in sight.

"Spartacus!" Natalie yelled, bursting past Alba. "Max is gone."

A moment later he emerged from his tent. Natalie threw the flaps of Gannicus, Gus, and Namir's tents. They were still out on their rounds.

"Fuck," Spartacus said under his breath.

Hadrian hobbled out of his tent clutching his side. "I'll alert the gladiators," he said.

"The perimeter scouts first. No one leaves." Spartacus turned to Alba and yelled, "You stay here."

Natalie and Spartacus each ran off in different directions as Hadrian hobbled up the hill.

"Take her," Cloe said, passing Aleni to Alba. "I'll find Gannicus."

"Be careful, Cloe!" Alba yelled after her.

Alba clutched Aleni to her as she paced the area, turning at every sound.

A radiant pink broke the horizon, and as the sun rose, Alba held on to hope. They would find him. Her son. They who knew this camp better than anyone. There was movement through the forest and Spartacus came toward her, his gait slow and heavy. Gannicus emerged with Cloe and then Natalie moments later. They were all slick with sweat, flecks of mud splattered up their legs.

"Nothing?" Alba asked as Cloe took Aleni from her.

"I don't know what happened," Natalie said. "He was there, sleeping between us."

"Who else knew that the baby slept there?" Gannicus asked. "Other than us."

There was a shift in Natalie's face. "Diana, she knew." Her jaw grew hard. "She was drawn to Max from the moment she saw him."

"She had a son that died," Alba said thickly.

Gus skidded down the ridge toward them. "One of the gladiators said he saw a woman headed north, with a bundle under her cloak, many hours ago."

Alba clutched her chest. "I should've had him with me," she said, her voice breaking.

Spartacus placed his hand on Alba's shoulder. Neither could look at the other.

"Alba," Natalie said, approaching them both. "I'm so sorry."

"It's not your fault," Alba said. "It's mine."

"No," Spartacus said sharply. "This is the fault of no one, save Diana."

The ground was tilting beneath her feet. Hollowed and weak she staggered forward. Hadrian and Gannicus were at her side, leading her gently back to Spartacus's tent. She dropped into a heap on the bed.

"I used to believe that it was only the slaves that knew trial and tribulation," Hadrian said, placing his large palm on her head. "But you have known more than enough for a lifetime."

She shut her eyes and pictured her son, every curve of his fingers and toes, every feature of his face, his father's clear blue eyes, her dark and curly hair. She would hold him in her memory.

"I will find him," she said to herself.

"You could pray," Hadrian suggested kindly.

"You don't believe in the Gods," she said.

"No, but you do."

"I'm afraid that there is no amount of praying that will bring me comfort in this," she said. "Please, leave me."

He did not leave her side, nor did Gannicus, until long after she had fallen into an exhausted sleep.

Thirty-Nine

In the late morning, when Alba finally stepped outside, it took her a moment to realize that all the tents were gone, their belongings organized into bundles.

"We're moving south to the city," Namir said.

It would be their largest traveling group yet. Gannicus had taken it upon himself to rally the gladiators, using his booming voice to instruct them. Spartacus stood nearby, his presence enough to accompany Gannicus's words.

Natalie and Cloe took turns carrying Aleni, while Alba walked in a bit of a daze, catching her feet on the roots and rocks.

The rebels took the city with ease and the walls swelled with their numbers. Gannicus and Namir set to organizing the wall patrols. All movement in and out was to be monitored. Natalie was with the gladiators ensuring that their entry into the city was as peaceful as possible, breaking up any bullying and forcefulness. Gus and Hadrian were charged with overseeing the inventory of supplies stored within the city's warehouses. Spartacus stood off to the side as all those closest to him knew their place, what had to be done. He had created this.

It had been almost a year since Alba had stepped foot within a city, and the uneven stones felt strange beneath her feet. Everything seemed amplified. The aroma of spices at the market stalls, the strong smell of freshly dyed fabrics, the clattering of the taverns. People everywhere in close quarters. The crowds were tightening in around her the deeper she and Cloe walked, brushing up against them, pushing them forward.

Hadrian was standing in the doorway of a storeroom where barrels of wheat were being counted. He didn't have to worry about the townspeople jostling him. The gladiators were cut a wide swath. His gaze was skeptical as he surveyed the bustling marketplace.

"Alba, Cloe," he called. As they made their way over to him, he glanced over his shoulder to check the progress. "We've taken a villa near the middle of the city. Make your way there."

Alba nodded absentmindedly as he gave Cloe directions on the most direct route. He didn't want them to linger.

It was the largest house in the city, the color of sand, rising above the others with its many floors and great pillars flanking the entrance. Two gladiators had already been placed on the steps, keeping watch.

Alba and Cloe walked through the empty villa, glancing at each other. It was all too familiar. The gardens and fountains, the opulence. It would not stay in this pristine shape for long. Upstairs there were clothes flung about the rooms, toppled tables and smashed urns, swords and daggers scattered down the hallway. Alba wondered if the family had made it out before the rebels blocked the entrances.

Spartacus and Alba took the master bedroom on the third floor with Hadrian and Namir on one side and Natalie, Cloe, and Aleni on the other. Gus was on the floor below with a dozen others.

Alba dropped her satchel on the oak chest and went to sit in a chair facing the window, utterly spent from the journey. On the third floor, the noise of the city faded and she was alone with her thoughts and the image of her son, cradled in her arms. There had been no time for wallowing in self-pity or mourning. No time to wonder how Diana could have done this—being a mother for even a brief time herself.

A calloused hand rested on the back of her neck and she shut her eyes.

"All I can think of is him," she said.

There was a knock at the door but neither she nor Spartacus moved. A second knock came, and the door opened. She felt Spartacus's grip on her neck tighten slightly as he turned, annoyed.

"Alba," Natalie said. "Come with us."

Cloe and Natalie led her down the back stairs of the villa and through a pillared hallway. There was the soft groan of metal as Natalie opened an ornate door into a room of white marble. They stepped inside, and a waft of warmth engulfed them. Steam from a freshly drawn bath. Torches mounted in sconces lined the stone walls.

Cloe and Natalie took off their dresses and stepped down into the water, the flames dancing across their backs. Alba slipped her dress from her shoulders and followed them. The water lapped around her, soothing her skin and cradling her body.

"I've something to confide in you both," Alba said as a memory washed over her. "The last time I took a bath was with Julius Caesar."

"I thought Spartacus was your first," Natalie said, taken aback.

"He was," Alba said. "It was to comfort me after . . . after Max had died."

"I always liked Julius," Cloe said. "At parties he would speak to me when others feared to because of my husband."

"He's the reason I am here now," Alba said.

"Julius?" Cloe said, dropping her head back to wet her hair.

"Publius had sold me to a pirate and had me chained. Julius set me free."

The water lapped the edges as Natalie turned. "At what price?" she asked. "What did he have you do?"

"Nothing."

Natalie studied her a moment.

"Come." Cloe pulled Alba gently toward her. She scrubbed Alba's hair until it shone.

"I've never been so clean in my life," Natalie said, stepping out and tying the sash around her robe.

In the bedroom Cloe patted Alba's hair dry, braided it, and pinned it into a low bun. They raided the noblewomen's closets searching for the simplest clothes they could find. In her search, Alba came across a white wool dress and a belt, the traditional dress for a woman to be married in. When they emerged from the room, Alba was wearing a pale blue dress, Natalie a deep purple, and Cloe, after trying on a beautiful pink dress that made her glow, a dull gray.

There was laughter and merry chatter from down below in the courtyard, the succulent smell of rabbits over a fire. They descended the back staircase, passed the garden, and walked into the atrium.

Spartacus was sitting with Hadrian, and Gus had Aleni perched on his knees. Spartacus glanced at the girls and then raised his head.

He came over to Alba. "You're all so . . ."

"Clean," she said.

Alba rose from her spot beside Spartacus and climbed the back stairs. A willowy figure came out of Gus's room on the second floor. As Cloe turned she gasped, slightly flushed.

"I didn't mean to startle you," Alba said.

As they climbed the last flight together, Cloe clutched Alba's arm and whispered, "It was our first time together—his first ever."

"And?" Alba said.

"It was . . ." Cloe shook her head in blissful glee. "He was so sweet and timid. He's quite strong, much stronger than Quintus ever was but . . ." Her face scrunched. "He did say that Spartacus had given him some advice."

"Spartacus? What did he say?"

"I'm not entirely sure, something about letting me guide him and not crushing me." Cloe smiled. "Whatever he said, it worked."

Alba took her friend's hands and said, "I'm so happy for you."

Forty

Over the next few weeks Natalie and Cloe kept Alba busy, giving her a purpose, an outlet, and a distraction. Every morning the three of them would go into the bountiful garden on the side of the house. With their hair tied back, their dresses light and loose in the warm summer air, they'd spend the morning digging, picking, and weeding, filling their baskets with beans, carrots, cabbages, plums, and figs. Gus and Namir would distribute the food to the rebels throughout the city so that they would not be such a drain on the citizens.

Alba nestled the last basket into the corner of the cart and Namir's forearms flexed as he lifted the handles and wheeled it toward the gate. Gus bit into a fig, his teeth white against the dark skin, as he used his other hand to steady Cloe's ladder.

"Gus, Natalie," Spartacus said, stepping down into the garden's olive grove. "We are hunting."

Natalie lowered herself down from the apple tree. "I will ready myself."

"As will I," Gus said, holding Cloe's waist as she climbed down.

"We will leave after dark—discreetly," he said. "Gannicus and Namir will keep watch of the wall."

Spartacus had to be much more careful now when he went on

raids. His face was well known, and there was a price on his head, which was no small amount.

Alba stayed behind in the garden, her white dress clinging to her damp back as she continued to work in the soil, the sun bearing down on her. She was reaching for a spade when she felt a figure staring down at her from the floor above. Bacchus. His eyes were fixed on her, his round, bald head slick with sweat.

Alba drove the spade into the ground and stood too quickly, her head spinning. She placed her hand on the wall to steady herself. When was the last time she had eaten? Though she was quite warm, she shivered as she made her way down the hallway. Spartacus was in the bedroom organizing his weapons. She lay down and shut her eyes for just a moment, but when she opened them to tell him to be careful, he was gone.

That night, Alba woke to cramps pulsing through her, stretching through her abdomen. Her whole body had broken into a sweat, her bum was wet, and a swelling discomfort sent waves of nausea through her. She patted the space beside her—empty. After lowering herself onto the floor, she crawled toward the door but in the darkness couldn't find her way. She banged her fist on something hard, hoping it was the wall.

The door was thrown open, and there was the glow of a torch as Hadrian sliced it through the air. "Alba?"

"I'm here," she breathed.

He came around to the side of the bed, the light catching a smear of blood that trailed behind her. He cringed at the sight.

"Why is there so much blood?" she asked through stifled breath.

He crouched beside her. "I'll get someone."

"No." She clutched his arm. "Stay with me."

He held her hand in his, the scar where he had been nailed to the cross a dark and shiny circle bump.

"Does it bother you?" She nodded at his hand.

"No," he said, and then he flexed his fingers. "Sometimes." He stood. "I'll not be a moment."

She lay back on the cool, marble tiles and it soothed her skin.

He came back with Cloe at his heels and she knelt beside Alba. "Oh, Alba."

"What's happening to me?" Alba stared up at her friend.

"I think you may have lost a child. The same happened to me once, but there wasn't quite so much . . ." She glanced at the blood.

"Will you help me clean it?" Alba said. "I don't want Spartacus to know." She pulled off her dress and held it out to Hadrian. "Burn it," she said. "Please," she added when Hadrian hesitated to take the dress from her. "He has enough on his mind."

Hadrian clutched the bloodstained dress, torn.

"He cannot know," Alba said just as Spartacus came into the room.

"Know what?" Spartacus said. His eyes widened in horror.

Alba lowered her head in anguish at the sight of him.

"She has lost a child," Cloe said.

"Why would you want to hide this from me?" he said.

"You have so many things on your mind," she said weakly. "So many burdens."

"You do not do me a kindness by keeping this from me," he said.

"Spartacus." Natalie came into the room, taking charge. "Lift her onto the bed." She had herbs in one hand and a bowl of broth in the other. She crushed the herbs and stirred them into the broth. "Drink, deeply."

The mixture was thick and coarse. Alba swallowed as much as she could until the repugnant aftertaste seized her throat.

"Keep it down," Natalie said as Alba convulsed. "Keep it down." She rubbed Alba's back.

Strength. It was her friends that gave her strength, standing over her now, watching her closely with such concern in their eyes.

. . .

Spartacus rose with the dawn. He sat perched at the edge of the bed for a moment before bending down to lace his sandals.

"Are you going to the outer wall?" Alba asked, sitting up.

"Yes."

"Can I come with you?"

He straightened, his shoulders tensing.

"I would like to get out of this house for a bit."

"Today is not the day."

"Will it ever be?"

With a small sigh, he acquiesced.

They set off together, their pace slow. As she walked, she kept her head down and focused on her movement, not wanting her mind to wander. Spartacus stayed right beside her and so it was easy to follow aimlessly alongside him.

It was with a start that she realized they were at the wall, the patrol spaced out atop it. Hadrian was sitting with his feet dangling over the ledge, eating an apple.

"Alba," he said in surprise as he glanced over his shoulder. He pulled her up to sit next to him and regarded her closely.

"I am fine," Alba said, tapping Hadrian's shoulder with her fist.

He inclined his head toward her.

The three of them sat side by side in silence as the sky was set ablaze with a radiant sunrise, casting its glow over the rolling fields. Alba shut her eyes to it and let the light wash over her.

On the way back to the house, Alba walked between Hadrian and Spartacus. Hadrian stopped to speak with some men selling fish at the edge of the market.

Alba turned to Spartacus and said, "Would you want to have a ceremony?"

"A ceremony?" he said.

"To become husband and wife," she said.

"Oh," he stumbled on his words, something foreign to him. "Yes, I would like that. Though I have never been witness to . . . I am not familiar with the nobles' customs."

"I don't want anything lavish. Just something simple. For us. With those we love," Alba said. "Tonight, even, while everyone is here."

"What are we doing tonight?" Hadrian said, catching them up to them.

"We are going to be married," Alba said.

"This evening?" Hadrian said.

"Yes."

He grunted and lifted his arm to smell himself. "Hm" was all he said, and then he took off.

"Hadrian!" Alba called after him, but he had slipped through the people and out of sight.

Forty-One

When Alba and Spartacus got back to the villa, Gus was waiting at the gate with a crossbow on his back and Namir was sharpening his knife.

"Where are you off to?" Alba asked.

"To hunt for the festivities," Namir said.

"You don't need to," Alba said, but neither was listening to her.

"There was a pack of wild pigs down by the river," Namir was saying as they set out.

Alba wrapped around the side of the house to the garden. Natalie and Cloe's tools and baskets were where they had been left the day before. She was partway through filling her basket with apples when Cloe came up to her and squeezed Alba's arm in excitement.

"What is going on?" Alba asked. "Why do you have flour on your face?"

"How're you feeling?"

"Fine. I'm fine," she said. "I didn't mean for this to be such a disturbance."

"We are excited. To be doing something different, something fun."

"What are you making?" Alba asked.

"A cake," Cloe said.

"I appreciate that but you don't need to. Spartacus doesn't worship the Gods so we won't be making an offering to them."

"He's the one who asked for it," Cloe said. "He has been asking me all about our rituals and customs."

"Alba." Natalie came toward her, taking the basket from her fingers. "Why don't you take some rest?" Natalie directed her toward the stairs. "Lie down."

"I don't need to."

"Just for a bit," Natalie said.

She was gently shaken awake a few hours later. Natalie and Cloe were leaning over her, already dressed with their hair done. Alba sat up and turned her gaze out the window. The sun was dipping toward the horizon.

"I've overslept," Alba said.

"No, you're fine," Cloe said. "Come with us."

They led her into their room. A simple white dress was on the bed, laced in a delicate trim. A crown of braided baby's breath was resting above it. It was tradition for the bride to be dressed by her bridesmaids. Alba undid the sash on her robe, and Cloe pulled the dress over her head. The fine fabric was so soft against her skin, it almost felt as though she was wearing nothing at all.

Alba's dark hair had grown just past her shoulders, and Cloe braided it into a crown. Natalie wrapped the belt around Alba's waist and knelt to tie the intricate knot of Hercules.

"Don't make it too hard for him," Alba said as Natalie's fast fingers fed the material through the loops again and again. It was tradition for the husband to undo the belt before he was to bed his bride.

Natalie raised an eyebrow and pulled it through one last time.

There was a knock at the door.

"Who is it?" Natalie called.

"Your humble servant," Hadrian said. "May I come in?"

"And see the bride before her husband?" Natalie glanced at Alba.

"It's fine," Alba said, and Cloe opened the door.

Hadrian walked into the room and brought his hands together as one would if they were praying. He came over to her and kissed her forehead. "We have assembled downstairs in the courtyard," he said.

Alba made her way down the stairs with Cloe and Natalie on either side of her. As she approached the courtyard, the scent of freshly cut flowers enveloped them, sweet and pure. Alba stepped through the archway, and the rebels parted, creating a path for her.

Spartacus stood at the far end with Hadrian and Gannicus.

They turned in unison to greet her. She had never seen them all so clean. Spartacus wore a white tunic and Hadrian and Gannicus a soft green.

Spartacus's eyes met hers and his chest rose. His hands, browned by the sun, were sure and steady at his side. Hers trembled slightly.

As she reached him, an older man cleared his throat, giving Alba a start. Stood before them was a priest, an actual priest. She glanced at Hadrian, but he just shut his eyes and nodded.

The priest started into the Roman chants of marriage as Alba and Spartacus stood before all of their friends. Then he stopped chanting and there was a pause.

"It is now that the groom exchanges his vows," the priest said.

"Vows?" Spartacus said.

"Words spoken to the bride about the impending union," he said.

"Ah." Spartacus took a moment to collect his thoughts. "Whatever trials and tribulations are set down upon us, I am given strength to know that I face them by your side. From our time in Thrace until now, I have always taken great solace from your presence in my life. I vow to always share in the weight of your burdens and the lightness of your joys."

Though the vow was unconventional, the priest nodded his approval. "And the bride must accept him," he said.

"I accept," Alba said.

"Now the ring," the priest said.

Gannicus reached into his tunic pockets and then placed something in Spartacus's hand. Spartacus slid a gold ring onto Alba's finger.

"Lastly, the ceremony shall be sealed with a kiss."

Spartacus leaned down and placed his lips softly on hers, which was greeted with an outburst of cheers and hollering.

Alba's face broke into a smile as did Spartacus's.

As she entered the atrium, arm in arm with Spartacus, she gasped, a wave of happiness and overwhelming gratitude coming over her. The cooking cauldrons, the chickens that grazed about, the misplaced chairs and stools had all been cleared away. Vibrant flowers hung in bunches all around them. The banquet table was overflowing with ripe figs, dates, olives, fish, loaves of bread, grapes, and cheese. There was even fruit drizzled with honey.

A feast.

Barrels of wine were brought up from the downstairs cellar and pried open as the cake was cut. Alba went around thanking each of them for the effort they had put in to create such a wonderful event with little notice.

Ava stood off to the side and Alba made her way over to her. "Natalie told me you hung the flowers. They're beautiful," she said.

"It is nothing," Ava said offhandedly.

Alba went over to where Hadrian and Namir were carving a roast pig.

"Where did you find the priest?" Alba asked.

"The temple at the edge of the city," Hadrian said, placing a large slice of meat on her plate.

"Did he come of his own free will or did you force him?" she asked.

"Define force," Hadrian said.

"You just did," she said.

"Alba, pardon my profanity but . . ." he said, bracing her for some vulgarity. "No. This is your day. I will hold my tongue. All I will say is that the man was pivotal to the ceremony and"—he put his arm around her shoulder—"as someone who has grown up with, we did not want you to have a wedding without."

She placed her hand on his chest and patted it before he turned to serve Cloe and Gus. Gannicus joined them resting his back against the table.

"You have all gone to so much trouble," Alba said with a bit of guilt weighing on her.

"It's not just for you but for all of us," Gannicus said. "It's nice to have a thing to celebrate, to rejoice in after so much blood and battle." His eyes traveled to where Spartacus was chatting with Natalie. "Never have I seen him so light, so at ease with himself as when you are around him. I am happy for you both."

She grinned. "Was it you who found this?" she asked, holding out her hand to show him the ring.

He nodded. "I had Cloe try it on for size," he said.

"It's perfect," she said. "Thank you, Gannicus." She kissed him on the cheek.

In the early hours of the morning Alba retreated to the shadows of the same stone archway where her breath had caught earlier that evening. As she leaned against it watching her friends she was filled with such emotion. Sadness and joy all at once. She had grown very attached to them, had come to care for them, and love them. Each time they went to battle the armies against them grew in size, the threat looming larger. Each time they went, her love for them had grown deeper and she feared now not only for Spartacus.

Natalie was seated next to Hadrian as Gannicus stood over them, regaling them with a story, his arms moving about wildly. Natalie shook her head in disbelief as Gannicus nodded and took a sip of his drink.

Namir was asleep on the steps, his head drooped against a pillar. Cloe sat with Gus, her head resting on his shoulder, the red glow of the embers softly lighting their faces.

Content, Alba shrunk from the archway and started to climb the back stairs.

She shrieked as her feet went from under her. She grabbed her crown of flowers as it tipped off her head. "Spartacus!" she said. She should have known that his eyes had been on her.

"Cloe told me that it is tradition for noblewomen to be carried to their bedchamber on their wedding night," he said, looking down at her.

She smiled. "Actually, it is the servants who carry the bride up the stairs and then they pass her to the groom at the door."

"Why the servants?"

"Because the groom does not wish to exert himself before they lay together."

He climbed the three flights of stairs and set her down in their bedroom. Then he knelt before her and began to untie the knot of Hercules, raising his eyebrows at the many loops.

"Who tied this?" he asked, his fast hands tugging at the fabric.

"Natalie," she said.

"Ah."

He slid the last bit of fabric through and pulled the belt loose.

Alba placed her crown of flowers on the table, and he came up behind her, wrapping his arms around her.

The weight of your burdens, he had said.

"I hate to think of him out there, living a life without us," she said. "With each passing day knowing us less and less."

"I wish we had longer, that he had memory of us, so that one day …"

"He might find his way back."

She felt him nod.

"He may yet," she whispered. "He may yet."

Spartacus held her tight.

Forty-Two

In the morning, while Spartacus slept, Alba took a cloak from the hook and went down to the courtyard. Smoke rose from the embers and she picked at some fruit left on the trays. There was a loud, stretching yawn behind her, and Hadrian rested his forearms across her shoulder blades.

"Did you take him to bed?" he asked.

"No," she said.

"Good." He nodded and his eyes fell to her footwear.

"I thought I might take a walk in the city," she said.

"Not alone?" he said. "There are people who know your face."

"Do you not have trust in them?" Alba asked.

"I do not wish to test it," he said.

She draped the cloak around her head. "I can be inconspicuous," she said.

"You have heard my thoughts on the matter."

But she did not agree with them. After he left on his rounds, she too left the villa. It was liberating to walk along the streets. The arrival of the rebels had made the city quite crowded, but the citizens went about their daily routines. The gladiators had worked hard to make sure that this was the case. It would be of no benefit to them if they were to bring the city to a halt.

Market vendors were set up in the square, the men loading their carts and wheeling their goods down to the docks. A few women worked together making an intricate design on a loom.

The streets swelled with people as the morning unfolded and she made her way back to the villa. A guard was stationed at the gate and he blocked her passage.

"What's your purpose?" he asked.

"This is my home," she stammered, taken aback.

"All entries must be cleared through Spartacus or the gladiator placed on wall duty," he said.

"I passed by you on the way out," she said.

"These are not my orders," he said.

"Who's on wall duty?"

"Bacchus!" he yelled.

Bacchus leaned over the wall, twenty feet above them. "What?" he grunted.

"Is she allowed to enter?"

"I can't see her face," he said.

Alba shut her eyes in frustration and pulled the cloak off her head.

Bacchus stared down at her, his hand on his knee. "Yes. She is fine," he said.

Alba walked through the entrance gate into the small courtyard as Bacchus hopped down onto the platform and descended the ladder toward her. She dearly hoped that he was not expecting her to voice gratitude for his consent to let her pass. "I've not been able to smell right since the night your friend smashed my face with that urn," he said, getting close to her, the stench of drink on his breath.

There was no one else in the small courtyard.

"I'm sorry to hear that," she said.

"I don't think you are," he said. He cupped the side of her neck with his thick, powerful fingers. "I know you are Spartacus's bitch, and for some reason the gladiators have taken to you, but I see you for what you are." He squeezed her neck. "A filthy Roman."

He pressed his lips to hers and she kneed him in the balls.

"You do not deserve to live among us!" he yelled as she ran into the large courtyard.

When Alba came down to the atrium, she had set the incident with Bacchus behind her, finding comfort among the others.

Hadrian had perched himself at the base of a column and was reshaping the leather soles of his sandals while Gus restrung a bow and Namir skinned a rabbit. Gannicus was fixing the wheel on the wagon that they used to distribute their garden's bounty throughout the city.

"You have gotten quite good at that," Alba said to Namir as his quick hands stripped the rabbit of its fur.

"Done it enough times," he said with a grin that quickly faded. "What's that on your neck?"

Alba pulled her hair down to cover the sore spot. "Nothing."

"That's not nothing," Gannicus said, straightening. "Who did that to you?"

Alba shook her head. Though she was appalled with Bacchus's actions, she didn't want to expose him, knowing he was a valuable warrior for them.

"It was Bacchus," Gus said, setting his bow aside.

Alba rounded on him.

"I saw from my bedroom window," Gus said.

Gannicus and Hadrian caught each other's eyes.

"It's not worth it," Alba called after them, but they ignored her.

"Alba," Gus said. "You and Cloe are not the only women he's forced himself on."

"It's true," Natalie said darkly.

. . .

When Spartacus came in later that night he strode toward them. "Is there a reason Bacchus's head has been parted from his body?" he asked.

Gannicus, who had just ripped a large hunk of chicken from the bone with his teeth, used the thigh to point at Alba's neck.

"I'm fine," Alba said, holding up her hand.

"Was that not the decree you set down on us if anyone touched her?" Hadrian said. "Gannicus and I were simply seeing it through."

It was a clear, warm night, and Alba leaned back on her forearms, turning her gaze toward the sky. It was speckled with the brightest stars she'd ever seen—a blanket of light above them. She stood and climbed the ladder. There was a gap between the wall and the roof. She ran along the ledge and jumped.

"Alba!" Spartacus said.

She slipped, then regained her footing and turned. "Aren't the stars magnificent?" she yelled down over them.

Cloe glanced at Natalie and they followed her up to the roof.

The men watched in trepidation as Natalie made the run first, landing with ease. Cloe jumped too soon, and Alba and Natalie had to reach out and grab her as she squealed in delight.

"They are spectacular," Cloe said. She laughed as Gus landed right next to her, followed by Namir, Hadrian, Gannicus, and Spartacus.

They lay on their backs, side by side on the roof, staring up at the stars, and as Alba glanced at Spartacus, she knew that she would never forget this moment. All of them together, all of them content.

A tear rolled down her temple and Spartacus took her hand in his.

A messenger came in the early hours of the morning, his fists on the villa door, declaring that he must have an audience with Spartacus immediately. After being checked for weapons, he was asked to wait in the courtyard.

He was greeted by Namir. This was not the first time a messenger had come, needing to discharge himself of some urgent news.

"I must speak with Spartacus," he said.

"You may speak with me," Namir replied.

"Commander Crassus is leading an army south. They move to cut down all who stand with Spartacus."

"How did you come by this information?" a deep voice said from the shadows.

"I've seen him," the messenger said. "Six days ago, traveling with his legions."

"What did he look like?" It was a woman's voice.

"He had dark hair and a curly wig. Sharp, chiseled features. And there was another man astride his horse beside him. His hair was golden in the sun."

Spartacus called a meeting in their bedchamber. The sky was a dark, menacing gray, with flashes of lightning illuminating the clouds. The room was dimly lit, their voices kept low.

"Crassus's army is moving south toward us," Spartacus informed the others.

Gannicus nodded slowly, his arms crossed in front of him. "Our time has run its course. We knew it couldn't last."

"It's not yet over," Hadrian said. "We have fight left in us."

"Can we go north around them?" Alba said.

"It wouldn't be possible, not with so many people," Gannicus said. "They'll have scouts lined from coast to coast."

"The rebels are scattered across the southern tip," Spartacus said. "We've become too fragmented."

"Marcus Crassus is smart, as is Julius," Alba said. "They will come down on us like nothing we have ever seen before." She paused, and a weight pressed down on her chest as she looked from one face to another, all of these people she had grown to love dearly. "I know that this is selfish to say"—Julius's words rippled through her, *every last one* —"but what if we warned them and left. Just us."

Spartacus lowered his head and shook it. "They will hunt me until I draw my last."

"If you lead them," Gannicus said, "they stand a chance."

"Only if the rebels are united," Hadrian said.

"Send out the gladiators to every village," Gannicus said. "We must bring together every able-bodied person willing to fight."

"Some of them speak of making the voyage to Sicily if the Romans ever were to come," Namir said.

"An island?" Hadrian said. "Well, that is a great idea."

Spartacus glanced at Alba.

"There is more. Another piece that the messenger shared," Spartacus said. "Crassus has pledged to Rome that as the commander of the legions he will eradicate us. Eight legions travel with him. Fully armed, fully trained."

Hadrian let out something like a wheeze. "We're fucked," he said—words Alba never thought she'd hear him utter.

And surprising her more it was Gannicus rallying them. "No," he said. "There is fight left in us still. How many times have we been outnumbered? How many times have we come out ahead?"

"Never against a man like this," Spartacus said. "He has more experience in battle than all the rest, and his resources know no limits. He has also . . . he's brought back decimation."

Gannicus cringed.

"Decimation?" Namir asked.

"It means that if you retreat in battle," Gannicus said, "ten men pick stones from a bag. If you pick the one black stone, you are killed by your comrades. Without weapons."

"That is barbaric," Natalie said.

"Why would he kill his own men?" Cloe asked.

"So that they fear him, more than they fear us," Natalie said. "So that no matter what, they do not turn around."

Forty-Three

It was decided. Natalie and Gannicus would travel together, as well as Gus and Namir, and Spartacus would be on his own as they set out to alert the rebels scattered across the southern tip.

Hadrian would stay behind with Alba and Cloe. He spent the day in town, cloaked on the edges to await how the ripple of news was received. When it came, it was not a ripple but a wave, washing over them with force. Not with the old excitement that the rebels carried with them into battle but panic.

Eight legions, Crassus, Julius. Their voices were tense and fearful but the message was clear. They needed to fight as one to stand a chance. Fragmented they would be cut down by the merciless legions. The alert was working. There was a current of urgency and the urge to act now. That was when Hadrian stepped forward to organize the people, directing their energies into swift preparation.

Alba was relieved when he came back to the courtyard in the early evening. With the others away, she had been restless, unable to sit still. Cloe had made a pot of rabbit stew for dinner.

Hadrian leaned over the steaming bowl and took a bite. "That's quite good."

"Natalie has been helping me with my cooking," Cloe said, lifting Aleni onto her lap.

Hadrian turned to Alba. "And has she been helping you?" he asked, his tone hopeful.

Alba furrowed her brow.

"Just because you can always get better," he said.

They climbed the stairs to their bedrooms, and Cloe paused with her hand on the metal pull of the door. She glanced at Aleni on her hip. "It's silly I know, but I'm nervous to sleep on my own," Cloe said as Aleni reached for her face with her chubby little hand.

They were all full of fear and nerves. Anticipation and worry. Alba didn't want to be on her own either.

Hadrian opened his door and held it for them.

As Cloe, Hadrian, and Alba lay down side by side, Alba noted how comical she would have found this threesome if it had been under another circumstances. Just a year ago, she would not even have fathomed it.

Gus and Namir were the first to return in the early evening on the third day. After quick embraces they reported that as they traveled back to the villa there was an eruption of movement, not just of the rebels but of the farmers and villagers. Some were fleeing farther south, others were attempting to hide. But many were preparing to fight, knowing the consequences if they did not.

Rome would be coming down on the rebels with a force never before seen against their own. It was a last stand. A fight for their lives. Though there was a massive shortage of slaves in Rome, the rebels knew they would not be allowed back in the houses. Not after this. Even their lives of servitude were over.

Natalie and Gannicus arrived just as the group was finishing their supper. Cloe was quick to ladle them each a bowl.

"He's not back yet?" Natalie said, freeing herself from the weight of her weapons belt.

Alba shook her head.

Gannicus and Natalie exchanged fleeting glances, worry flashing across their eyes.

"What?" Alba asked.

Natalie hesitated. "There has been a price set on his head," she said.

This was not news. There had been one since the beginning.

"How much?" Hadrian asked, scooping himself a second bowl.

"One that would pay for this villa twice over," Gannicus said solemnly.

Hadrian set the bowl down. He did not touch his food again.

Once they had been discharged of their news, no one spoke much. His absence weighed on them all, filling the air they breathed, the space between them. The flames shrunk and the red glow of the embers dimmed, but nobody moved to add another log to the fire.

"Let's get some sleep." Gannicus's deep voice cut through the darkness. "We'll need to be well rested when he returns."

It was with a slow, somber rustle that they got to their feet. Alba bid the others good night, her hand on the latch of her door. She waited until the last door had clanged shut before going to the top of the stairs where she sat with her chin resting on her fists.

Time slipped by, but she did not move.

"I couldn't sleep either," Hadrian said, sitting down beside her. "This is why I never liked having friends. These moments."

"It's a good thing you don't have many then," Spartacus said, climbing the stairs, his steps weary.

Hadrian shot to his feet. "Let me get you food."

Spartacus shook his head. "Sleep." His hair was matted down and his cheeks flush with exertion.

After embracing Hadrian, Spartacus and Alba went into their room.

"Will it be enough?" Alba asked.

"I don't know," he said with the slow rise and fall of his shoulders.

He lay down, and she gently stroked his head as he drifted into a heavy sleep. In the night, she could feel him there, warm beside her, his body so familiar to her now. She ran her hand over the muscles in his chest, his shoulders, letting her eyes linger on every curve, trying not to think that it could be for the last time.

Then he caught her wrist, his eyes on hers. She lowered her body onto his, stomach to stomach, and as she took a deep breath, he wrapped his arms around her.

As they emerged from their rooms dressed for battle, Alba had to steady herself to descend the stairs. She stepped behind a pillar and took a breath, trying to force down the deep melancholy that had taken hold of her face. She wanted to hug each one of them close to her, to tell them so many things she hadn't yet. She was so grateful for their friendships and the peace they had brought her, the happiness and devotion.

"No." She heard Namir's voice in the atrium. "I was silent once before—I shall not be again."

Hadrian was dressed for battle. "I am worth ten of those men on the field of battle," he said.

"You are," Gannicus said. "But at present you cannot even grip a sword properly."

"I'm a gladiator," Hadrian said firmly. "I was born to fight."

"No man is born to fight," Spartacus said. "That urge, that need for violence is instilled in him as a means of survival, to defend, to protect. Himself, his land, the ones he loves."

"I belong at your side," Hadrian said.

"Not this time," Spartacus said. "It is my wish for you to remain at Alba's side."

Hadrian looked over Spartacus's shoulder to where Alba leaned against a pillar watching this all unfold. It seemed this was one request Hadrian could not refuse, for he hung his head, silent. Spartacus cupped Hadrian's neck with his hand and placed his forehead to Hadrian's. A silent understanding passed between them.

Alba packed a small satchel to travel with, only the essentials.

"I knew it was coming," Cloe said.

"We must be brave for them," Alba said.

"And for yourselves," Hadrian said, coming into the room. "We will cloak ourselves as we leave the town. It's best if we are discreet. It will be a long, arduous journey. Harden your minds to it."

"What about our bodies?" Alba said.

"The body will follow," Hadrian said. "We'll be leaving shortly."

Spartacus was in the courtyard arranging the gladiators. His gaze flickered toward Alba and he followed her behind an archway.

"I wish I did not love as I do," he said. "It would make it all easier."

"It's your love that drives you, that fills you up. Don't see it as a weakness."

It was a heart-wrenching sight. Her dearest friends, saying their goodbyes. Cloe held Gus's cheeks in her hands until Aleni reached up, grabbing at his face too. He leaned down and kissed her little blonde head.

"I'll keep an eye on him," Gannicus said to her.

Cloe kissed Gannicus on the cheek. A gesture that startled him.

"Natalie," Alba said, taking her hand. "You have been so incredibly warm."

Spartacus put his hand on Natalie's shoulder. "Stay in the middle, near—"

"I will stay near you," she said.

"No," he said. "I will be a target."

"Then I shall be as well," she said it firmly, without hesitation, an intensity in her dark eyes.

Namir stood off to the side, his head bowed, despondent.

"Hey," Hadrian said, lightly slapping Namir's cheek. "You are a warrior."

He nodded solemnly.

"You are focused." Hadrian pressed his finger to Namir's temple. "You are alert. Use your size to your advantage as I have taught you."

Namir nodded again.

"Good," Hadrian said, and slapped him once more. Then he turned to Alba and Cloe. "It's time."

They covered themselves in cloaks, and Gus passed Aleni to Cloe. Alba felt like she was going to be sick as they walked through the courtyard.

At the gate she turned. Spartacus held her gaze until Hadrian placed his hand on her back and she continued on.

The townspeople were readying themselves, sharpening their weapons, assembling their armor. There were no vendors in the market, no tradesmen or barterers today. Hadrian didn't take them down the main streets. They cut through an alley with fabrics hanging down around them and out a side door.

As they made their way toward the forest, Hadrian said, "We will not speak. If you wish to communicate, do so with hand gestures." He outstretched his hand so his palm faced the ground. "If I do this, drop down." He waved his hand twice. "This is find cover quickly." He waved his hand once. "This is run and don't look back," he said. "Understood?"

Cloe and Alba nodded.

For half a day they walked in silence. They met a tall, steep ridge with great roots and rocks buried into its side. Cloe made a swaddle for Aleni and tied her to Hadrian's back. Once she was secure, he started to climb. Alba and Cloe followed behind, helping to push and pull each other up, using the rocks as footholds. If this had been the old Alba, her arms would have fatigued. She may not have made it. But she was stronger now and she willed herself forward.

As they crested the ridge, Hadrian was sitting on the ground, catching his breathe. His gaze was fixed on something in the distance.

Alba and Cloe turned to follow it. Way down below stood the rebels on one side and the Roman legions on the other, in perfect formation. Neither was moving.

It was unsettling and ominous. Alba had to force her eyes away from it.

"Come," Hadrian said, passing Aleni back to Cloe. "They are doing their job. We must do ours."

FORTY-FOUR

No matter how much distance they tried to put between them and the battle, they could not escape the desperate yells and clashes of metal on metal.

On the third day, they came across a man's body, his face blood-smeared and broken. His muscled forearm bore a *B* etched into the skin.

"Atreus," Hadrian spat. "Coward. He's deserted."

"Can you blame him?" Cloe said.

Hooves thudded the ground behind them. Hadrian turned over his shoulder, his hand on the hilt of his sword. "Natalie!" he yelled.

She reared the horse around. In front of her, a body lay limp across the horse's back. It was so still. The yells and clashes went silent as Alba reached for his face, covered in sand, sweat, and blood.

"He's alive," Natalie said. "But not for long. He tried to kill Marcus, went through two of his centurions before they descended on him."

"Without him, they will fall. You must go," Hadrian said.

"Alba," Natalie said. "You go."

"No, you have brought him back from the brink before," Alba said. "It is you who can do it again."

A thought crossed Alba's mind. She pulled Spartacus's shoulder pads from his lifeless shoulders, his sword from its sheath.

"What are you doing?" Hadrian said.

"He has no use for them now." Alba slid them onto the dead man's shoulders and placed the sword on his chest. Spartacus's sword and armor, purple with gold pleats, would be instantly recognizable to any who came across it.

"Until he draws his last breath they will hunt him," Alba said. "Let this be his last."

"Passing in history as one who was defeated?" Hadrian stood over her.

"Passing into history as one who died for his people, who gave his life to their cause."

"He may yet if I do not go," Natalie said.

"Leave the name of Spartacus behind you," Alba said. "Call him by his birth name, Alex."

"How fitting," Hadrian said. The meaning of Alexandros was *defender of mankind*. "You have done well, my brother." Hadrian leaned down to kiss Spartacus's blood-crusted temple. Then he stood aside for Alba. She could feel the heat from his body. She kissed his warm forehead, his hair damp with sweat.

"When Neme and Max call out to you," she whispered. "Do not go to them. Not yet, my love."

Hadrian rested his hand for a moment on Natalie's leg.

"Don't look back."

On the fourth day, men and women jostled by each other, panicked, their tempers short, their words gruff. Some were headed north, others south.

Gannicus and Gus caught up to them, their horses utterly spent. Gus swung his leg over it and hopped down. He hugged Cloe and then cupped Aleni's cheek in his large hand.

"Hadrian." Gannicus's chest heaved as he slid from his horse. He clutched a stitch in his side and his horse collapsed. "They're coming down from the north. More soldiers led by Pompey."

"Namir?" Hadrian said weakly.

"I don't know," Gannicus said. "Our lines have gone ragged. They'll be upon us soon."

"They hunt to kill?" Hadrian asked.

"Capture."

"Capture?" Hadrian said, horrified.

"I do not know to what end," Gannicus said.

"Why would they call Pompey home?" Hadrian said.

"To make sure that none get out alive," Alba said. "To quash us once and for all. He'll take the credit for this win."

"We stand a better chance if we separate," Gannicus said. "Traveling in a group is dangerous. I'll take Alba. You take Gus and Cloe."

"No, I'll take Alba," Hadrian said.

"You'll linger, waiting for Namir," Gannicus said.

"I won't. I swear it," Hadrian said, the pain of his words etched in his face.

"Keep your wits about you." Gannicus slid Hadrian's thick leather bracelet so that it covered the shiny *B*, tightening the laces to keep it in place.

Gus took Aleni from Cloe and secured her high on his shoulders where she wrapped her pudgy arms loosely around his neck. She was such a calm, sweet child, her pale blue eyes filled with bright intelligence. Throughout this whole ordeal, she had barely uttered a peep as if understanding the severity of the situation.

Alba took Cloe's hand and held it as they climbed the shallow valley together. At the top, she released it only as they were forced to veer from the other.

Gannicus took Hadrian's forearm. "See you on the other side, brother."

. . .

The farther north they traveled, the more people thinned. Where had they all gone? Into hiding or captured. Alba tried not to think of it, lowering her gaze from the few people they did pass. She couldn't stomach the trembling fear and desperation in their eyes.

They came to a steep ravine, and using the jagged rocks and roots, they climbed. It was nerve-racking, and a couple of times she had to make a leap of faith, letting go and launching to the next root. There was a narrow opening carved into the earth. Hadrian carefully pulled the brush to the side.

"If Pompey's men are coming down from the north, it will be too dangerous to travel by day," Hadrian said.

They shimmied into the crevice, and he pulled the undergrowth back, concealing them. It was a small, unassuming place. Her body was pressed against his, her forehead touching his shoulder. The feel of his skin, his body lying next to hers, brought her comfort, and she shut her eyes to the rising and falling of his chest.

She was woken from a deep sleep, her head heavy, in a daze. Hadrian's hand was over her mouth in fear that she might have forgotten where she was and gasp or cry out. She had not forgotten.

Slowly he peered out through the brush. They slid out of the crevice and continued upward.

It was a dark night, pitch-black, the moon buried beneath the clouds. She couldn't even see the outline of the trees, and the ground beneath her feet started to tilt in her disorientation. Hadrian took her hand in his, walking slowly, until they found a stream. They followed the sound of the trickling current, lapping gently against the rocks and tree roots. As the darkness turned to gray, Hadrian surveyed the ground. He found some berries and mushrooms for them to eat.

"Have you ever slept in a tree?" Hadrian asked while sizing up the ones around them. Alba had climbed many trees in her childhood but had never slept in one. He cupped his hand and lifted her so that she could reach the lowest branch. He nestled himself into the branch across from hers. "Tie yourself to it like this. Tighter."

They were shaded by the canopy of leaves above them and shielded by those below. Her thighs were pulsing and she had pulled a muscle in her foot. She flexed it, and the rough edges of the bark pressed into her back.

Hadrian shifted and tilted his head up toward hers. "Alba . . . " He hesitated, his voice low. "If we are captured. I fear for you . . .of rape and worse. If I am able, would you like me too . . ."

"It will be quick?"

"Very."

She nodded. "Yes."

For nights and days they traveled like this, scavenging what they could from the earth. When they stopped to rest, she had to quiet her mind, to push away the fear. Every cracking tree branch, every scurrying animal parting the leaves sent a small shot through her exhausted mind and body. Every sense was heightened, amplified. Never had she been this stressed for so long. She could feel herself cracking, unraveling. They didn't discuss the hunger and fatigue or the imminent threat of death that engulfed them. They barely spoke at all for fear that someone might hear them.

Fear. Prolonged and unrelenting. It coursed through her veins and shortened her breath.

It was Hadrian's steadfastness that saved her, his calm presence, sure and steady. It was he who kept her from faltering. A dozen times she wanted to tell him to go on without her, but she could not, because she knew he would not.

One night she clutched her ribs, unable to fall asleep beneath the damp brush. On the hard ground she turned her head, ever so slightly. "Hadrian," she breathed. He did not move. "I'm scared." A warm tear rolled down her temple.

Slowly, carefully, he reached his hand through the brush and rested it on her stomach. The weight of it calmed her and she was able to sleep.

Every day as the sky grayed they would search for an indent in the ground and cover themselves with brush and leaves. One morning, Hadrian could not find enough brush for cover or a thick tree to sleep in as light broke over the horizon and they were forced to continue on into daylight. He had just found a spot when voices cut the still air, abrupt and terse. A Roman patrol.

Hadrian took Alba's hand and they tucked up against the base of a wide tree. Alba followed Hadrian's lead skirting around it, but as the Romans approached, they parted. One on either side of them and yards away. Hadrian went still, gripping Alba's hand so tightly it hurt, the other clutching his dagger.

One of the soldiers stopped. He held his hand up.

Alba held her breath.

A rabbit dashed out in front of the soldier. Alba jolted, her back scraping against the bark.

The scouts continued onward. Once they were out of sight Alba squatted down and clutched her head.

Hadrian lifted his shirt to wipe the sweat from his brow. The outline of his ribs was visible through his taut skin.

FORTY-FIVE

They needed to cross the Via Appia, a well-patrolled road the Roman soldiers used to travel south from Rome. They crested a hill to get a better vantage point and lay on their stomachs. The Roman scouts were dark ants in the distance, but it was not them who caught Alba's attention.

She let out a gasp as she processed what she was seeing. Hundreds, no thousands of crosses. Thousands of bodies nailed to them.

Captured rebels.

"Those bastards," Hadrian said.

On their stomachs they watched. For hours. The movements of the patrol, the timing of their switches. Alba was now used to being still for long periods, but it was her eyes she needed now. To be alert and sharp. Focused. Patterns were something she was good at finding.

"When that pair makes their next change," Alba said, pointing to the men in front of them, "we will make our way swiftly through the middle."

Hadrian nodded.

They descended the ridge with haste and made their way toward the road. As they approached the crosses, the horror of it gripped her.

Nothing could have prepared her for the smell of death, the pallid faces, or the drooped limbs.

As they drew nearer, she kept her head down. She couldn't look at them. She needed to pass through the crosses as quickly as possible.

It was a few moments before she realized that Hadrian was not beside her. She turned in a panic.

He was yards away, his face lifted upward. Transfixed.

Why had he stopped?

Then Alba saw it. A pair of long, slender legs crusted with blood. Alba's eyes traveled upward, and she let out a small groan. Guttural. Such deep sadness pressed down on her. Consuming her. She took a staggering step backward. Even from the backs of their bloodied heads she knew. It was Gus, Cloe, and Gannicus.

Her body drained as she stumbled toward them. All the happiness she had ever known, gone.

Hadrian stood at the bottom of Gannicus's feet, browned from blood and dirt. Gus's wheat-colored hair no longer shone in the sun. He placed his hand on Gannicus's foot. His voice was thick in his throat. "I'll see you on the other side."

Alba didn't know how they made it across the plain and into the forest. It was a wonder they weren't spotted.

Mounting hunger and fatigue weighed on her every step, but it was her friends that sat at the forefront of her mind. Her hands were quivering slightly.

"Alba," Hadrian said. "Your feet."

She didn't realize she'd been shuffling, dragging them through the brush. She focused on picking them up when Hadrian's hand went against her stomach. She'd almost stepped in a rabbit's snare.

The succulent smell of meat billowed toward them in wafts of smoke, tantalizing them with its aroma. Nauseated with hunger, Alba cupped her hand over her nose. A wail nearby sent shivers down her spine. A child's voice.

"That's Aleni," Alba said, turning to Hadrian. She'd never heard fear in that child's voice, but there was no doubt in her mind that it was her.

"We can't," Hadrian said.

"We must," Alba said. "I'll not leave without her."

Hadrian led Alba to the top of a ridge. Aleni's hair was instantly recognizable—a vibrant golden blonde, gleaming even in this shaded area of forest. Having just started to walk, she took wobbly steps past the men, women, and children who lived in several little hovels, crowded together. One of the older children pushed her and her little face hit the ground. She grunted in frustration and pushed herself up again.

Hadrian lowered his head and Alba knew. He wouldn't leave her here with these people.

He started to stand, and Alba pulled his thick leather bracelet so that it covered the *B* on his forearm. Even peasants living deep in the forest would know of the famous gladiators from the House of Batiatus.

"What will you do?" Alba whispered.

"I'll speak to them first so that if it goes badly it will not weigh on my conscience."

As they entered the clearing, the men stood, their wary and hostile stances quickly turning smug when they realized it was just the two of them. Alba scanned the children, unable to see Aleni among them.

"The blonde child in your midst is mine," Hadrian said. "She's coming with us."

One of the women came forward, her face streaked with tired lines. "No," she said. "She's my child."

"Quiet," one of the men barked, his eyes fixed on Hadrian. "They're rebels."

"Do you have quarrel with the rebels?" Hadrian said, resting his hands on his belt.

"That depends on what they have to offer."

"I have nothing to give you," Hadrian said.

"I beg to differ," he said, nodding at Alba.

The men's eyes became desirous at the thought. How anyone could want her in this state was beyond her. Her hair was matted and stringy. She was all bones and angles and did not smell good.

"You misunderstand me," Hadrian said. "What I mean to say is, I will give you nothing."

Alba glanced at Hadrian's hands, turned in like large claws. She hadn't seen him handle a weapon since he'd been nailed to the cross. It was only a flicker of a glance, but it drew the eyes of the man.

"Well then"—the man shrugged as if the decision was out of his hands—"we'll have to take."

Hadrian lowered his head with a slight huff, disappointed.

"We mean no quarrel," Hadrian said, trying again. "Give us the child and we'll leave you peacefully."

"Whether or not things are peaceful is up to you," the man said.

Aleni came into the clearing and caught sight of Alba. She ran toward Alba in delight, her arms outstretched. One of the men held his walking stick out. It caught Aleni's feet and she skid across the dirt. As Alba reached for the child, Hadrian reached for his sword.

Alba had forgotten. He was a warrior first and this was second nature to him. Even in his weakened state, the peasant men were no match to him. His movements were deft and precise, his sword a blur as he cut each of them down.

Screams of panic pierced the dank air as the women wailed out. An elderly man took shelter behind one of the tents.

"Your pockets," Alba said to the old man. "Empty them."

The man started to fumble with the pouch tied to his tunic.

"Now," Hadrian yelled.

The old man ripped it free and tossed it to him.

Hadrian slid his sword back into the sheath and Alba glanced at his bracelet. It was still covering the mark. Blood splattered his arms and chest as it rose and fell.

She put a loaf of bread, a hunk of meat, and some clean cloth in a satchel and slung it over her shoulder. She didn't have the strength to carry Aleni. Thankfully Hadrian picked her up.

They walked and walked until they met a wide river. Hadrian put Aleni down and sat on a large rock. Alba ripped the loaf into little chunks for Aleni and gave her a small piece of meat to suck on.

Hadrian's gaze was on the water, his body still.

Alba went to its edge and wet the cloth. She wiped the blood, sweat, and grime from Hadrian's neck, arms, back, and face. With his head bowed, he didn't seem to notice her hands on him.

She placed her hand on his shoulder. "Eat," she said. When he didn't move, her grip tightened. "Hadrian."

He reached into the satchel for some meat but then pulled his hand back and flexed it.

"Is it all right?" she asked.

"Yeah." The word came out as a sigh. He shook it a couple of times and then reached in again.

Aleni scrunched her face as Alba gently dabbed away the dirt and grime embedded in her soft skin. She placed her pudgy hand on Hadrian's knee to balance herself, determined to stand. He glanced absent-mindedly at her little fist, so white and smooth against his darkened skin.

Forty-Six

With a bit of food in their stomachs, they set out, Aleni perched high on Hadrian's shoulders. She didn't fuss or cry, and her pale blue eyes followed their interactions with bright curiosity.

The farther north they walked, the farther away they were from the threat of danger. They had successfully made it through Pompey's scouts and patrols and had navigated themselves through two armies. Though their paranoia eased, they didn't lower their guards. There would still be rewards out for the rebels.

At a stream they stopped and Alba bent over to lift water to her lips. As she drank, a realization came over her and she leaned back. The soft rise of her belly was unmistakable. A thing gone unnoticed until now.

"Hadrian," she said, placing her hand instinctively on his. She turned to face him as horror filled her.

"What?" he said.

"I . . ." Unable to say the words, she pulled his hand to her stomach and then squeezed her eyes shut. As realization dawned on him, she pushed his hand away and said, "I don't deserve another child." Her words were quiet, barely a whisper.

"What are you saying?" he said.

"I couldn't even keep the one I had," she said. "He's out there somewhere in this world, and he'll never know me, never know his father or the love we had for him."

"You know I am a man that says what he believes. I don't mince words," Hadrian said. "What happened was out of your control. It wasn't your fault. You do deserve this child."

They crossed rolling hills, gently parting sheep as they cut through a herd. A man stood above them on a hill watching as he leaned against his staff. Hadrian nodded at the shepherd and the man nodded back. He turned to follow his flock, moving with a slight gait.

"My father was a shepherd," Hadrian said. "He was a small man, older when he had us. He was gentle and kind. We grew up in a small hovel, my brother, sister, and I. He never told a lie a day in his life. He was an honest man . . .to a fault." He paused, deciding which direction they would take. "The Romans came to our village to stock their army and ordered a man from each family fight for them for two years. When they came to our hovel, my brother and I were out with the herd. My father said that he was the only man that belonged to the house."

The words weighed on Hadrian. "You never saw him again," she said.

He shook his head. "When my brother died, I vowed never to love someone again, fully and unconditionally for the pain of losing is too great. But then there was Spartacus and Natalie and Namir, who forgave me all of my faults and stubbornness."

"Who would have thought at the end, it would be me and you," she said.

A small smile. "Not in a million years."

They came to the walls of a large, bustling town. Alba and Aleni waited crouched down in the forest, shielded by darkness, while Hadrian skirted the edge searching for a way to bypass the patrols that had been set up at every entrance. He wasn't as stealthy or as swift as Alex, and Alba prayed he wouldn't be spotted.

She was filled with relief when he rejoined them.

"Can you climb?" he asked.

"How high?"

"Twelve, maybe fourteen feet," he said.

"Yes," she said, trying to convince herself that she could.

Hadrian tossed a rope with a hook attached to one end over the ledge of the wall. He tested his weight on it, and then Alba quickly helped him secure Aleni on his back. Once he had made the climb, he gave the signal for Alba to start. Partway up the wall, there was an owl hoot, the signal to stop. She held herself still with her feet planted against the wall, her arms shaking. She was about to lower herself back down when there was another hoot. She started to climb again.

They decided to stay in the taverna district. Alba was not excited about the notion but knew that it was necessary. It was a busy, boisterous area where unsavory people came and went. There was less regulation here and fewer questions. Being the man, Hadrian would have to negotiate on their behalf but he'd never used coins before.

"Ask the man how much a room is and then offer him less. A bit less so that he respects you but not so low that he resents you. If he asks why you are in the city just say that you have business here," she said.

"What if he asks how long we are staying?" Hadrian said.

"Tell him until the business is done."

Alba and Aleni waited in the alleyway while Hadrian negotiated. Nearby, a group of men were playing dice on the surface of an upright barrel. Other men crowded round to watch. One man sat slumped against the wall fast asleep and a few children with dirty faces sat in front of a rug littered with trinkets.

"Want to buy something for your child?" one of them asked Alba.

The noises, the yelling and crassness, were grating on her. She needed to lie down. To rest.

Hadrian signaled to Alba and she was grateful to climb a staircase to a room on the backside of the taverna where it was quieter. Hadrian had negotiated for clean sheets, and Alba took the grimy, slick furs from the bed while Hadrian cleared away a few dirty cups and plates.

"I'll go to the market in the morning to get some fabric," Alba said, unfolding the clean linens. "Make us all some new clothes."

"Alba . . ." Hadrian said reticently.

At the tone of his voice, she turned to face him.

"The Roman Senate has ordered a census of all the children born this year. Any non-Roman child can be taken and placed under their ownership if they cannot prove a clean lineage."

"They wish to restock their slaves," Alba said darkly.

"Yes and no one will question it. Not after . . ."

"What they did on the Via Appia."

He nodded gravely.

"Then we'll stay here for a few days and continue onward," she said.

"I think it best we wait here until the child is born," he said. "Remember how large you became last time. It's not something we could hide."

"Are you saying that . . . that I will have to stay in this room?"

"I think it best until the baby comes and we can travel again," he said. "I'm sorry, Alba."

That night as they lay side by side in bed, Alba had to quiet her mind to the new sounds all around them. The banging doors, the pounding of feet on stairs, the babies crying out into the night, and the hollering from below in the tavern. In the early hours of the morning, she tossed and turned, restless.

Hadrian's eyes were open. He too could not sleep.

"Your mind is on the others?" Alba said.

"I cannot help but think, all that time we were surrounded by so many, and now it is just us," he said, turning to look at her. "Is all that we did in vain?"

The next morning Hadrian went to the market. He and Alba had made a list of the essentials that they needed. Fabric, food, soap. They could all use a good cleaning.

There were many rumors about what had happened to Spartacus but most believed him to be dead. The tribute Alba having made for him had worked. It also made finding him or Natalie almost impossible. How to find a man who needed to stay hidden? And that was if he had survived his wounds.

Being forced to stay in the room brought back painful memories for Alba. Flashes of her childhood isolation crept to the surface. She found herself pacing, standing up, sitting down. She tried to pray, but it wouldn't do. It no longer brought her comfort.

She was grateful when Hadrian found some decent fabric for them. Something to keep her busy, to give her a purpose, and to settle her mind. Aleni was delighted when he pulled a well-made doll from his pocket and set it in her small hands. She hugged his leg and he patted her head.

Aleni kept Alba sane. Her open face was filled with such tender happiness. That and trust. In Alba and Hadrian.

They fell into a routine. Alba spent the days cooking, cleaning, and sewing while Hadrian would lurk in the alleys and side streets listening and watching for any sign of their friends. When Hadrian would be away for many hours, Aleni would wait by the window in the early evening watching for his arrival. He always returned before dark. "Albie!" she would say, excited to point him out as he came up the alleyway.

At night Alba would wrestle with her thoughts and the images that flashed through her mind. The crusted blood that coated Cloe's leg. Gus's limp foot. Hadrian staring up at his friend. She pressed her hands against the sides of her temples, trying to squeeze out the thoughts, needing to block her mind from it.

The night the baby came they were blessed by the Gods. Alba woke, her back drenched with sweat, a pang surging through her as a bolt lit the room and thunder rippled across the sky. She clenched her teeth determined not to cry out.

With a sudden inhale Hadrian woke. "Is it time?" he asked, sitting up.

She nodded.

The pain was less intense than when she had gone into labor with Max, but the cramps still coursed through her body. It took everything she had not to wail. Her whole body clenched as Hadrian rubbed her thighs just as Natalie had done.

They had gone over all the steps. All of the things that they would need and what had to be done. When the baby slid out, bloody and slimy into Hadrian's arms, he beamed at her. "You have a son," he said. "A healthy baby boy."

The baby cried out as the thunder cracked and the room was lit.

Alba dropped her head to the pillow exhausted.

"Well done, Alba," Hadrian said.

He cut the cord and wiped the child clean. It was only then that Alba realized that Aleni was standing at his elbow.

She named him Luka. He was smaller than Max had been. His hair was the color of hay and his eyes a hazel. Aleni was enamored with him. Every morning when she woke she went to his cradle and stood on her tiptoes.

"He's sleeping," she would whisper or, "He's awake."

Hadrian was growing restless. They both were. He didn't like the city, the pace, the bartering. It was wearing on him. He was a man who liked the open fields, the forest, and the rivers.

At times he wouldn't sit still, pacing back and forth at the end of the bed.

"Hadrian," Alba said, trying to draw him from his walking trance. "Hadrian," she said, again placing Luka in his cocoon of blankets. "Where are your thoughts?"

He shook his head. He didn't want to burden her with them.

"You wish to leave this place," she said.

"Not yet," he said with a glance at Luka. "I've found a small apartment for us. Somewhere quieter but near the market."

"So that I may venture out again?" she said, hopeful.

He nodded.

The apartment was not large, but compared to the previous cramped room, it was a welcome relief. There was a room to make meals and eat, a sitting area, and a separate bedroom where they all slept. She fed Luka and put him in his cradle.

"I'm going for a walk," she said after unpacking what few possessions they had.

"What if... what if he fusses?" Hadrian asked.

"Rock him back and forth."

"But he is so small. So fragile."

"He is sturdier than you think."

To step outside and stretch her legs was bliss. The uneven stones beneath her feet. The people, everywhere people. So many faces. It seemed they were converging on her. But they weren't. They were going about their own business and she was going about hers.

She couldn't stay out long on her own. Hadrian would worry and Luka needed to be fed again.

That night when the children had been put to bed, Alba went to sit next to Hadrian.

"I've been thinking. Let us leave the city," she said. "Make a home somewhere, the four of us. We are not city people you and I. We have tried but it's not taking."

They both knew what this meant. If they left the city, all chance of finding Spartacus, Natalie, or Namir would be gone. They would have to put that hope behind them and move forward. Not on. But to a new place of peace. To start afresh and to be content with that.

"Are you sure?"

"Yes," she said. "I am sure."

"You once told Spartacus of a dream you had. You wished to have a family, to fill your home with warmth and happiness. I wish to own land and to work it. To have animals and a garden."

"Let us do these things together," she said. "The four of us."

Forty-Seven

Alex faded in and out of consciousness until their horse collapsed in exhaustion. Natalie sat next to his lifeless body, the weight of it too much for her to carry. A shepherd hobbled up to her, offering his help. Natalie was wary of the man but she was desperate. Together, they dragged Alex into his cart and wheeled him to his modest hovel.

In the dim light Natalie cleaned Alex's wounds and forced him to drink small amounts of broth. The shepherd boiled water for her and cut linens, found herbs for her on the hillside. Natalie's greatest concern was that as pale and still as he was, he did not sweat. He didn't move at all. Was she doing him a kindness by keeping him alive? She desperately clung to him, the last friend on this earth she had, and so for months she tended to him. She was scared to be alone.

The shepherd was kind and unassuming. Natalie made him an ointment to sooth his muscles, seizing up in his old age. After months of careful tending, Natalie was brought to tears when one evening she felt Alex's hand on hers.

A few weeks later, with a heartfelt thanks to the shepherd, they were on their way and set out to find the others. The shepherd told them of the atrocity along the Via Appia. They needed to be very careful. Alex covered his head, knowing that his face would be recognized by many. He was slower and more methodical with his movements, his body sore and stiff from being bed bound for so long.

When they came upon a town, they didn't go through the regular entrances, wanting to avoid the Roman patrols and citizens eager for even meager rewards. Instead, they found back alleys and sewer openings. Even in the heat of the bustling markets Alex kept his head cloaked, the fabric itchy on his damp neck. He was negotiating for the price of fish when Natalie appeared.

"Alex," she said sharply with a quick head tilt.

The vendor selling the fish yelled out a lower price as Alex followed her swiftly through the stalls.

There were days when patrols and random searches suddenly erupted in the market. They always had to be alert. Alex thought this was why Natalie had called him away. She stopped and stood against a wall. Alex followed her gaze to the empty window of a launderer busy with activity. Women were pulling in lines, folding clothes, and hanging tablecloths, napkins, and linens. The drying fabric swelled in the breeze of the alley.

After some time, Diana appeared briefly at the sill.

Alex's fist clenched.

"Wait," Natalie said, placing her hand on Alex's chest.

In the early evening dim, a few of the women started to trickle out of the building, and as Diana emerged, they straightened. They trailed her at a distance through the alleyways, adept at tracking people discreetly. It was a maze she knew well. She went into a large communal house where other women lived with small children.

Natalie glanced at Alex. "I'm afraid your presence will not go unnoticed in there."

"Hm," he grunted, having surmised that himself.

He was studying the building, the outline of windows and the rooftop, silhouettes in the darkness.

"I'll meet you in there," he said.

"I don't think it's wise," Natalie said. "She cannot see your face." He was also still in a weakened state, not strong enough to climb the side of a building. "I'll go. If he is with her, I'll get him." She turned to him, her dark eyes intense. "Trust me."

There was a woman with beady eyes and stringy hair shelling peas just inside the entrance. Natalie nodded in greeting as she walked past her.

"Staying the night?" the woman asked.

"I'm visiting a friend," Natalie said.

"No visitors allowed," the woman said, shifting the bowl from her lap to the bench. "Only paying customers."

"I'll not be long," Natalie said.

The woman stood. "Only paying customers."

Natalie needed to avoid making a commotion of any sort, not when so much was at stake. After placing a coin in the woman's hand, Natalie ascended the stairs and counted the doors as she passed. Fairly certain she was standing before the right one, she stopped and knocked.

The door opened and Diana's round eyes widened.

"I'm not here to cause trouble," Natalie said. "I'm only here for the boy."

"He's not yours," Diana spat. "You have no right to him."

So he was alive. Natalie was filled with a surge of joy but she needed to remain calm.

"How can you speak of right and wrong?" Natalie asked. "You took him from his mother and father. Two people who love him."

"It is because of families like hers that I am like this. They are the reason we cannot hold seeds in our bellies. She did not deserve to live among the rebels," Diana said. "She didn't deserve that beautiful little boy. Leave us be. He'll only be a burden on you. He'll have nothing to offer until he reaches manhood."

"Nothing to offer?" Natalie repeated. Was this woman counting on Max to care for and provide for her as she aged? "What about Max's father? Did he not give everything he had to free the slaves? He is the reason you are here now."

"And where did that get him?" Diana said. "Buried in the earth. Dead."

"Not quite," Alex said, perched on the window ledge.

He tugged the sheets from the bed and in a swift movement covered Diana's face. He held the cloth tight as she gasped for air and controlled her fall as her body fell limp to the floor.

Natalie glared at Alex, annoyed. It had never been his intention to let Natalie try and speak sense to the woman.

Alex shrugged apologetically and she shook her head in frustration.

His gaze fell to the doorway. There was little boy standing in the frame. His hair had become darker and curlier than Alba's, but his eyes were the same vibrant blue as Alex's.

Those eyes took them in now, studying them, and the body they were trying to shield from his view.

Natalie bent so that she was at his level.

"Max," she said. "I am Natalie. You're safe with us."

Alex knelt beside her and did his best to soften his deep voice. "I'm your father," he said. "I love you very much."

"Me?" the boy said, rolling back on his heels, uncertain.

"Yes, you."

With Diana's death they had to leave the town quickly. They added her small collection of coins beneath the mattress to their pockets.

As they journeyed to the next town many miles away, Max walked between them. If he slowed or fell behind, Alex would stop and offer to pick him up, but Max refused. He was shy around them and determined to keep up with his short, pudgy legs.

One day the boy placed his small fingers in Alex's hand. The gesture startled Alex, and if it had not been for his honed reflexes, it might have shown. Alex wrapped his large hand tenderly around Max's and glanced down to smile at his son.

Alex taught the boy to call him Pa.

One day he called Natalie "Ma."

"No, son," Alex said. "This is Natalie."

The sharpness of the statement startled Natalie. So bluntly were his words spoken and without hesitation. That night they had found lodging near the market. Natalie tucked Max into his little bed and leaned over him to kiss his forehead.

Alex was in the chair by the window with his feet up, staring into the darkness, his thoughts elsewhere.

"May I speak with you?" she said.

"Of course," Alex said, lowering his feet and turning to give her his full attention.

"I know that we cannot have what you had with Alba. I have resigned myself to that," she said. "But could we go back to what we were before, at the ludus?"

He lowered his gaze, and she braced herself for his words. "It would not be fair to you," he said. "You deserve someone who loves you with their whole heart."

"What if I told you I didn't care?" she said. "I will take what is left of yours for it is more than most others ever experience. I've never known someone who made me feel as you do. So at ease and safe."

He took her hand in his. "I love you, Nat, and until my last breath, I would be honored to live by your side but not in the shadow of love."

"What if I were to find comfort in the arms of another? Would you not be moved?"

"Of course I would, but I wish for you all the happiness in the world," he said. "I have since I first knew you."

"Because you do not know the truth," she said, her voice breaking. "The first time I saw you I left you for dead. To rot and spoil in the pit. You have always felt strong kinship to me for saving you, but I nursed you back to health only because I was ordered to."

He studied her face a moment. "I know," he said gently. "Through the haze I saw you there kneeling next to me in the pits."

"You knew that I left you?" she said. "Why did you not say anything?"

"Because you did nothing wrong. It was not a matter worth discussing. It didn't change how I grew to feel for you."

"You don't know how this has weighed on me."

"Let it rise from your shoulders. They have carried too much."

After days of searching the countryside for the right place to make a home, Alba and Hadrian found a small house built at the top of a rolling wheat field glowing in the golden sun. The soil was rich, and there was a river nearby.

"What do you think?" Hadrian asked Alba.

"It's perfect," she said.

He paid for it with coins, and Alba didn't ask him where he got so many.

Though the land around them had much promise, the home, on inspection, was falling apart. A light breeze came through the cracks in the walls, the floor was uneven, and the wood beams above them were rotting.

"Can we patch it enough to get through the winter?" Alba asked.

"I'll have to go back to the town and get some tools," Hadrian said, inspecting the beams and roof.

It would be a half-day journey.

"It'll be faster for you if I stay here with the children," she said.

"Are you comfortable with that?" he asked.

She assured him she was and tried to sound confident.

"I'll leave first thing in the morning," he said. "You remember all I taught you?"

"I do," she said.

"In the spring I'll rip this down, build something better," he said.

"We will build it together," she said.

Natalie and Alex made their weekly trip to the market, Alex holding Max's hand in his. Max had outgrown his tunic, and his shoes no longer fit. Natalie perused a few vendors comparing their colors, prices, and quality of the fabric before settling on a deep blue for the boy.

"A wise color choice," the vendor said. "It will go nicely with his dark hair."

Alex kept a watchful eye from beneath his cloak. The patrols had decreased, but he was still cautious in these busy areas. Through the crowd and bustling market, he spotted the back of a head, a head so familiar he would know it anywhere.

"Nat," he breathed, releasing his son's hand.

He strode through the crowd, his gaze fixed on the man. Alex was jostled from side to side as he cut through the people with a single purpose. It took everything he had not to run. He couldn't risk bringing attention to himself.

Hadrian slipped through the vendors, ducking under some hanging laundry, and down an alley. Alex elongated his stride. Hadrian stopped and leaned down, pretending to tinker with the wheel of a cart, but Alex knew that his friend had reached for his dagger.

Hadrian turned suddenly, clutching the dagger, his stance alert, aggressive. Then his face opened in shock.

The force of Alex's embrace almost knocked Hadrian backward. They held each other for a long moment. When Alex pulled away, Hadrian's eyes had misted over, and he grabbed hold of Alex's shoulders as if he could not believe what he was seeing.

"Natalie," Hadrian said warmly, his eyes passing over Alex's shoulder.

It was then that he noticed a small boy standing in front of her. Max backed up into Natalie's legs as Hadrian came swiftly toward them.

"Max." Hadrian bent down and picked the boy up so that they were at eye level. "How are you?"

"Good," Max said cautiously. He was many feet off the ground.

"Good . . . good," Hadrian said with a wide smile, and he put the boy down. "I know someone who would love to meet you."

Alex's eyes filled with hope and longing.

Hadrian placed his hand on his friend's shoulder. "It's a half-day's journey."

"Take me."

Alba was down on her hands and knees, the tail of her braid falling over her shoulder as she dragged the bin along beside her. She had cleared away most of the debris on the floor, preparing the space for Hadrian. Aleni sat on the nearby bench, kicking her feet as she played with her doll.

Aleni's feet went still. Those young ears heard the voices first, full of laughter and excitement. There was one voice that cut across the others, deep and resonate. Alba gasped, and shivers danced down her spine. She got to her feet and pressed her hand against her chest, her breath laboring under the emotion as she made her way to the door.

The setting sun spilled golden over the fields, and the people approaching glowed against it. Alex saw her first, and his stride lengthened as he came up the hill. Her face broke into a smile as she ran toward him and into his arms. She was lifted off the ground as he hugged her tightly to his chest.

When he set her down, warm tears fell down her cheeks.

"It is too much," she gasped.

"There is more," he said, taking her by the hand, steadying her.

Natalie stepped forward with a small boy resting on her hip.

"Am I dreaming?" Alba said. "How did you . . ." Alba reached out to her son, but he turned in toward Natalie.

"Max," Natalie scolded. "This is your mother."

The boy looked skeptically at Alba.

"It's fine," Alba said. "He does not know me." The words pained her to say. "It's good to see you, Natalie."

Alex took Max in his arms. "Max, this is Alba. She loves you very much."

After a moment, Max reached out and touched Alba's face. She shut her eyes to his small, pudgy hand.

"Aleni," Natalie cried out.

Aleni started as Natalie rushed toward her, but she held her ground.

"How are you? Dear, sweet child," Natalie asked.

Aleni stared up at Natalie with a crinkled, cautious face.

"I was a good friend of your mother's," Natalie said. "I will tell you all about her."

Alex put Max down, and the little boy went over to meet Aleni. Alex placed his hands on his hips and lowered his head. "Hadrian told us of Gannicus, Cloe, and Gus."

Alba nodded solemnly. "We'll make a tribute to them once we put the garden in."

"And one for Namir," Hadrian said.

"Are you sure?" Alba asked.

Hadrian nodded, his chest rising and falling. Then he turned to Alex and clapped him on the shoulder. "Would you like to meet your son?" With a quick glance at Alba, he said, "I hope you don't mind—I told him about Luka."

"Not at all," Alba said.

"I would," Alex said.

"I've gotten very good at holding him," Hadrian said. "The trick is not showing any fear. The child can feel that, you see."

Alba grinned.

As they climbed the rolling hill, Alba stopped to watch Max running toward the house with Aleni.

When Hadrian asked Alba if all they had done had been in vain, she did not have an answer for him then. But as she watched him and Alex pointing out a spot to put in a well and Natalie bending down to pick a few flowers, she knew now.

No, none of it had been in vain.

Acknowledgments

A massive thank you to everyone who has supported my writing, whether that's by showing interest in it by asking how it's going, reading snippets or offering encouraging words even if they had no idea what the book was about. I really appreciate my creative writing group's feedback on the early chapters of this book.

Made in the USA
Columbia, SC
09 March 2023